THE *SEA BREEZE*

THE *SEA BREEZE*

S J T Riley

Matador
Unit E2 Airfield Business Park,
Harrison Road, Market Harborough,
Leicestershire. LE16 7UL
Tel: 0116 2792299
Email: books@troubador.co.uk
Web: www.troubador.co.uk/matador
Twitter: @matadorbooks

ISBN 978 1803132 235

British Library Cataloguing in Publication Data.
A catalogue record for this book is available from the British Library.

Printed and bound in the UK by TJ Books Limited, Padstow, Cornwall
Typeset in 11pt Adobe Garamond Pro by Troubador Publishing Ltd, Leicester, UK

Matador is an imprint of Troubador Publishing Ltd

To my wonderful wife, Loly

ONE

A FATAL SURPRISE

Tugging at the canvas sails, the sea breeze scuffed the low-crested waves south-eastwards towards Land's End and the open Atlantic beyond. To the north, the Welsh coast and the Irish Sea lay bathed in grey daylight. Looking the other way, a curtain of damp mist had fallen, leaving only the cries of seabirds to warn them of anything untoward. Changing tack now, the yacht's bow pointing towards some as yet undisclosed haven, the rocky cliffs began to push through the mist in partial and uncertain shape.

*

'He's back already?'

The question was more one of surprise than interrogation. The yacht rocked lightly at its mooring; the woman's voice left trailing.

'Not unless he's taken a dip. He told me to go back and pick him up in the dinghy.'

The reply came from the sailor sitting opposite who, without looking up, continued reading the newspaper laid out on the small cabin table between them. They were speaking Dutch.

'I know.'

With the late evening, the mist had closed in after them.

'A real pea soup, as Freddie would say,' Johann had remarked in English an hour or so earlier, on slipping down the hatch after having tied up the dinghy on his return from ferrying Freddie ashore.

They had dropped anchor in the middle of the cove and Freddie had wanted to go as soon as the light had started to fade. He'd refused to give any reason or explain why he was carrying so much money in cash in his holdall. They guessed it must be for some stolen piece of art: a painting, perhaps. Since then Anna had waited quietly, a little apprehensively. This was not their usual business, and they had no reason to be here. Would he even come back? She had to trust him. *Only nerves*, she kept telling herself. But their situation was altogether too unsettling.

'He's got a lot of money on him, Johann.'

'Too much.'

'For what?'

'A surprise, he told you, didn't he?'

'But why here? We've never been here before.'

'And why did he have a bunch of flowers?'

'No idea!'

The boat tipped slightly.

'Someone's coming aboard, Johann. Go up and see who it is. Please.'

Worry edged the request.

Pulling himself out from around the table, the sailor shot up the steps and through the hatch; the woman getting to her feet, first waiting, listening to the sounds on deck, then following him, anxiety taking control of her.

'Nothing, there's nobody.'

'Behind you!' Anna cried out.

A man, his head covered by a black sou'wester, was standing on the deck, steadying himself with a hand on the mast whilst below in the water two others in a dinghy drawn up alongside the yacht stared up at them.

'Who are you?' the man in the sou'wester asked, surprise in his voice.

'Get on with it!'

The light Cornish growl from one of the men in the dinghy with a captain's cap abridged any possible discussion aboard the yacht. The man in front of him scrambled out of the dinghy and onto the yacht, tipping the little boat to one side with the loss of his weight and letting out a curse from the man left in it. Still, in what seemed to them no more than a flash of seconds, the woman and her companion found themselves overpowered and penned in against the stern rail by the three strangers with nothing else but the empty sea around them.

'So, who are you then?'

This time the man with the captain's cap asked the question, more direct and menacing now that they were in control. For the moment, their simple presence gave them authority. Anna, her hands clasped around the rail behind her, stared back at them defiantly. Johann stood next to her, nursing a heavy blow to the head.

'Well?'

'Don't you think we should be asking you?' Anna parried in perfect English, a haughty tone providing a mask of courage, and adding, 'You're on my boat.'

'Your boat? Really?'

'You can't be serious?' Anna objected.

'Take a look below, Kenny.'

The man with the sou'wester turned towards the hatch as directed and made to go down below deck.

'You, just stay put!'

The sharp warning from the man with the captain's cap made Kenny turn back but not quickly enough to avoid colliding with him, thrown backwards by a lunging kick from Johann that sent the two men falling through the hatch.

'Johann!' Anna screamed, tearing at the third stranger. 'Jump!'

The sailor hesitated, looking at the woman.

'Go on!' she urged whilst frustrating the other's movements, adding, 'This isn't your business.'

'Get him!'

The two men thrown down the hatch were back on their feet and on deck but not in time to prevent the sailor, a plimsoll already on the stern railing, from taking a diving plunge overboard. The white splash of water was lost almost immediately in the darkness. Two gunshots cracked out in rapid succession.

'You idiot!'

'But Captain?' The third man stood with the automatic revolver still in his hand, defiantly.

'You fool, Tabby. You'll have a rope around our necks yet. Go and fish him out and pray to God he's still alive.'

But the energetic strokes of the swimmer had ceased.

'Go on! Give him a hand, Kenny. And give me the gun, Tabby.'

The so-called captain gave the man with the sou'wester a push.

'I'll deal with the woman. Give me that rope.'

The dinghy disappeared in the mist, discernable only by the clumsy splash of oars. Aboard the yacht, with several rapid movements, Anna found herself bound and gagged, and left alone momentarily as the man carried out a search below deck.

'So why did he jump ship, eh? If there's nothing aboard.'

The man had returned on deck and stood looking down at Anna, an expression of muffled fear in her eyes. Angry, he was uncertain what to do. Clearly, they were on the wrong boat.

'Well?' he snapped, seeing the dinghy reappear.

The dumb shake of heads only fuelled his irritation.

'Well?' he repeated.

'Sorry, Captain, there's nothing out here.'

'So you missed then, Tabby. Thank your lucky stars.'

'I didn't miss.'

'So where's the body?'

Tabby pointed his thumb downwards.

'Don't be daft. Anyway, who gave you the gun?'

'Pengal.'

'Pengal! Thank your soul that it wasn't him who fired. We surely would have a body on our hands. Kenny, come up and give me a hand with the woman.'

The man with the black sou'wester climbed aboard the yacht and the two of them took hold of Anna, lifting her down into the yacht's own dinghy.

'What are we doing?'

'We're taking her with us. Her friend must have reached the beach by now. Sooner or later, he'll come looking for her, and then we'll know what they're about. Working in our waters won't do, will it now?'

A muffled screech sounded from within the yacht.

'What's that?'

'Just a bird. Leave it.'

'That's no common bird.'

'Leave it, Tabby, and take up the anchor before you jump off.'

'What for?'

'So it'll float out with the tide. Now get into the other dinghy and follow us back.'

'So where's Skinner and our yacht?'

The man with the captain's cap paused for a moment, holding the oars still in his hands.

'That's a good question, Kenny. How the hell could you have messed that up?'

*

Ten minutes or so earlier, within the darkened grounds of a large house high up on one of the headlands of the cove, Alfred Chessington, or Freddie as he liked to be called, shoved the necklace, still in its velvet pouch, into his overcoat pocket and headed towards the path that would take him back down to the cove and the *Sea Breeze* where he'd left Anna and Johann waiting for him. He'd bring them up to the house in the morning. That would be a surprise for them! Before his appointment with Pengal a little earlier he'd gone inside, succumbing to a curiosity to revisit its familiar rooms, but the torch-cut darkness had revealed little to satisfy his memories, old of ten years or so.

He was breathing hard. Yeats, the bastard, had double-crossed him; and instead of walking away with both the necklace and the money he'd brought to pay those who'd stolen it for him, Freddie only had the necklace. Still, it was something and much better than nothing at all! Yeats had agreed with Freddie when they'd met some days before to ambush Pengal, once he had taken the money for the necklace and was walking away. Instead, Yeats had decided to play his own game and ambush Freddie instead. Fortunately for Freddie, his sixth sense had been alive, and he had come off best from the scuffle, leaving Yeats unconscious on the stone slabs of the terrace to the villa, a sacrifice almost to the moonlit sky that had broken through the mist.

Freddie continued holding the necklace in his hand as he walked; the touch of its diamonds through the soft velvet bag a more real reminder of Jennifer, his long-dead wife, than the cold and empty house. He had paid handsomely for its theft. Even more than the amount for which he had stupidly sold it before the War after Jennifer had died. Stolen goods! Still, he had it. That's what counted. The man Pengal had been on time, meeting him at the gates to the grounds of the house and handing over the jewellery in exchange for Freddie's money. Yeats' treachery had left Pengal free to disappear with the money, back into the night, back up the road to Westcliff and, Freddie had imagined, back on the road to London.

Passing through the gap in the wall the crack of the two gunshots in the cove below sent a shiver of alarm down Freddie's spine. What was happening? Yeats' treachery, now this! Their boat was alone in the cove, or had been before darkness had set in. And there were no guns aboard. Silence had fallen again, effortlessly and completely, like quicksand. Freddie started to run, the descent pulling him down faster and faster until, losing his footing at a sharp bend in the path, he fell headlong into the undergrowth, cursing loudly before his head hit a stone and he lost consciousness.

TWO

A TELEGRAM FROM AN OLD FRIEND

'Damn! Not again.'

Robert Lynnford sat back in his chair, exasperated. The heavy typewriter was giving him a lot of trouble. The metal fingers studded with the letters R and O had clashed again in mid-flight, remaining locked together like two exhausted wrestlers, halting the writer's rhythm for the third, fourth, perhaps fifth time in the space of as many minutes. He had already had to replace the ribbon.

Well-founded hard fact as it was, he would have readily conceded that the real source of his irritation was not the machine but the task. Every job has its downside and for him this was writing newspaper copy. Making stories was what stimulated him, not writing about them; investigating crime mysteries, not reporting them. A distinction that, in his view, Paul Kombinski, the editor of *The London Herald*, didn't always fully appreciate.

And at the request of his editor, he had spent the morning at the Central Criminal Court, the Old Bailey, reporting on the trial of an affair he had helped bring to light earlier in the year. The proceedings had been adjourned for lunch, allowing Lynnford to nip back to the office in Fountain Street. He looked up at the wall clock above his desk. Almost one-thirty. He should be getting back.

The door opened.

'Ah, so you're back then?'

Maxwell, his colleague, with whom he shared an office, filled the door frame, a large smile on his face. Maxwell was *The London Herald*'s sports writer.

'Lunch?'

Lynnford shook his head, freeing the recalcitrant typewriter keys. The tap, tap recommenced, the words appearing on the unrolling sheet of paper, slowly at first, as mind and matter took time to rebuild their acquaintance, and then more fluidly, as the writer's confidence in the machine re-established itself. But he lacked inspiration. The clatter stopped abruptly, this time without mechanical failure for excuse. The placid and monotone descriptions of the morning's proceedings had taken their toll. He sighed. The thrill of the mystery had evaporated long ago.

'Let them have their courtroom drama, but please, Heaven help me, let someone else write their script!' he cried out in semi-voice.

'Something wrong, old boy? The Mayfair necklace?'

Maxwell had taken his seat and, with his feet elongated across the desk beside his typewriter, was surveying Lynnford's hapless figure, not without some mirth in his eyes.

The Mayfair necklace was Lynnford's current investigation, but he wasn't getting anywhere with it and Maxwell's jibe only served to fuel his irritation. The necklace had been stolen from a banker's Mayfair apartment in Hanover Square during the summer. Lost for leads, the policeman in charge of the investigation, Detective Chief Inspector Sheffield, had enticed Lynnford to give him a hand with the carrot of a mystery. Its history alone was enticing. A string of South African diamonds, the necklace, known as the Exmoor Jubilee, had been given by a wealthy tea merchant to his wife in celebration of their twenty-fifth wedding anniversary and in honour of her birthplace on the north Devonshire moors. But after some promising ideas tied up with a female companion of the banker and former resident in the apartment who had also disappeared without trace, and about whom the banker had been less than eloquent, Lynnford had come up against a frustrating brick wall.

'Come on, Lynnford! I'll buy you a round at The Golden Fox.'

Maxwell got to his feet, adding, 'I've put a bet on a tip, seventeen-to-one on the two-fifteen at Doncaster. We can follow the race on Maureen's wireless. It'll change your ideas.'

'Good idea. I'll throw in a sandwich.'

Lynnford pushed back his chair, getting to his feet.

'I'll get Jack Worth to go down to the Old Bailey for me. What's the horse?'

'*Sweet Dreams*. Come on, there'll be a crowd at this time.'

Maxwell picked up his hat, placed it firmly on his head and led the way out. Lynnford followed, closing the door behind them.

*

The Golden Fox stood some way down a narrow road off Fountain Street, just a few yards from the offices of *The London Herald*. A public bar, the clientele was limited to local traders, residents, and "people from the Press". Maxwell drank there regularly, perhaps a little too regularly. Still, as he maintained, the bar was an excellent environment for stimulating the circulation of sporting information, some good, some bad. And Maxwell had developed a good nose for a sound tip, particularly on the dogs. Maureen held the bar and laid down the rules on all that could or could not take place within its walls. She was in full swing, conducting the lunchtime symphony, as Maxwell and Lynnford stepped inside.

'Two gins and a pale ale.'

'Just a minute, lovey.'

Maureen turned towards a young man squeezed in against the bar some places further along.

'What's yours?'

'Make it a whisky soda, if you please.'

Maureen nodded, snapping shut a beer tap and placing a dripping pint glass on the counter in front of the man next to him.

'Ten pence to you, young man,' she called out as she reached up and pulled down two fresh glasses, opening again the beer taps with a deft clip of the hand.

'Here, keep the change.'

Collecting with a sweep of her other hand the two sixpenny silver pieces, she dropped them in the till behind her and held up a tumbler to one of the upended bottles of spirits fixed to the back wall, filling it with a shot of whisky and turning round in time to close the two beer taps.

'One and six,' she called out, placing the glass of whisky on the bar. 'Help yourself to soda.'

'Turn the wireless on, Maureen, there's a dear. The one forty-five at Newmarket is set to start.'

Lynnford and Maxwell edged their way up to the bar. Two stools were vacated and seized by Maxwell.

'What will you have?'

'A glass of bitter, Max, but listen, I'll get these. Two halves of bitter, Maureen, and two rounds of cheese and pickle sandwiches when you're ready.'

Maxwell pulled out from his jacket pocket the day's edition of *The London Herald*. The paper had been folded back with the racing pages facing outwards, Monday 22nd October 1951. The two-fifteen Doncaster race had been marked out with four thick red lines. Maxwell went through the running order, commenting rapidly on each horse's form. He paused when he came to *Sweet Dreams*.

'*Sweet Dreams*, seventeen-to-one. A long shot, perhaps. But if my tip's anything to go by, she's going to show what she's really made of and sprint away in front of the pack, all seven furlongs. A nice set of horses,' he summed up, putting the paper down on the counter.

Turning back the cuff of his jacket sleeve, he checked the

time on his watch. Ten minutes past two. Picking up one of the sandwiches on the plate he took a large bite, looked at Lynnford and smiled.

'There'll be some surprises today.'

'Who's your tip, Max?'

Maxwell tapped his nose with a sly glance at Lynnford. He had a whole network of contacts; people working in the stables and on the racing courses, in the stadiums and sports clubs. This was his bread and butter, the source of his sports copy and for the rest a useful supplement to his pay packet. By dint of sharing the same office Lynnford had made the acquaintance of most, if not all, of Maxwell's regular noses. At seventeen-to-one, somebody certainly was going to be surprised. If the tip was good, then somebody was holding back something on either the horse or the rider.

'Who's riding her?'

'The lad from Kerry. Pete Henessey. It's about time now. The Newmarket race finished some minutes ago.' Maxwell looked at his watch again. 'Turn it up there will you, Maureen?'

Maureen reached up to the radio and a man's voice suddenly leapt out from the wall, '*I think they're just about ready now. They're under starter's orders. Stand by for the start of the race. And they're off.*'

The commentator's voice seemed to breathe a sigh of relief before taking up the canter, his voice full of excitement and suspense.

'*Now Sweet Dreams has taken up the gauntlet,*' whistled the voice some minutes later.

'*She's whipped outside Wild Sands and there's one down,*' the commentator cried out in dismay but without breaking rhythm.

'*Midnight Delight has come to grief. The jockey has taken a tumble in front of Wild Sands who falters, and Sweet Dreams is in front and crosses the line followed by Wild Sands, Midnight Delight running without her rider and Royal Pardon comes in third.*'

The commentator's breathless voice trailed off with the names of the remaining horses.

'*Sweet Dreams*, yes you are!'

Maxwell banged his fist on the counter in triumph, giving Lynnford a friendly cuff across the back of the head. He drained his glass and called out to Maureen, 'Two double Scotches for two happy men of the Press and the sooner you make it the happier they'll be.'

He turned to Lynnford. 'You'll join me for a little celebration, won't you?'

Lynnford looked as though he was making signs to leave.

'Oh, don't bother yourself. You've got time. Anyway, you've sent young Jack Worth off to report on the Osborne case.'

'All right, Max. I'm not likely to miss much. The case won't finish before the end of the week, anyway.'

'That's the spirit. Thanks, Maureen, you're a dear. Here, take one for yourself.'

Maxwell placed a note on the bar.

'Don't mind if I do.'

Maureen took out some coins from the change and dropped them in a jar next to the till.

The pressure on the bar was beginning to ease off. It was still full, but it was no longer heaving. Bit by bit, the customers were drinking up and making their way back to their offices or, in some cases, just back out on to the streets. A ray of sunlight shone through the upper skylights, casting a hazy smoke-filled spotlight on one corner of the bar. Maxwell continued, 'Osborne? Isn't that the government minister who killed his wife, changed his identity and married again?'

Lynnford smiled.

'Almost. A senior civil servant in the Treasury. Killed his first wife in a fake road accident and poisoned his second.'

'A psychopath?'

'No, he was just greedy. Expensive tastes and no money of his own.'

'That's a bit rich from someone in the Treasury. You'd think they'd be happy enough with all the tax we pay. What's his defence?'

'We'll see this week. I guess he'll try and discredit the witnesses and maintain his original alibi. But we'll see.'

Lynnford drained his glass. His interest in the Osborne case had long since gone.

Maureen was now mopping up in preparation for the afternoon call for last orders. She picked up the two empty Scotch glasses left standing on the bar with one hand, and, with the other, gave the counter separating her and the two departing journalists a broad wipe with a damp cloth.

'Thanks gents. Pass by tomorrow,' she called out, her mind already elsewhere.

Outside The Golden Fox, Lynnford waited for Maxwell as he went inside Gates, the betting shop next door to the public house, to cash in his winnings, Lynnford's feeling of tedium quickly reasserting itself after the brief excitement of the race. *London can be awfully dull*, he mused. *And Maxwell*, he worried, *needs to be careful in making use of his dodgy tips to supplement his monthly pay packet.* Once Maxwell came out of Gates, his face flushed with his winnings, they walked back to *The London Herald*.

*

The offices of *The London Herald* extended the full length and breadth of Number 18 Fountain Street. It was a substantial edifice, whose imposing character was only lost by the two similarly dimensioned adjacent buildings. Immense windows fronted each building on either side of a Pharaonic entrance, leading the visitor up a short series of marble steps, bordered by columns at the foot of which sat two watchful foxes, a fox and a vixen with curled bodies. Fountain Street was a symbol of Edwardian ambition and creativity built upon Victorian wealth. Above the steps to Number 18 an elegant sign spelt out in solid characters the title of *The London Herald*. The newspaper had moved there in the 1920s and had remained ever since.

'Mr Lynnford! Telegram.'

The information was bellowed out across the entrance hall by George, whose face filled the little opening to the glass-fronted reception. George was still very much a military man and fulfilled his role as *The London Herald*'s senior clerk with an iron rule that knew no favours and which fully gave Mr Kombinski, the paper's editor, his peace of mind.

'Thank you, George.'

Lynnford tore open the envelope and unfolded the telegram. It had been sent from a post office in the West Country, from a town called Westcliff. The message read:

EMPTY YACHT AND SAILOR FOUND FLOATING
IN SANDY COVE WESTCLIFF THIS MORNING
STOP CALL ME (WESTCLIFF 2912) SAM STOP

'Good news?' Maxwell enquired.

'Hmm?' Lynnford appeared absorbed.

'Your telegram. What does it say?'

'It's from Sam.'

'A friend?'

'Sam goes back a long way. Royal Air Force.'

'And?'

'He wants me to call him.'

'A story?'

'Maybe, Max.'

On the face of it, not much of a story, Lynnford reflected. *Certainly nothing to please old Kombinski. Possibly something for the local rag on its front page. But it has to be something more than an accident. Sam wouldn't have bothered me for less. He must be holding something back, something he didn't want to put down in the telegram*, and it was Sam's reason for this that was most intriguing Lynnford. *I'll have to see what more Sam can tell me before making a decision. And where exactly is Westcliff?*

Jack Worth was waiting for him in his office.

'Already, Jack! What time is it?'

Lynnford looked up at the clock. It was only three-thirty.

'What happened?'

Jack scratched his head. He worked in *The London Herald* as a messenger boy under the authority of George, but his ambition was to become a journalist and Lynnford never tired of calling on him to help him out in his work, under the nose of the head clerk, it had to be admitted. He was a young lad of seventeen but still looked more like a boy of fourteen and so had taken to wearing a waistcoat, that he always wore buttoned up, with the idea of better showing his age. Unfortunately, it had the opposite effect, tending to exaggerate his youthful appearance.

'They were arguing some point of law I couldn't make out. Anyway, Mr Justice Huntingford called it a day. They'll start again tomorrow morning, at ten-thirty on the dot.'

'So much for that, then. Doesn't look as though I missed much.'

Lynnford cast a glance at Maxwell before adding, 'Fine, Jack. Nice work. Better get back to George before he strings me up for having taken you away again without leave.'

Well, that's smoothed things out rather nicely, Lynnford concluded to himself as he walked over to his desk and sat down. The unfinished copy he had been writing at lunchtime was still stuck in the typewriter, lying limply along the carriage. He tore it out and picked up a fresh sheet of paper, placing a sheet of carbon paper between it and some copy paper, and rolling the whole through the typewriter until the top was aligned neatly with the metal paper guard. *Osborne case opens at the Old Bailey – trial set to continue for a week*, he quickly typed and in a few short lines resolved his earlier mental impasse with a column that was as quickly sent up to the editor. He then picked up the telephone and put a call through to the number on the telegram. And a few minutes' conversation with his old friend was all that was needed to convince him that there was indeed a story to feed his curiosity and, as Sam remarked, sea air to blow London's cobwebs out of his mind. As soon as he replaced the receiver, he set about planning his visit to Westcliff and late in the evening he was already aboard the night train from Paddington railway station.

THREE
WESTCLIFF

Sitting with his back to the engine, Lynnford gazed along the line of carriages, watching with pleasant surprise as the early morning countryside rolled out like a newly laid carpet. Nine o'clock. He checked the time by his wristwatch. The Exeter train was approaching Westcliff; for some time it had been following the course of a river to its left. Suddenly, with a rush, the brown-green moor fell away, leaving in its place the open coastline. Lynnford looked to his left and saw the wide-open sky meeting with the sea in the distant horizon, a gigantic canvas painted in blues and greys. He pulled down the window. The fresh sea air smacked him in the face. He could almost taste the salty sea-spray. The rattling of the carriage wheels was very much louder now and somehow their crescendo, pounding in his heart, raised the sense of excitement as a new adventure unfolded before his eyes.

Two shots, one after the other, Sam had told him. So it could not have been an accident. He had been out walking on Sunday night along Watchman's View, around eleven o'clock, when he had heard them. At the time he had dismissed them. A farmer shooting vermin, he had preferred to think, he had told Lynnford. The body had been discovered early the next morning, floating in the sea, by a party of weekenders holidaying in a chalet in the cove and who had stayed over to Monday. An accident was the official story, but then why, Sam had asked Lynnford, had the body been so quickly put under lock and key. And no weapon. The empty yacht, the *Sea Breeze*, had been taken in tow to the harbour in Westcliff. Still, Sam had not told Lynnford everything. He had been holding something back whilst they had been talking on the telephone and Lynnford had been scribbling down notes, Lynnford was sure. Something that Sam had not wanted to articulate, something that Lynnford was certain was his friend's real concern. Sam had agreed to meet him off the train.

The train pulled into the station at Westcliff, the railway terminus, and halted amidst a squeal of brakes and a hiss of steam. A glass canopy supported by heavy iron girders painted in dark green spanned the three platforms.

Lynnford walked along the platform and through the ticket hall towards the exit, carrying his suitcase, looking around for the smooth jet-black hair and tall, slightly built frame of his friend without spotting him. He stopped inside the hall, put down his suitcase and consulted his watch again. Maybe the train had arrived early, or at least earlier than Sam expected. But no, it was Sam who had fixed the time. Nine-fifteen, and it had already gone nine twenty-one. He must have been held up in his shop and Lynnford decided to make his own way there, directly. He stopped a porter returning through the ticket hall with an empty trolley.

'Mortimer's newsagents?'

'In the high street?'

Lynnford nodded.

'Opposite the post office.'

The porter waved towards the open entrance.

'Left, across the bridge. Left again and up the hill. At the top, turn right.'

'Is there a taxi?'

'Most of us walk.'

The porter allowed Lynnford to detect a certain disdain.

Outside the station building, the sea, only twenty-five feet or so away across the promenade, was being whisked up by a strong wind; and Lynnford, standing at its edge, felt its tremendous power, tamed seemingly only superficially by the stone-walled sea defence that marked the boundary between land and sea. The air was clear and fresh. Two large grey and white seagulls descended onto the blue-painted railings of the promenade. They perched there, watchful, whilst their peers remained high up in the sky, circling and screeching at full cry.

Turning round to his left and looking up, he saw the town rise steeply before him, on the other side of the river mouth. Leaving the railway station, he started to walk towards a bridge that carried the road over the river. A short parapet, one or two feet high, ran the length of the bridge on either side, but not high enough to offer much protection against the wind blowing across it from the sea. The wind gusted around him, tugging furiously at his suitcase and at his raincoat, trying to work its way inside or, worse, topple him over.

Crossing the bridge and turning off the promenade, he started the steep climb amidst a mounting series of terraced side roads that fanned out along the hillside. The wind was now blowing behind him, pushing his coat against the backs of his legs.

*

Hiding like a wounded animal from its predator, Gwen Mortimer shivered with worry. He was there, standing on the pavement outside the newsagents; Sam's friend, Robert Lynnford. At least he had been a second ago when she had last peeped through the half-closed blind, some distance away from the glass lest he should detect her presence. The handle had rattled up and down some minutes earlier, the door resisting his pressure but the disturbance drawing her irresistibly forward, a hand nervously to her mouth ready to silence any unwanted cry. Crouching to one side of the door now, the side with the hinges so that, should it break open, she would remain protected, hidden, temporarily at least, she waited, her back to the wall, listening and hoping that he would tire and go away. But how long could she keep it up? She couldn't hide from him for ever.

In his early thirties, a suitcase on the ground next to his feet, Lynnford hadn't changed. The look of puzzlement as he stared at the front of the newsagents without seeing her had twisted her resolve. Nine-thirty gone; the shop should be open. What must he be thinking? Was she doing the right thing? Couldn't he just go away? Now!

A scrape of feet and voices, children's voices, caught her attention. Someone leant a bicycle against the wall, the rubber-covered handlebar seeming almost to touch her back. Oh no! He was talking to the children.

'Hello there. When does it open?'

'It's open!' the two voices rang out, almost colliding into the door. The handle rattled furiously.

'Careful! It's locked.'

'But it can't be.'

'Come on! Too bad. We'll be late,' a girl's voice warned.

Georgina and her brother, Gwen thought to herself. *Late again for school.* The bicycle was lifted off the wall and dragged away.

'Hold on!'

The girl and her brother stopped. Gwen imagined them looking up at Lynnford, impatiently, astride their bicycles, their feet flat on the pavement, waiting to go.

'The Harbour View Guest House. Have you heard of it?'

'Of course! That's Mrs Knight.'

The boy rang the bell on his handlebar as if confirming his sister's answer or, somehow, celebrating the landlady's name.

'And do you know where it might be?'

'We'll show you.'

'No, John, we're already late.'

Instead, the girl rushed out some simple directions before she and her brother hurriedly rode off, Lynnford's thanks trailing after them as he, too, walked away from the shop. Gwen Mortimer waited a few minutes before getting to her feet, aching slightly, and brushing the creases out of her clothes. She unlocked the door, raised the blind and looked across the street.

Yes, that other man who had been there before Lynnford had arrived was still there, pretending not to look her way. She didn't know how long he'd been there, but she had first spotted him standing on the pavement across the street, in front of the post office, when she had come down into the shop that morning, ready to open up, until, on seeing him, she had thought better of it and had left the shop door locked. She didn't recognise him. He wasn't local. Had it been his voice on the telephone? Whoever it might have been, the warning the caller had given her had been clear enough. Sam wasn't safe until Lynnford had been sent packing. At the time of the telephone call Sam had already been missing for an hour or so. Gwen had not seen Sam since. Why had Sam been so stupid? And what trouble had he got them into? Couldn't Robert Lynnford just go back to London and leave them alone? But she knew he wouldn't. Not if he was still the same. She sighed, exasperated, locking the door once again and bringing down the blind.

*

A detached Victorian house stood on a corner looking down towards the harbour below. Two square bay windows flanked the entrance. The heavy-looking front door was painted bright red and net curtains were hanging in the windows. Two separate signs spanned the porch; a small sign carrying the inscription "Bed and Breakfast", and a second larger sign with the words, "Harbour View Guest House" and underneath, "Mr and Mrs Peter Knight, registered proprietors, established 1930". Down in one of the ground-floor windows, a small white board was hanging with the word "Vacancies".

The door was open. Lynnford rang the bell and stepped inside. He was met by a woman in her late forties, rather short and broad, with dark curly hair. She was wearing a housecoat and holding a cloth which she was using to dry her hands as she walked towards him.

'Yes?'

The woman let the crumpled cloth fall on a nearby table placed under a mirror.

'Good morning. Mrs Knight?'

The woman nodded.

'Do you have a room? My name is Lynnford, Robert Lynnford. Sam Mortimer told me you might have a room.'

'Sam? Yes, of course. Come in. Please forgive the welcome. I'm in the middle of cleaning the kitchen. Just down from London?'

'Yes, that's right.'

'The train from Exeter is a nightmare, or so they tell me. Never had much call for it myself. I expect it was much worse coming all the way from London. Anyway, don't let me keep you waiting in the hall. I'll show you to your room.'

And Mrs Knight beckoned Lynnford to follow her up the stairs.

'You haven't seen him by any chance this morning?'

'Who?'

Mrs Knight turned round to look down at Lynnford on the stairs.

'Sam. He'd arranged to meet me at the station and the shop is closed.'

'Closed?'

'I've just come from there now.'

'Maybe Gwen, his wife, has been taken ill. She's been a bit off lately. At any rate, there's not much business for them at this time of day, once the morning rush is over.'

What rush can that be, so far from the metropolis, Lynnford mused as he continued up the stairs, following Mrs Knight into a room that led off the landing.

'It has a good view over the harbour.'

Mrs Knight was holding back the net curtain in order that he could better see.

'It does indeed,' he agreed.

The guest house commanded a dominating view over the rows of houses leading down to the seafront. To the left, a headland extended out into the sea.

'Watchman's View,' Mrs Knight explained, referring to the headland. 'So you're the newspaper man?'

She let the curtain fall back into place. Surprised, Lynnford feigned a clumsy look of ignorance.

'Sending a telegram from a small-town post office isn't the best way of keeping a secret, Mr Lynnford. All I'll tell you is don't come here upsetting things you don't understand. We can run our own business, thank you very much.'

'So some things are private, at least.'

She ignored his remark.

'The room is five and six a night.'

She pressed out the creases in her housecoat as she summed up her terms and conditions.

'You don't need to pay now. I'll take it when you leave. Breakfast is included. I can provide dinner. It'll be extra. You eat with us. But you must let me know at breakfast. Although, today I'll make an exception seeing as you've just arrived.'

'Yes, thank you. I think I will. I don't know how long I'll be staying. Maybe a few days. Possibly until Friday. Perhaps a little longer.'

'That's fine by me. The season has long since finished and you're the only guest, although we expect a couple of salesmen later in the week. Let me know if you need anything. I'll be in the kitchen.'

Left alone, Lynnford went back to the window and, gazing out over the town, wondered what had happened to Sam and his wife, Gwen.

FOUR
A SIMPLE AFFAIR

'Hello!' Lynnford called, standing outside the kitchen.

Mrs Knight was not alone. The gruff voice of a man, talking to himself, accompanied her steady counting aloud. She interrupted herself on hearing Lynnford and called out in reply, 'Come in!'

The kitchen was large and served for more than the preparation of food: office, laundry and workshop. Still wearing her housecoat, her cleaning finished, Mrs Knight was sitting at the kitchen table engaged in updating her accounts amidst a series of open ledgers lying on the table. A white colander, full of shelled peas, had been pushed to one side. Next to it, the pile of empty green pods lay on an old newspaper, for the moment unattended. Another table was piled high with laundry, neatly folded, with a basket of washed clothes ready for ironing on the floor.

'Just one more turn and that should do it.'

This from the man whose upper body was bent down under the sink and who, after a last gasp of effort, pushed himself out from under it and stood up. Mrs Knight looked up from her accounts.

'Oh! It's you, Mr Lynnford. Did you want something? This is my husband, Peter.'

She indicated the man standing beside her.

'Pleased to meet you, sir.'

Mr Knight smiled with some embarrassment.

'Excuse my hands. We're having a small problem with the waste pipe. Always troubling us it is.'

His shirt sleeves were rolled up to the elbow. Turning on one of the taps, he washed his hands rigorously under the cold water. 'A bad business,' he commented abruptly, his back to them. 'The man in the cove,' he explained.

'Nothing that we can't sort out ourselves, Peter.'

'Nothing that anyone will sort out if they have their way,' he retorted, adding, 'mind you, Mr Lynnford, it's a bad business but don't count on anyone in Westcliff to bother about it. Isn't that right, Joyce?'

'No it's not! You should be ashamed of talking like that in front of strangers. You heard what Sergeant Evans had to say, didn't you?'

'Him!' Mr Knight snorted with contempt.

'It was an accident,' Mrs Knight continued.

'My foot! Where's our trade going to go if we allow accidents like that? I'll tell you what's wrong with this town, Mr Lynnford. It's not the strangers but the people who live in it.'

'If the sink's fixed, Peter, you can get on with the garden. Mr Lynnford's not here to listen to us squabbling.'

'Please, I don't mean to be a nuisance.'

'Hah!' Mr Knight could not resist a loud guffaw as he strode across to the back door. 'When were newspapers never a nuisance?' he exclaimed, letting the door slam shut behind him.

'Sorry, I seem to have come at a bad moment,' Lynnford apologised.

'Don't mind my husband.'

'The police station, Mrs Knight, could you tell me how to get there?'

In the absence of Sam, Lynnford told himself, where else could he go for information about the reason why his friend had asked him to come down to Westcliff?

'Carry straight on up the hill. Turn left. It's opposite the church.'

'Thank you.'

Lynnford turned to go.

'Dinner is at six-thirty,' Mrs Knight called out after him.

*

'The sergeant is very busy.'

The constable in the police station looked doubtfully at Lynnford.

'Possibly, I might be able to help him,' Lynnford replied.

The uncertainty in the youthful officer's expression increased.

'And you are, exactly?'

'Lynnford, Robert Lynnford.'

'Mr Lynnford?'

The policeman's repetition, subtly transformed into a

question, made clear his expectation of something more informative.

'If I might take down the details, sir?'

And, as if to underline his meaning, the constable opened the large register lying on the counter in front of him, ignoring Lynnford's impatient sigh. But, before any further procrastination was possible, they were interrupted by the arrival of the station's sergeant walking into the lobby with a gust of wind scuttling in on his heels.

'Quiet morning, Constable? Good day, sir.'

Walking behind Lynnford, the sergeant rattled out his pleasantries, his footfalls resonating loudly on the stone floor. Raising the hatch set in the counter he folded it back on its hinges and passed through to the other side.

Heavier than the constable and with a well-developed stomach, the sergeant's uniform was impeccable and buttoned up to his neck. Three large white stripes were emblazoned on each coat sleeve. Loosening the strap from under his neck, he removed the helmet he had been wearing and placed it on the counter.

'Well then, what have we here?'

The sergeant seemed to heave up the words from the depths of his stomach but still with the ease of someone accustomed to exercising untrammelled authority.

'The gentleman would like to see you.'

'Really? Well, here I am. What can I do for you, sir?'

'The sailor in Sandy Cove.'

'I beg your pardon?'

'I heard the body of a dead sailor had been fished out of Sandy Cove yesterday morning.'

'That's correct.'

'And I was wondering what progress you had made.'

'Progress?'

'Have you been able to identify the body yet?'

'No, not yet. And what's your interest? I didn't catch your name.'

'Lynnford, Robert Lynnford,' Lynnford replied. 'So, not a local then? The dead sailor,' he added.

'No, not at all. Like you, sir.'

'And any idea why?'

'Why what?'

'Why he was killed?'

'Is it any of your business?'

'Nothing secret is there?'

'Certainly nothing that a nosey newspaper man from London needs to know about.'

'From London! How did you guess, Sergeant?'

'I didn't guess, Constable. Can't you see the grime? And smell, if you've no eyes.'

'There's no need to be offensive, officer.' Lynnford lowered the tone with an engaging smile.

'Each to their own, sir,' the sergeant replied, adding, 'I don't see any need for strangers to interfere in my business. Least of all the London press. Good day to you.'

So saying, the sergeant turned his back and opened the door to an office behind the counter. Yet no sooner had he done so than he jumped back in shock. With a screech and a vigorous flap of wings that brushed a strong set of feathers against his ear and the side of his face, the bird, whose heavy weight had just landed on the policeman's shoulder, released its claws and hurtled back into the air, through the doorway and into the station lobby.

'Ouch!' The sergeant could not resist the exclamation of surprise and mild pain.

A parrot! The blue feathers spanned out, balancing its short flight and bringing it to rest on a filing cabinet in the far corner of the lobby. The bird sat perched on the edge of the cabinet, eyeing the three men disdainfully with its head cocked to one side, its blue-feathered wings brought down along its sides, cloaking a bright yellow and red chest. A white mask circled its face, setting off a shiny beak.

'Not a suspect, Sergeant, I hope?' Lynnford smiled with irony.

'What? No, of course not.'

Still ruffled by the shock, the police officer had recovered himself sufficiently to start trying to tempt back the bird. Looking up to it, he held out some seeds in the palm of his hand, calling less than patiently to it, 'Polly, Polly, come on down.'

'It's a beautiful bird,' Lynnford remarked, observing the pantomime.

'And very expensive, so they say, sir,' the constable joined in.

The parrot turned its head away but then bent down, putting its beak in the sergeant's open hand only to then, with a squawk, shake it from side to side, scattering the seeds in all directions. The sergeant took his hand away quickly with an oath, letting the remaining seeds fall to the floor.

'Apparently they don't take to new owners,' the constable explained.

'Has it been lost?'

'She was all we found on the *Sea Breeze*.'

'That will do, Constable,' the sergeant interrupted.

'Along with the dead sailor,' Lynnford added, addressing the sergeant this time.

'He was in the water.'

'The bird or the sailor?'

The sergeant did not reply.

'Perhaps you'd have preferred that they had killed the bird and not the sailor, Sergeant?'

'Listen, Mr Lynnford, there hasn't been a murder.'

'Two shots, no weapon and an empty boat. Surely, your detectives must be busy investigating what happened.'

'There hasn't been a murder.'

The irritation provoked initially by the bird's escape now continued to bristle over the sergeant's face at Lynnford's unwelcome persistence.

'An accident until proof to the contrary. Let's see what the coroner finds,' he added.

'And so do you have a date for the inquest?'

'Everything's in hand. It's a simple affair that us simple folk in Westcliff can sort out without your help, sir. Now, good day to you. I'm sure you'll be wanting your morning cup of tea.'

*

Captain Jacobs, sitting with his back to the fire in a terraced house down by the harbour, let his hand run through his beard whilst he examined with a puzzled air the three passports set out on the table in front of him. The light in the room was poor. He was still unsettled by the events of Sunday evening when he and his men had boarded the *Sea Breeze*, mistaking it for the yacht they had been expecting, the *Sea Bird*.

'We have the woman. That's one passport, a Dutch passport. Anna Chessington, *née* Braam. Chessington, that's an English name. It rings a bell, but I can't place it,' he mused aloud for the benefit of his two companions.

'The second Dutch passport belongs to the sailor who's dead. And thanks to Tabby's stupidity, he won't be coming back for the woman. This is his passport. So, where is this man?' Jacobs asked, indicating the third passport. 'Alfred Chessington, British and married to the woman. That name, why can't I place it?'

It was Tuesday. A day had gone by since the mess-up in Sandy Cove but there was still no sign of the man to whom the passport belonged. Maybe he hadn't been aboard the yacht, but it seemed unlikely.

'What makes you think he's still hanging around, Jacobs?'

'The woman, Pengal. And the yacht.'

Pengal had recognised straight away in the passport photograph the man to whom he had handed the stolen necklace, the Exmoor Jubilee, outside the big house up on the headland on Sunday evening but he wasn't going to say anything about that to Jacobs. It wasn't his business. Still, like Captain Jacobs, Pengal was wondering what could have happened to him. Why hadn't he gone to the police when he'd seen what had happened aboard his boat? Something was amiss but he hadn't shared his concerns with the captain, asking, simply, 'And what do you think you'll get out of him?'

'Well, her off our hands for a start.'

'I can do that right now, no problem.'

'That's not our way, Pengal,' Jacobs retorted. 'And, anyway, we've been told to keep her here. Why did you ever come back to Westcliff, Pengal?'

The other's reply was lost in a raucous bout of coughing that made him double up in pain. The captain and the third man in the room looked on, waiting for it to end.

'Why did you give Tabby the gun, Pengal?'

Pengal stared back at the third man in the room, a blood-stained handkerchief in his hands and scorn in his eyes.

'Well, Kenny, there's a new world out there. It's no longer yo ho ho and a bottle of rum, three bags full, sir. Isn't that so, Jacobs?'

'And what were you up to on Sunday night, Pengal? Leaving us to ourselves. That's what I'd like to know,' Jacobs asked. 'Maybe we wouldn't have bungled the boat and mixed up the names if you'd been there.'

'Very true, but it wasn't anything that concerns any of you. Personal business, see?'

'Maybe, Pengal. We'll see about it later.'

Captain Jacobs stacked up the passports like a hand of cards and slipped them into his pocket.

'For now, let's not forget what we're about. Everything else is going to plan. The *Sea Bird*'s now in Sandy Cove, we've taken off the goods that Skinner brought in with her and the crates to be loaded aboard will arrive this evening. Kenny, you'll take us all up to the tower in your van.'

'You're a fool to leave the woman in the cave, Jacobs.'

'She's safe enough, Pengal.'

Pengal gave another cough, short and dry this time.

'It's me I'm worried about. Not her.'

'So you should, Pengal. Now shut up and leave me alone with your damned croaking.'

FIVE
A BRUISING ENCOUNTER

Back down on the waterfront, Lynnford looked out across the old harbour, taking in the white silhouette of the *Sea Breeze* moored alongside the harbour master's office; a single-storey timber building with a red and white pennant flying from the top of its pointed roof. He had still not found Sam, or his wife, Gwen. Concern was beginning to eat away at him and, indeed, the disappearance of his friend, to whom he had spoken not much more than eighteen hours earlier, was beginning to worry him more than Sam's own story of the dead sailor and of the empty yacht before him.

He had just come down from a long spell outside Sam's newsagents with no sign of life within. Nobody who he had asked had been able to explain why the shop was closed or where Sam and Gwen might be. Ill or asleep in their flat above the shop, someone had suggested. Nobody had seemed too concerned. On walking down the hill, a fisherman had

40

pointed out to him the *Sea Breeze* in the harbour, tied up alongside the harbour master's office.

The wind had dropped. The sun was shining strongly, bathing the harbour in an air of tranquil security. Held in by the harbour walls, the sea water lapped quietly as it swelled lightly against the fishing boats, free of their previous night's catch and now anchored down in the mud bed below; the captured water gently pushing them up and down. The air was fresh with a cold edge. Lynnford breathed in deeply, submerging his senses with its smell and pungent, salty taste.

A movement caught his eye. On the far side of the harbour a man's head had surfaced from the deck of one of the fishing boats. The man looked around, as if to reassure himself that nothing had changed since he'd last been on deck, and then dropped out of sight again, back down below deck, leaving Lynnford once more alone with his thoughts.

Still with Sam uppermost in his mind, he turned his attention back to the *Sea Breeze*. Not too large. A cabin was raised above the deck in its centre, with a single mast poking up into the air, high above the roof of the harbour master's office. A heavy-looking beam went back from the mast almost to the boat's stern where there was a cockpit with a wheel.

'A fine boat, that she is.'

Lynnford turned round, a little surprised, as he had thought himself alone.

'She's a beauty to handle, so the coastguard tells me. And I can fair believe it.'

A tallish, thin man in his forties had joined Lynnford, leaning against the railings a yard or so further along. He was wearing a blue jacket over a heavy white woollen jumper, rolled up to his neck. A black-peaked captain's hat was perched on the back of his head. A cold pipe was jammed between his teeth.

'You'll be wanting to take her away. Is that it?'

'I'm sorry?'

'The yacht,' explained the man.

Lynnford smiled.

'I'm afraid she's not mine. Although I'm sorry for that.'

'I thought that you being a stranger like, and that you seemed to be taking such an interest in her, you might have come to claim her.'

'Why? Has she been abandoned?'

Lynnford feigned ignorance and the man nodded. Lynnford continued, 'That's a strange place to abandon a boat, up alongside the harbour master's office.'

'That's my office. I'm the harbour master, Mr Yeats.'

'Indeed? Well, good afternoon to you, sir.'

Lynnford raised his hat and introduced himself. The harbour master knocked the bowl of his pipe against the cast-iron post standing between them.

'You must be the newspaper man, then?'

'Word gets around quickly.'

The harbour master replenished his pipe, releasing a cloud of smoke through his mouth once he had relit it. He seemed in no hurry and more than ready to talk.

'So, you're a friend of Sam Mortimer?' he continued.

'That's right.'

'A good man. He and his wife have the newsagents in the high street.'

Lynnford turned the conversation back to the *Sea Breeze*.

'It's a fine boat. You said it handles well?'

'I did. It's a Danish cruising yacht. Only a few years old by the looks of it. Forty feet long at the water-line. A lot of space inside with berths for six but easy for a crew of two, even one, to handle. Look, the rig is very compact.'

The harbour master paused again as if inhaling, with the tobacco smoke, the information and reflecting on it himself. Glancing about him as they talked, Lynnford noticed out of the corner of his eye another man, this time standing on the opposite pavement, looking his way. Before he could really make him out, the man had quickly turned away. Heading off in the direction of the railway station, he soon disappeared up one of the side roads, leaving Lynnford with the uncomfortable feeling of having been observed. Mr Yeats seemed to have also noticed the man but made no comment.

'So you'll know about the body?' he asked, instead.

'The dead sailor? Yes, that's what interested Sam.'

'An accident, that's what the police say.'

'I've just come from the police station.'

'Of course you have. Or it could have been suicide. Why not? It can be a lonely life, sailor.'

'True,' replied Lynnford, 'out there in the middle of the ocean. I never fancied having to bail out over the sea, I can tell you.'

Mr Yeats looked up, interest in his eyes. 'Pilot?'

Lynnford nodded and returned to the dead sailor.

'But there were two gunshots, weren't there? That can't be suicide.'

The harbour master shrugged.

'Maybe he missed the first time! Anyway, it's not my business. It's for the police. They must know what they're doing.'

'Still.'

'It's a small town, Mr Lynnford. Don't ask too many questions.'

'And where is his body now?'

'Over there. In my office. Or at least, in the storeroom.'

'Really? Isn't there somewhere better? A morgue?'

'They'll take it there tomorrow. They've only just fished him out, poor devil.'

'A little too casual, don't you think?'

The harbour master shrugged again.

'As I said, we're a small town, Mr Lynnford. Don't expect too much of us.'

'So what about the boat, is it from here?'

The harbour master shook his head.

'She comes from a Dutch port, Rotterdam most likely. The police are waiting for something concrete from the Dutch authorities. But so far nothing's come in.'

'A missing Dutchman, then?'

'Most likely.'

'What about the logbook?'

'It's missing. In fact they found nothing of interest on board except, I bet you can't guess what.'

'A parrot.'

'How did you guess?'

'Sergeant Evans has already introduced me!'

'Yes, of course!'

The harbour master laughed and Lynnford noticed some fresh bruising to his face.

'Have you been in a fight, Mr Yeats?'

The harbour master put his hand to his cheek.

'Oh you know, the harbour's a rough place, full of thieves and smugglers!' he replied with a smile.

The harbour master leant back on the large rusty oil barrel behind him and took a little weight off his feet. He continued drawing on his pipe, puffing out little clouds of white smoke from time to time. He continued, 'An exceptional bird. Electric blue feathers and a yellow and red chest. As tall as my forearm. She almost took off the poor coastguard's hand.'

Their conversation moved on and after several minutes discussing the size of the morning's catch, fish prices and the upkeep of the harbour, Lynnford decided to take his leave. In return, the harbour master gave a little salute before turning his attention back to the sea, his own thoughts going nervously back to Sunday evening. The bungled loss of the necklace still made him angry, but more worrying was the disappearance of Freddie Chessington. What could have happened to him? He could only hope that the second gunshot had been for him. But then where was his body? And the gunshots had come very soon after their scuffle. He had to be hiding somewhere. And if he was alive, it wouldn't be long before he would come after him. Well, he would be ready for him. Until then, he had to keep a cool mind.

*

Walking quickly along the promenade, Lynnford headed towards the headland that separated the town from Sandy Cove, Watchman's View. Mrs Knight had told him of a path that would take him quickly across the headland and down into the cove; the path that Sam must have taken on Sunday evening. Arriving, however, at a boatyard at the end of the promenade with the rocky cliff face rising up behind it, he realised that he would have to find some other way. He looked around for someone to ask but the boatyard, although full of boats drawn up on wooden supports, was otherwise deserted. He decided to retrace his steps.

It had already gone three o'clock and the public house that he had spotted earlier on his way along the promenade, The Blue Harp, was closed. Still, as he approached it, a side door opened, and a young man came out carrying a crate of empty bottles. The crate fell with a crash onto a similar crate outside the door. Oblivious to the clatter, the young man was about to turn back inside when Lynnford held him up.

'Hello there! Excuse me!'

The man turned round.

'Can you tell me how to get onto the headland? There's a path that'll take me over to Sandy Cove, isn't there? Where can I pick it up?'

'Go up to the high street and turn right. Where the road turns away to the left once the shops end, you'll see a stile. There's a sign pointing to Sandy Cove. The footpath goes all the way. You can't miss it.'

'Thank you.'

'Here, you can go this way.'

The lad pointed to an alley running alongside the public house.

'It'll save you walking all the way round. Turn left at the top.'

A gutter ran down the middle of the cobbled alley. A cast-iron bollard had been erected at the entrance to stop traffic making use of it as a shortcut. Halfway up, he heard the crash of another crate of bottles, making him turn round. The young man and the side entrance of The Blue Harp were lost from sight. He was, however, not alone. A man in sweater and loose corduroy jacket was walking up behind him. A fisherman, Lynnford guessed. His pace seemed to have slowed on seeing Lynnford look over his shoulder, but he was not certain. The noise from the crashing bottles could just as well have caught the man's attention as it had Lynnford. He carried on up the alley, pursued all the time by the sound of the other man's boots echoing his own footfalls.

Twenty yards or so from the top, a woman came into view, walking past the opening on the other side of the rusting metal barrier. A familiar silhouette. Surprised, he realised who it was.

'Gwen!' he cried out.

Distracted, the woman turned to look briefly down the alley. Her hair, tied in a bun and protected from the wind by a light headscarf, framed the practical, no-nonsense air of Sam's wife. It had to be her, but she seemed not to recognise Lynnford and turned away, carrying on along the pavement and disappearing from view. He began running lightly, in an attempt to catch up with her.

Gaining the top, and just about to turn into the road, he almost collided with someone but it wasn't Gwen. It was another man, but also someone he recognised; the man who he had spotted earlier when he had been talking with the harbour master, Mr Yeats. Now he could see him properly. His face seemed to cover his head. Hairless and strongly featured, he was surely bald under his cap. But there was no recognition in his eyes, only a malicious smile that gave Lynnford no time to avoid the hefty push that sent him off balance and staggering several paces backwards into the grasping hold of the man who had come up behind him. A sharp kick to the knee brought him to the ground and a succession of blows rained down on him, into his back and stomach. All he could do was cover his head with his hands, but not sufficiently to withstand the piercing blow from a bottle swung at him from behind.

'That's enough!'

The voice seemed a million miles away but the torment stopped instantly. Someone leant over him, panting heavily, his breath close to Lynnford's face, smelling sour.

'Now go back to London and leave us alone,' the voice whispered close to his ear. 'He wasn't from here, the dead sailor, so no one cares about him. Get it? Just like you, see?'

Unconscious, Lynnford heard no more; unaware that he had been left alone.

SIX
GWEN AGREES TO HELP

The shops were already preparing to close when, an hour or so later, Lynnford, after staggering to his feet and out of the alley, reached the top of the hill and entered the high street. Passing by a butcher's, he glimpsed within two men dressed in white coats with blue and white-striped aprons speckled with dirty red stains and capped with round-edged straw hats busily engaged in clearing and wiping down the heavy marble slabs of the window display. And behind them, in the brightly lit shop, the light reflecting off the white-tiled walls, a woman similarly attired was occupied serving a final customer. The sense of normality was reassuring, giving Lynnford a sense of safety. A few shops further on, he spotted the post office and opposite it, Sam and Gwen's shop, squeezed between a florist and a gentlemen's tailors. The sign on the board running the length of the shop's short frontage read, "Mortimer's: Newsagents, Fine tobacco,

Stationery and Confectionery". A man walked out of the shop. It was open!

A bell tinkled as Lynnford closed the door behind him. It was a real Aladdin's cave. Every possible space was filled with something: the counter, the shelves, the drawers and even the walls and the ceiling. The counter presided in the middle of the shop but with only a little space left free on which to transact business. On either side of it were stacked packets of cigarettes, lighters, pipes, pipe cleaners, matches and tins and pouches of loose tobacco. In front, and on the shelves behind, stood rows of bottled sweets. Everything to tempt the customer was on display, only that the remaining space was so small that serving anything that was not within immediate reach required the utmost dexterity.

Gwen was occupied with a woman holding a handbag tightly under her arm. Yes, it was her that he'd seen. She was trying to dislodge a children's puzzle placed on a shelf high up on the wall, close to the ceiling. For this she was using a long pole with a small metal hook attached to the end; poking at the end of the box to which was fixed a small metal ring that had been stuck on with Sellotape. The effort was exercising her patience.

'Hello, Gwen, do you want a hand?'

She did not reply, ignoring Lynnford. With a final twist of the pole, she caught hold of the box and, a little recklessly, brought it down.

'There you are, Mrs Williams. One second and I'll wrap it up for you.'

Walking back to the counter she turned to stare coldly at Lynnford but this quickly transformed into a look of shock, and she made faces to him to keep out of the way. Once more behind the counter she pulled off the metal ring from the box and then began rolling out a sheet of brown paper with an air of forced concentration, carefully wrapping up the puzzle and handing it to the woman.

'That'll be four shillings.'

Gwen took the money with a distracted air as she accompanied the woman to the door and saw her out, pulling down the blind and locking the door after her.

'Lynnford!' she cried, aghast. 'What happened to you?'

'I'm all right, Gwen. Just cuts and bruises. I've had worse.'

He gave his clothes a brush down as he spoke, as if to dismiss the incident, and added, 'Nothing more than a little roughing up. Sam told you I was coming, didn't he?'

'Yes he did, but you can't stay.'

She turned her head as she spoke, pushing up the sleeves of her cardigan and wringing her hands nervously.

'What's wrong, Gwen? Where's Sam?'

'Nothing's wrong. Sam's fine. We're both fine.'

'But where is he? Why have you been closed all day?'

'What are you talking about? I've been open all day. Why should we be closed?'

Lynnford shook his head, slowly.

'What's wrong, Gwen? Something's wrong. Where's Sam?'

'You can't stay.'

'But where's Sam, Gwen?'

'You shouldn't have come.'

'Why not? What's going on? He was supposed to meet me at the station this morning. I spoke to him yesterday afternoon. The shop was shut up all morning. I came up here.'

'Can't you hear what I'm saying?'

Gwen's hands, released from their agitated embrace, slammed flat down on the hard wooden counter.

'Just keep away. Leave us alone.'

She stared back at him defiantly for a moment or two, before dropping her head and raising her hands in a convulsion of tears; yet shrugging away from Lynnford's attempt to console her.

'Please, Robert, just go.'

'Gwen, tell me what's going on.'

'I don't know. The whole town's gone mad. We should never have come back.'

'Back?'

Gwen nodded.

'This is where I grew up. The chance came up of this shop and Sam couldn't leave London quick enough.'

'And where is he now, Gwen?'

Gwen closed her eyes with a sigh.

'I don't know.'

And she reached out across the counter, taking one of the packets of cigarettes and breaking it open.

'I spoke to him only yesterday, as I said.'

'I know. I haven't seen him since.'

'Gwen, this is ridiculous! What's happening?'

'They're watching the shop. They must have seen you come in. God knows what's happened to him already. I don't know what they're up to, but Sam must have sniffed out something. They're mad at him for having brought you down.'

'Who, Gwen? Who?'

'Everyone! I don't know who. The man outside. No, he's gone now. Let's hope so.'

She seemed tired all of a sudden, a release of exhaustion. She continued, 'I should, but I don't. Someone, I couldn't recognise the voice, telephoned last night threatening Sam's life if I talked to you.'

'A bluff?'

'Not anymore. Things have changed. Look at you, and how long have you been here? A few hours only!'

'Have you gone to the police?'

'And tell them what?'

'That Sam's missing.'

Gwen laughed.

'And that's just what Sergeant Evans will say. Your old man's gone missing. He'll be back soon enough when he wants his dinner.'

'Gwen, don't worry. We'll find him. It's just a bluff. I'm sure. They just want to keep him away from me. Stop me talking to him. He knows something they don't want him to tell me.'

'I hope you're right. You know, the worst thing about the War is that it stopped.'

'Gwen!'

'Peace! It's only brought violent men home.'

'Not everyone, Gwen.'

'Let's hope not. Anyway, it's too late now.'

She shook her head as if events were out of her hands.

'You're here. You'd better come upstairs and let me see to those cuts.'

Gwen lifted the wooden flap of the counter and beckoned Lynnford through to a narrow set of stairs that led up to the flat above the shop. Piles of unsold newspapers tied with string were stacked on the floor, along with half-opened boxes of cigarettes.

Sitting on the edge of the bath and stripped to the waist, Lynnford winced as Gwen dabbed gently the different cuts to his face and arms with cotton wool soaked in antiseptic liquid. A dark purple bruise around the small of his back seemed to have a life of its own.

'You'd better get that seen to.'

'There's nothing broken.'

'You don't know.'

'I was speaking to the harbour master before I got jumped on.'

'My God, it wasn't him!'

'No. But he looked like he'd been in a bit of a fight too. He mentioned thieves and smugglers, although I believe he was joking.'

'Listen, Robert, the police here, you can't expect too much from them. At least not if it's tied up with local smuggling.'

'Isn't that their job? Aren't they supposed to be dealing with it?'

'Yes, but we might as well have turned the clock back several centuries for all the difference they make. They tolerate it, Robert, unless it gets out of control. It's what makes the town tick. They know that.'

'Well, it seems to have done just that, got out of hand, I mean.'

Gwen pulled a face, saying nothing.

'Smuggling? Is that why Sam brought me down? Is that what it's all about?'

'I don't know.'

'Listen, Gwen. I need to get aboard the *Sea Breeze* and look it over. See if I can find something that might help explain what's going on. Can you give me a hand?'

'Lynnford, the doctor!'

'The boat first. So?'

'I don't know.'

Gwen bit her lip.

'Gwen, our best chance of helping Sam is to understand why he brought me to Westcliff.'

'Nobody brought you here, Robert.'

'Perhaps not, but still it was Sam's idea.'

Gwen hesitated, still doubtful.

'What do you want me to do?'

'Keep an eye out whilst I'm on the boat. Nothing more. I don't want the harbour master surprising me should he decide to take an evening stroll to inspect the harbour.'

'Oh, I don't think you need fear that.'

'And I shall need a torch and a pair of thick socks or better still boat shoes. These brogues of mine would make too much noise.'

'I'm not sure about the shoes. But the torch and socks are no problem. What time?'

'Let's make it seven-thirty. Does that suit you?'

'That gives you just over an hour. You'd better get a move on.'

'Wouldn't it be better that I stay here with you? Just in case.'

'It'll be worse if you stay any longer. You don't want to give the Knights in the guest house anything to talk about. I'll make a scene as I throw you out. That'll put anyone out there, if there is anyone, off the scent. Here, let me help you with your shirt.'

Downstairs in the shop, Gwen opened the door and Lynnford felt her hand push him out. Losing balance, he fell to the ground and heard the door slam shut. Nothing said, but the message was clear should anyone be watching. He winced. His wounds were still raw. He got to his feet and brushed down his clothes for the second time that day.

SEVEN
ABOARD THE *SEA BREEZE*

At twenty-five minutes past seven that evening, Lynnford met Gwen, who was waiting for him at the same spot where he had been talking with the harbour master in the afternoon.

'Here you are.'

She handed him a small packet. Her tone was impatient. Inside there was a heavy-duty cylindrical torch and a pair of thick woollen socks.

'Still no sign of Sam?'

Gwen shook her head.

'Will they do?'

'Perfect,' Lynnford replied.

'Let's get going, then.'

The promenade was deserted and cast in darkness. The only lights came from The Blue Harp. The air was cold and damp, and became progressively more so as he and Gwen left the shelter of the promenade and allowed the harbour's eastern quay to project them into a state of splendid isolation, away from the promenade and with the sea water almost surrounding them. Only the noise of the water below, quietly lapping the stone walls of the quay, betrayed its presence and the reality of the world around them.

They ducked underneath a police cordon and walked up alongside the *Sea Breeze*. The boat was rocking gently in the water, its side riding up and down two large rubber tyres that must have come from an old lorry and were now being used to stop the sides of the boat from scraping against the quay wall.

Lynnford sat down, dangling his legs over the side. The cold stone surface of the quay felt damp through his trousers and against the palms of his hands. Replacing his shoes with the socks that Gwen had given him, he tied together the laces and hung them around his neck. Gwen watched in silence. As he let himself down onto the boat's deck, she moved away a few paces, just sufficiently so that she could keep in view both the boat and the length of the quay leading back to the promenade.

Dropping down onto the deck of the yacht, the quay wall now above him, he did not waste any time. Seeking out the cabin door, he grasped the round wooden doorknob in his hand, pulling it towards him. The action had little effect. The door gave a little in the centre but held firmly at the top and bottom. Flicking the torch on, he quickly inspected the door and saw that two bolt locks had been fitted to it; the bottom one secured by a small padlock.

With his free hand he felt inside his pocket and pulled

out two fine metal picks. Working these tools inside the lock, he quickly released the mechanism, and the metal barrel of the lock sprang open. Slipping off the padlock, he slid across the bolt, and then the second. Stepping down into the dark cabin, he turned round and brought the door to without a sound.

He stood in pitch blackness. He flashed on the torch and swung the light around the galley cabin. It was not large. Two wooden benches ran port and starboard, and in the middle was a small square table. The table was bare, as was the rest of the galley. *It must have been cleaned up*, thought Lynnford, as he passed the torchlight methodically around the cabin a second time, lighting up the dark corners. From the galley there was little to show that anyone had ever been aboard. Fore and aft, two small cabins were each fitted with a single bed and a bunk bed with some items of clothing in a locker under one of them, one or two shirts and an old sweater thrown carelessly into the drawer. A tall perch stood in one corner, surrounded by a mess of bird seeds and droppings. *The parrot!* Lynnford smiled to himself. In the second, a canvas bag, the sort typically used by sailors, was propped up against the end of the bed. Lynnford placed the torch on the mattress and carefully emptied the bag. Its contents had been neatly packed. Some clothes and a small toiletry bag containing only a razor, soap and a toothbrush. Whoever it was had, for some reason, preferred to keep his clothes packed in the bag rather than in the locker under the bed, which was empty. Lynnford replaced everything in the bag and stood it back up against the end of the bed.

Outside, up on the quay, Gwen was getting cold. With nothing to do but watch and wait, she was getting irritable, her worries over Sam preying on her. The sound of footsteps made her start; footfalls rubbing leather sole against the gritty stone surface of the quay. Squinting in front of her, along the quay, she thought she could make out a vague form, but nothing more. With a slight movement of her foot she knocked an empty tin can over the side. It banged noisily onto the boat and then rolled off, falling into the water with a splash.

'What's that? Hello there.'

A torchlight flashed briefly in Gwen's face.

'Oh, it's you, Gwen Mortimer.'

The light went out and she saw before her the anxious face of the harbour master. *What's made him come out this evening*, she wondered.

'Good evening, Mr Yeats. How are you?'

'Fine, Mrs Mortimer. Did you hear that?'

'What?'

'I thought I heard something.'

'I'm sorry. That was me. It was just an old tin can I kicked out of the way.'

She looked apologetic.

The harbour master walked past her and shone his torch over the walls of his office and then down onto the deck of the *Sea Breeze*.

'What brings you out here, Mrs Mortimer?'

'I don't know. Sam's not come home.'

'You won't find him here. Didn't you see the cordon?'

Gwen heaved a sigh.

'What do you think, Mr Yeats? That I'm going to sail the boat away in the middle of the night?'

'No, of course not, but this damp air's not going to do you any good. Come along. Sam will turn up soon enough.'

He rubbed his hands vigorously together.

'Let's go back into the warmth. I'll stand you a Scotch in The Blue Harp.'

'No, I'd better be going home, Mr Yeats. Thank you all the same.'

*

Sam woke with a start, breathing heavily through his nostrils. The blindfold around his head and the tape over his mouth were hurting him. He must have dozed off. Yet through the ebbing drowsiness, he recalled the sound of a familiar voice. It had been a woman's voice speaking to a man, almost above him it had seemed. *Gwen!* And he tried now to call out her name but his lips stuck in the tape around his mouth. He strained his legs, trying to find the strength to stand, but a chain stopped him. The voices had receded and Sam hit the floor with his bare heels in frustration. And, despite the darkness, he knew where he was being kept! He was in the hold of a fishing boat that was tied up alongside the quay in Westcliff. There could be no doubt about it. The timbers around him were impregnated with the smell of fish and he had felt the fall and rise of the boat with the tide whilst, from time to time, the clear sounds of the harbour had drifted across the water to him in his prison. No one had come to see him since his capture and he was now starving with hunger.

Some distance away from him, up on the quay and behind the harbour master's office, three figures crouching in the dark relaxed on hearing the receding footsteps of the harbour master and Gwen Mortimer.

*

Lynnford, standing motionless down in the galley of the *Sea Breeze*, also heard the footsteps recede with relief. The search of the boat had so far produced little of interest. Most of what there had been must have been carried off, he guessed, and either taken to the police station or stored in the harbour master's office. He pushed to one side a hatch that gave access to a narrow kitchen. It was clean and tidy. In a drawer, there were a few utensils and in another, a set of metal plates. A cupboard contained a few tins of food and an open packet of coffee. He reached inside and picked up one of the tins and examined the label. It was not in English, possibly Dutch or Danish. He wasn't sure. About to replace it, he noticed the corner of a card poking out from behind the remaining cans and leaning against them. Putting down the tin, he retrieved the card, realising instantly on touching it his mistake. The sharp edges and smooth surface could only be a photograph. What luck!

But his heart took another beat. Muffled noises from somewhere close by drew his attention again. Someone else or perhaps even two or three people were outside on the harbour quay, moving silently around. They seemed to be struggling with a load. He switched off his torch and waited. Thankfully, they were not approaching the *Sea Breeze*. The silence returned. More discreetly this time, he flicked on the torch, shielding its light so that he could examine the photograph.

The shades of white and grey revealed a young man and woman sitting astride two bicycles in the sunshine. They had stopped for the pose, and their feet were planted firmly on the ground. Both had broad smiles and looked very happy. The man, in a light jacket and trousers with an open cotton shirt, and who Lynnford guessed to be about thirty or thirty-one, was bent forward with his hands on the handlebar. The woman, who looked much younger, in her early twenties, was standing upright. She was wearing a blouse and summer skirt. There were some buildings in the background, but he could not make them out. He turned over the photograph, and on the white reverse side was scribbled a date: 1936.

Lynnford flicked the glossy paper between his fingers. Who were they? They could be anybody. Smugglers didn't usually leave family snapshots lying around. Still, it was something. He slipped it into his inside pocket and, taking one last look around the galley, stepped up onto the deck, closing the door behind him and securing the lock.

The quay was now deserted. Whoever he'd just heard had gone. Gwen and the harbour master had long since disappeared. And he had hoped for a hand from Gwen to lift him up onto the quayside! He reached up and rested his fingers on the cold slabs. His arms were not quite at full stretch, yet too much to give him an easy pull upwards. He looked around for some other option and his eyes fell on the two large rubber tyres lining the quay wall and which offered a sort of step up from the yacht's deck, albeit a moving one.

Steadying himself, with his two stockinged feet on the rough tread of one of the tyres, he reached up again to the edge of the quayside, tightening the muscles in both arms, the injuries from the afternoon still hurting, and, pressing firmly on his hands, slowly pulled himself up. But, turning to swing his legs over and up onto the quayside, an arm gave way, his hand slipped, and he fell down on his chest, his right leg slipping down the wall, almost pulling the rest of his body with it. He felt his leg sting with pain. And then another sound struck his consciousness, the splash of oars. Was that them? The people who he'd heard moving around before? The noise seemed to be coming from outside the harbour, on the other side of the quay but he wasn't sure. He just needed to get away as quickly as possible and hope he hadn't been spotted. Pushing all his weight as far over as he could, he struggled to retain his balance and lift himself fully back onto the quay. A little winded by the fall, he stood up and, after having struggled back into his shoes, walked towards the promenade and the flickering lights of The Blue Harp.

*

'What happened to you?'

The harbour master was sitting at the bar and had called Lynnford over with a friendly salute on seeing him enter the public house.

'What do you mean?'

Mr Yeats pointed at Lynnford's leg.

'You look like you've had a nasty fall. And your face is not in such a good state either. Are you all right?'

Lynnford looked down and noticed for the first time that his trousers were ripped around the knee of the right leg. A small flap of material hung down one side and a damp-looking, dirty patch surrounded the tear. As if it had just happened, Lynnford became aware of a dull, throbbing pain in his leg.

'Oh, it's nothing. I slipped over just now, crossing the road and hit the kerbstone. Damned silly thing to do. But I don't think there's any real damage.'

He shrugged off the matter. The harbour master smiled, patting Lynnford on the shoulder in a gesture of sympathy.

'So, still on your own?'

The Blue Harp was quiet. Not that it was empty. The room seemed to absorb sound, as if the very walls soaked it up. It was in fact quite full; the regulars sitting around tables or huddled together in wooden alcoves. The bar was lined with men in small groups. One or two sitting alone, quietly smoking, half lost in their thoughts. The young man from the afternoon was not behind the bar.

Lynnford shook his head, not understanding the harbour master's question.

'Sam and Gwen Mortimer. Aren't you with them?'

Lynnford shook his head again.

'No, not this evening. Tell me, Mr Yeats—'

'Yes?'

'The sailor. How old did you say he was?'

'What sailor?'

'The sailor from the *Sea Breeze*.'

'I'm not sure that I did say. Mid-twenties, something like that. Why?'

'Nothing, I was just wondering.'

'Curiosity killed the cat, Mr Lynnford,' the harbour master cautioned with a wink, putting his glass down. 'Still, would you like a look?'

'I beg your pardon?'

'Would you like a look? He's lying in a back room in my office. That's if you don't mind seeing a corpse in the middle of the night,' he finished off with a dry laugh.

Lynnford would have liked nothing better. But he could not think of any reason to give the harbour master for accepting his invitation at such a strange hour, since he guessed that he could only have made it in jest, and so he declined.

'You're right,' the harbour master replied, adding, 'who knows, he could be a vampire!'

'Maybe tomorrow morning? In the daylight, before the body's moved to the morgue, if you don't mind, of course.'

The harbour master raised his glass as if in agreement and Lynnford took the photograph he'd found on the boat out of his pocket.

'Would you know who these two people are?'

The harbour master examined the photograph and then gave Lynnford a look of enquiry.

'No, are you looking for them as well?'

'Funny thing. I found it in the street just now when I fell over,' he made up, adding, 'I thought if someone recognised them, I could give it back.'

The harbour master smiled.

'That's the end of the high street true enough, up by the town hall. Look, you can just make out St John's Church. But who they are, I've no idea.'

He turned over the photograph.

'1936! They must have long since gone. Maybe somebody else can help you, Mr Lynnford. I must be going.'

And the harbour master finished off his drink in a gulp.

'Good evening to you.'

Before leaving he paused with his hand on Lynnford's arm and, pointing to his leg, gave him some friendly advice.

'If I were you, I'd get that cleaned up before you get an infection.'

EIGHT
SAM TURNS UP

He must have been asleep a long time. Yet it was still dark. Something had made him wake up. Lynnford turned over and stretched out his hand, fumbling for the light switch. Inevitably he knocked over the lamp in his blind search and it fell to the floor, out of reach.

Pushing back the bedcovers, he sat up, scratching his head and looking around to see what could have made him wake up all of a sudden. Picking up his watch, he tried unsuccessfully to make out the time and so, getting out of bed, he walked over to the window and drew back the curtain. A small red hole in the blackness down below immediately caught his attention, making him look harder.

A fire! There was a fire down by the harbour, maybe one of the boats. What if it was the *Sea Breeze*! With a start, letting the curtain fall back into place, he turned back into the room, and dressing quickly, tumbled downstairs, pulling on his jacket as he took the steps in haste. In the hallway, Peter Knight, already standing in a pair of black wellington boots, was struggling into an overcoat.

'You heard it then?' he gasped, adding, 'It came from down in the harbour.'

'What?'

'The explosion! Are you coming down?'

His question was superfluous. The door banging behind them, the two men hurried out of the house and down the hill to the harbour.

'Look!' Peter Knight cried out as they turned onto the promenade. 'It's old Yeats' office.'

The harbour master's office seemed cut adrift in the water, a floating funeral pyre, the bright light set against the dark sky obscuring the outline of the surrounding harbour. Sparks were being sent up amidst large clouds of billowing smoke. Timbers from the roof crackled and crashed. Those remaining carried flames along their length, flaring up and dancing a merry fury. *It must then have been the explosion that woke me*, Lynnford mused as he took in the scene.

A crowd had gathered around the entrance to the quay, held back by a dishevelled policeman. Gwen was in the crowd. She turned towards the newcomers. She appeared apprehensive.

'You finally woke up then?'

The question seemed more addressed to Peter Knight.

'We got down as soon as we could,' he replied. 'Joyce has stayed up in the house. Do they have any idea about what started it?'

Gwen shook her head.

'The landlord of The Blue Harp raised the alarm,' she explained. 'He was about to go to bed after clearing up in the bar when he thought he heard someone breaking bottles outside the back door. He looked out of the window and saw the fire. The sound of glass must have been the windows breaking with the heat. That was about one o'clock.'

'What time is it now?'

Lynnford didn't wait for a reply. The dial of his watch showed twenty-five minutes to two.

'And about ten minutes ago the kerosene dump on the other side of the harbour master's office went off with an almighty bang.'

'That's what must have woken us,' remarked Peter Knight grimly.

'Where's the fire service?' asked Lynnford.

Gwen scowled.

'The nearest fire station is ten miles away in Overcombe. And the road is poor and treacherous in the dark, but they should be here any minute now.'

Lynnford looked out towards the fire. A chain of people had been set up. Four or five match-like figures, all furiously engaged in passing buckets from hand to hand, cold water splashing on bare hands in their haste. Fanned out in a line, the person at the end had the job of pulling up water from below. They had a hopeless task.

Peter Knight tugged at Lynnford's coat sleeve.

'Come on. We'll give them a hand.'

And, accompanied by two other men from the crowd, they ducked under the police cordon and raced forward, the breeze blowing across the quay strengthening with their every stride.

One of the two men with them picked up a collection of buckets stacked up near the scene and, handing them out rapidly, went down on his knees, stretching down with a bucket in his hand to collect up the water below. Lynnford recognised the barman from The Blue Harp.

'Here, take this!'

Lynnford threw him a short pole with a hook, gesticulating at the other line to show how it was being used to lower the bucket down to reach the water.

Some minutes later, someone shouted out, 'Look! They're here.'

'At last!' cried out an exhausted voice and Lynnford, looking back in the direction of the seafront, saw a fire engine carefully manoeuvring its way onto the quay. The policeman had pulled down the cordon and was giving directions to the driver, whilst holding back the ever-pressing crowd.

'The *Sea Breeze*! Look lively! The boat's caught fire.'

Some cinders had blown onto the deck of the yacht, glowing red hot in the dark. More menacingly, one of the remaining roof timbers, flames continuing to run along its length, had twisted round, and having become dislodged, came crashing down on the quayside, spraying the boat with more red-hot cinders. Lynnford ran up to the *Sea Breeze* and launched a bucketful of water that quenched some of them, sizzling as the cold water hit the hot wood. Seconds later, another timber beam in flames came crashing down on the quayside, just missing the yacht, but showering yet more hot cinders onto her deck.

'We'll take care of that.'

A jet of water shot out from behind them, splashing the deck and cabin of the boat. The firemen had finally been able to set up their equipment and run up a hose to within a few yards of the blazing building. The fire engine had been left, marooned further along the quay. Lynnford stepped out of the way, almost bumping into the barman from The Blue Harp, an empty bucket still in his hand.

'That was a close thing.'

The young man nodded. Not finding any words of his own to reply, he managed at least a faint smile before walking away.

With the hose, the fire was soon under control and eventually extinguished. Still, the worst had been done and really there was nothing much left of the harbour master's office. Only the walls remained standing.

'The fire's out,' Lynnford heard the fire officer-in-charge declare to Mr Yeats. 'But you should have someone keep an eye on it until the morning just in case.'

'What about the body?' Lynnford called out.

'There was somebody inside?' replied the fireman, alarmed. 'We were told it was empty.'

'He was dead already,' explained the harbour master. 'A sailor we'd fished out of the sea. We were about to take it up to the morgue.'

'That's correct,' confirmed Sergeant Evans, who had just joined them.

'Well, the body will be calcinated now. Perhaps you should have one of your officers keep watch, instead, Sergeant.'

'Don't worry, Mr Yeats will find a reliable volunteer.'

'Easy enough for him to say,' muttered the harbour master as he walked back along the quay towards the promenade, worn out and angry. 'Not good enough to see my life burnt to a cinder, I have to become the most unpopular man in Westcliff by finding someone to keep watch.'

'Why not volunteer yourself?' suggested Lynnford, walking alongside him with Peter Knight and, perhaps foolishly, trying to lighten the harbour master's gloom.

'You think that's funny?'

Mr Yeats turned towards Lynnford, only then realising who he was.

'You again!'

Surprise turned quickly into suspicion.

'What are you doing here?'

'Helping out.'

'But before?'

'Before what?'

The conversation was momentarily interrupted as the three men became mixed up with several other men who had been helping to fight the fire but who were walking more quickly than them. Although weary, like Lynnford, they were trying to make light of their recent toil.

'That's one problem less,' one of them quipped.

'The body?'

'Yes, lucky they left it there. It won't do anyone any harm now.'

'Ashes to ashes.'

A muffled guffaw greeted the remark.

'And old Yeats can have himself a new office.'

Another burst of laughter.

'Oi! Mind what you're saying.'

Provoked, the harbour master made a sudden lunge at the man nearest to him, swiping at him with a loose fist that fortunately missed.

'Steady on!'

Lynnford grabbed hold of the harbour master whilst his victim stepped back with surprise. But recognising his assailant, the man released a coarse, inoffensive laugh that was echoed by his companions as they carried on their way, leaving behind Lynnford, Peter Knight and the harbour master. The harbour master shrugged off Lynnford's hold.

'They didn't mean anything, sir,' Lynnford consoled him. 'What were you saying before?'

But the harbour master did not reply and walked on, looking for a victim for the night's vigil, leaving Lynnford with an uneasy presentiment.

'Look! There's a body on the beach.'

The group of men that had pushed through them, now almost at the end of the quay, rushed over to the railings, pointing down to the short stretch of beach on the other side that the tide had left exposed. The harbour master, running up, joined them.

'Whoever it is looks the worse for wear,' he observed dryly.

'Let's get a closer look, Peter,' Lynnford suggested.

As they reached the end of the quay, Lynnford spotted Gwen. She was climbing over the railings.

'It's Sam!' she exclaimed on seeing Lynnford with Peter Knight and slipping down the sloping wall to the patch of beach.

'It could be anyone, Gwen,' Peter Knight called out, trying to restrain her excitement.

'What's going on?'

Sergeant Evans appeared, having pushed his way through the crowd.

'You'd better go down and see who it is before they do your job for you,' the harbour master directed.

But Gwen, already down on the beach, was ahead of them and had raised the man's head in her lap before the others, sinking in the deep shingles and scattering pebbles with their feet, could catch up.

'Sam!' she cried.

'That's all right, Mrs Mortimer, let us take care of him.'

And the policeman gently eased her to her feet whilst Lynnford quickly examined the body before the harbour master pushed him out of the way.

'He's alive!'

'Thank God!'

'Drink.'

The harbour master nodded, confirming Lynnford's observation and adding, 'As full as a barrel of rum and no mistake!'

'But he doesn't touch the stuff.'

'Everyone drinks, Gwen. Your husband's no exception.'

'How long has he been here?'

'Not long, Mr Lynnford. But if you don't mind, this isn't your business. Please stand back.'

'Sam Mortimer's my friend and I have owed him my life on many an occasion, Sergeant.'

'That's as maybe. We've all been through the War, sir.'

'So how long—'

'Not long, Mrs Mortimer. Some time this evening. Look, he's stone dry. Mr Knight, help us lift him up.'

'Hold on, Evans!'

The police officer looked at the harbour master.

'What is it?'

'That smell.'

The harbour master had raised one of Sam's hands to his nose, a look of shock and disgust crossing his face.

'What do you think that is, Evans?'

The police officer took the hand, exchanging glances with the harbour master as he breathed in.

'Kerosene. Crikey, it's all over his trousers as well!'

Sergeant Evans turned to Gwen.

'When did you last see your husband?'

'I haven't seen him all day.'

'All day? Are you sure?'

'Of course I'm sure.'

'What's he been doing?'

But the police officer did not wait for her reply, seeing Lynnford fall again to his knees and slapping his friend about the face, in an effort to bring him round.

'Please sir, if you don't mind. I've already warned you.'

'Yes, Mr Lynnford, you should keep away,' the harbour master interrupted, taking hold of him by the shoulders.

'Shouldn't we bring him to?'

'Yes, yes, of course. But we're taking him directly to the station. A doctor can look at him there.'

'The police station? He needs to come home!'

'I'm afraid not, Mrs Mortimer.'

'But he's got nothing to do with the fire.'

'That's not what it looks like. Now clear a space.'

'You can't!'

But Lynnford caught hold of her, whispering in her ear, 'Don't make things worse. In the police station he'll be safe enough. At least he's alive.'

And the two of them stood aside, watching as the harbour master helped Sergeant Evans carry Sam up onto the promenade and onto one of the benches, waiting for the ambulance to arrive. Lynnford felt the grip on his arm tighten and then relax. Gwen, leaning against him, let her head fall on his shoulder, fear and confusion taking their toll.

'Don't worry, Gwen, it'll all turn out fine, I'm sure,' Peter Knight tried to console Sam's wife. 'Come and stay with us at the guest house, at least for the few hours that are left tonight. Joyce will be happy to have you stay.'

Gwen nodded, unable to say anything more.

One by one, the onlookers and those who had been helping to fight the fire moved away. The fire engine had been packed up and, reversing back onto the promenade, drove off. Soon there was no one left on the quay except for the solitary figure appointed by the harbour master to keep watch until daybreak.

NINE
A DELIVERY LATE IN THE NIGHT

A little earlier that same night, some miles distant.

'What time is it now?'

Captain Jacobs was impatient. He'd been through it many times before, but he never gave too much thought to the past. The cold wait had got through to his bones, making him miserable and unpredictable.

'Where is it?'

He thumped the side of Kenny's baker's van with his fist.

'Who are they taking me for?'

Pengal got out of the van and joined him, lighting a cigarette.

'They're not going to take any chances. This isn't a few crates of whisky.'

'Damn you, Pengal, I know what it is.'

The captain stared up at the broken moon, hanging unbalanced in the night sky above the top of the stone tower beside which they had parked the van. Several hours had already gone by.

'They need us, so why are they messing us around. And where is Tabby? I said, all of us, didn't I?'

Pengal said nothing, ignoring Jacobs and drawing heavily on his cigarette. The two men stared down the track ahead of them, but the darkness did not let them see much further than fifteen yards or so.

'Kenny, wake up!'

Jacobs banged again on the side of the van.

'Get out and go down to the road. After this, we don't want them missing the turning.'

'They said tonight. They'll be here.'

'Shut up, Pengal. I don't need you to tell me what to do. If I find Tabby's gone off on one of your little jobs there'll be all hell to pay.'

'He's got a mind of his own.'

'If he had a mind, he'd have stayed at sea.'

'Captain!'

Kenny was running back towards them.

'They're coming.'

'At last.'

The engine noise from the unlit lorry coming off the road and out of the blackness seemed almost a careless abuse of the solitude of the place. The lorry stopped. The driver's door remained shut. The other door opened, and someone got out, dropping to the ground.

'I'll give him my mind,' muttered Jacobs, taking a step forward.

'Don't!'

Pengal's command was harsh.

'Just stay put.'

A bright light flashed in their faces. The three of them, Jacobs, Pengal and Kenny caught like frightened rabbits against the side of the baker's van. The torch moved slowly from one to the other, inspecting them in turn.

'They're in the back.'

It was a woman's voice.

'Who are you?'

The captain's surprise was cut short.

'Just get them out, now.'

'A woman?'

'Don't waste my time.'

The silence was ominous. They felt themselves being picked to shreds as if several carnivorous birds had alighted on them.

'Come on.'

Pengal led them round to the back of the lorry, lifting the canvas flap and pulling himself up. Inside, there were seven wooden crates, some long, the others small and square. The captain joined him, about to remove the lid of one of them.

'What are you doing?'

The alarm in Pengal's whispered voice was clear.

'They could be giving us potatoes for all we know.'

'We just take them. No questions this time.'

Pengal began pushing one of the crates to the tailboard.

'Come on, Kenny. Give me a hand with this.'

Jacobs jumped out.

'I'll go and open up the tower. We'll take them in there. Except for two small ones. We'll take them with us.'

'Just put them on the ground,' the woman interrupted him. The torch still hid her face from them.

'We're leaving now. Just get them off the lorry and make sure you deliver them correctly. You have your instructions.'

Her voice snapped shut.

Five minutes later, the three men were left standing next to the seven crates as the lorry reversed noisily back down the track, its occupants lost inside.

'Come on! Let's get them into the tower.'

Captain Jacobs resumed his authority, adding, 'If we don't hurry, it'll be almost daybreak.'

The captain gave a last look around the inside of the lower room of the tower where five of the crates had been arranged along the walls. He appeared satisfied.

'We'll bring the woman from the *Sea Breeze* here. It'll be safer than the cave until we've finished. There's room upstairs. Kenny, you can do it tomorrow after your morning deliveries.'

He pulled the door shut and followed Kenny and Pengal to the delivery van.

Minutes later the dull thud of a distant explosion broke the silence. Instinctively, the three men bent their heads, cowering and fearing illogically that the blast had come from behind them.

'What's that?'

Jacobs was the first to speak as they recovered and looked up.

'It looks like Westcliff.'

A red glow had sprung up, singeing the shadowed horizon.

'Well, it's nothing to do with us,' Jacobs reassured himself, adding, 'Good thing we've got everything stored in the watch tower apart from those two crates.'

And he indicated the two small crates that had been put in the back of the van ahead of them. In the dark, he didn't notice the sly smiles of Pengal and Kenny and their look of connivance.

TEN
SANDY COVE

The sea stretched out before his eyes, placid all the way to the distant horizon. The sun was shining brightly, still high in the mid-autumn sky. From the top of the cliff, Lynnford could see the waters breaking gently and silently from blue to white over the rocks below. Far out, the only movement he could discern was the almost timeless voyage of a sailing boat crossing the sea from east to west. It was about half-past eleven in the morning, and he was on his way to Sandy Cove, following the path across the headland that he'd been looking for the day before. Maybe he'd find there some clue as to what Sam had not wanted to tell him on the telephone for fear of being overheard.

Some way back, he had had a full view of Westcliff harbour. Smoke had been still slowly rising from within what remained of the burnt-out shell of the harbour master's office and, a little apart, from a smaller black patch which he had taken to be the place where the barrels of kerosene had been stored before they had exploded during the night. What looked like two official cars belonging to the police and the fire service had been parked at the entrance to the quay, their occupants busily inspecting the site. The fishing fleet had disappeared, but the *Sea Breeze* had been still there, moored to the quayside, unharmed by the night's drama except, possibly, for a few scars to its varnish left by the burning cinders.

He had had little sleep, still worried about Sam. Tossing and turning in his bed, his thoughts had broken over, like jagged rocks in a coastline sea, the burnt-down building, the fate of the sailor whose charred body had been inside, and his puzzlement over whatever Sam had been holding back, without being able to resolve his interrogations or the links between them. With daybreak, he'd been none the wiser.

And now, as he stared across the sea, he couldn't resist the increasingly pressing concerns over Sam's role in the fire. Why had he been set up? Lynnford couldn't for one moment believe that his friend had started the fire himself. What reason could he have had? He'd tried to see Sam in his police cell earlier in the morning, but he'd been refused access just as Gwen, who he'd met on the steps to the police station, had been. His thoughts then shifted momentarily to Sam's wife. After the fire, the three of them, Gwen, Peter Knight and himself, had returned exhausted to the Harbour View Guest House. Joyce Knight, who had been waiting for them, had not appeared too happy at her husband's offer to Gwen that she should spend what was left of the night with them in their guest house. What had that been about? Fear of being tainted by association? If so, he thought, it was not a good sign. Still, albeit possibly in a similar vein, it had been Joyce who had not hesitated in giving him information and her opinion about the family that ran the farm in Sandy Cove and the holiday chalets and cottages that were part of it. Mrs Hope and her son, she had said, were no more than a local nest of low-born smugglers that stretched back in time over several generations. To which her husband, on hearing this, had been unable to resist an amused smile.

With a shake of his head, as if to focus more keenly on the task ahead, Lynnford resumed his walk. The path began to descend and shortly a gap in the trees brought him into full view of the cove: a pool of water littered with autumnal petals of light reflecting the sun-filled sky above, its two densely wooded headlands coming together like the half-open pincers of a crab. So closely the tips of land appeared to each other from where he was that Lynnford thought that if he were to stand on one, he would be able to stretch out with his hand and touch the other. Behind them, the cove widened out into an almost perfect circle; rocky outcrops joined by a sandy beach in the shape of a half-moon against which the captured sea ebbed and flowed. What he took to be the Hope family's farm and holiday chalets were clearly visible; set back from the beach on the side furthest from him, surrounded by some fields.

A glint of light below him caught his eye and drew his attention to a yacht idling in the deep water close to the rocks. Her sail was down, and she was bobbing gently up and down with the sway of the water, evidently at anchor and seemingly unattended. The boat was so directly below him that he felt almost as if he were perched up on top of the mast staring down on the white cabin, varnished decking, cockpit and wheel. She was the spitting image of the *Sea Breeze*, and, if he had not just seen her moored in Westcliff harbour, he would have sworn it was the same boat. Surely, there isn't another dead sailor floating in the water, he half kidded himself. That would be too much of a coincidence! But one never knew. And so, whose boat was this, he wondered.

With these thoughts he quickly completed the remaining path into the cove and found himself on the beach, the path having melted into the sand. Soft sand hills, spiked with grass, undulated before him, obstructing his view of the farm. About half way up the beach a line of seaweed stretched out along its full length, the strands of green and brown kelp glistening in the sunlight.

Setting off along the beach, keeping just below the level of the seaweed where the damp sand was firmer, Lynnford soon came upon a track that led to a tarmac-laid road. Once on the hard surface, he kicked the sand off his boots and, looking around, immediately found what he wanted; a gate leading into the farm. A large sign with the inscription, "The Beachcomber, family farm and holiday chalets and cottages", hung from a post planted in the ground next to the gate. Another sign, fixed to the gate itself, read "Private property – access for residents only". A cattle grid passed under the gate. Lynnford lifted the iron latch and pushed open the heavy gate.

'Can't you read?' a rough voice growled behind him.

He turned round, fully expecting to encounter a large, boorish man, towering over him. Instead, it was a smallish, but heavy-set man, in his late thirties, roughly dressed and who, whilst retaining his hostility towards Lynnford, stood some distance away. He appeared to be watching and waiting, now that he had issued his warning, rather than menacing a physical attack.

The man was dressed in corduroys, boots and a fraying jumper pulled over a collarless shirt. The cap on his head framed an unshaven face. One hand was resting on a walking stick. The other held loosely the lead of a light-golden Labrador, standing close to his legs.

'Sit!' snapped the man and the dog sat back immediately on its hind legs. Its head remained firmly and silently pointing up at the stranger.

'Good day to you, Mr Hope. It is Mr Hope, isn't it?' Lynnford greeted the man, taking a step back into the lane whilst keeping a hand on the uppermost bar of the gate.

'My father died some years back,' the man replied in a gruff tone. 'Who said you could go trespassing on our land?'

'I'm sorry. I didn't mean to,' replied Lynnford, determined to be conciliatory. 'I just wanted to have a few words with the owner.'

'Well, he's here. What do you want? Police?'

Lynnford could not resist laughing, interjecting rapidly, 'No, I can assure you I'm not. I'm visiting some friends in Westcliff. I came over for a walk. They said that you let out chalets for weekends and holidays.'

Lynnford pointed in the direction of the headland, 'And I thought I'd take a look. It's a splendid spot.'

'We're closed.'

'Yes, so I see. But I'm not looking for anything right now. As I said, I'm staying with friends in Westcliff. I just wanted to see what you have to offer.'

'There's nothing to see. We're closed.'

Certainly, the man seemed disinclined to talk. Yet he still did not make any move to walk away, standing his ground. *Perhaps*, thought Lynnford, *he's less than impressed with my story and anyway has no interest in attracting business at such a dead time of the year*. He changed tack.

'You have a farm as well, I see? That must be a lonely life, I imagine?'

Again, the usual conversational clues were ignored. The man made as if to pass Lynnford and leave him stranded on the wrong side of the gate.

'I'm sure business can't be easy with so many guest houses in Westcliff?' he added quickly.

Lynnford sensed the man relax slightly, although his immediate reaction was to spit on the ground.

'That's true indeed,' he agreed, patting the dog's neck.

'It seems a little unfair on you. They can take business all year round but here you're stuck to the summer. Nobody's going to want to spend the winter in a wooden chalet.'

The man shrugged.

'There's some that do.'

'But it's not worth your while opening up the site for an occasional visitor like me, is it?'

'That's right enough. It's the council. Full of Westcliff folk. They give out licences two a penny for a small backhander. But you've got to be one of them, mind.'

Lynnford had touched a raw nerve and the man was beginning to lose a little of his coldness.

'That's a nice boat you have there.'

Lynnford pointed in the direction of the yacht that he had just seen, although from where they were standing it was hidden from view by the sand dunes. The man gave a start.

'What boat?'

'The smart yacht anchored just off the beach, close to the rocks.'

'That's not my boat.'

'Someone staying in one of the chalets?'

The man frowned.

'There's no one here. I told you, we're closed.'

'The skipper and his crew?'

'Oh, a boat like that doesn't need many hands to sail her.'

'Really?'

'Like I said, we're closed, and we don't take any visitors until next year.'

He made to push past Lynnford. Only Lynnford's tall frame and his hand on the gatepost were in his way, and the man really would have had to forcibly push him out of the way if he wanted to rid himself of the visitor by entering the field. Lynnford continued, 'It's funny, I saw a boat just like it this morning lying in Westcliff harbour, just outside the harbour master's office. Almost its twin. I thought it was the same boat.'

'That's the one they took away the other day,' the man replied, stepping back.

'Yes, didn't they find a sailor in the water, here in the cove? A rather dreadful accident, so they say.'

'That's what they say.'

The man looked away and shrugged, adding, 'None of my business.'

'And the police? What are they doing? Have they arrested anyone?'

'What for? For an accident? Right enough, the local bobby came down and asked a few questions. But they're not going to find anyone.'

'No?'

The man made a noise of contempt but said nothing more. Instead, he took the opportunity to try once again to dislodge Lynnford from his position in front of the gate.

'So sorry,' Lynnford apologised. 'I've been holding you up. You must have a lot to do.'

And he fell back to allow the farmer to pass by and open the gate. As he passed by, he added, 'Only I thought that really if it's not too much trouble I would very much appreciate a quick visit.'

The man shrugged his shoulders and let Lynnford follow him through the gate. The field was empty. The man took Lynnford to the other side where a similar gate closed off the field.

'There's not much to see.' The man indicated with a sweep of his hand a field to their right that led down to the beach. 'Take a look. Close the gate after you.'

He was about to leave Lynnford to his own devices when a woman suddenly appeared, seemingly almost on their shoulders. She was standing above them in the garden in front of the farmhouse that climbed the field.

'Frank! What are you up to?'

'I'll be right over, Mother.'

'Who's this?'

'He wants to look over the huts. He's walked over from Westcliff.'

'Chalets, Frank! Well, don't just leave him there. Perhaps he would like to see inside one of them. No wait, don't bother, I'll see to it myself.'

So saying, she disappeared and reappeared a few seconds later in the field, several wild-looking cats scattering away as she approached. She was in her late sixties but clearly still very active. She was dressed neatly, and her eyes passed quickly from one to the other as she spoke.

'Good morning to you, sir. Please excuse my son. He hasn't any manners.'

And before Lynnford could say anything she carried on, 'Normally we're closed for the season, but we can also make an exception.'

Lynnford felt her son scowling behind his back.

'Really, I've just come down out of curiosity. I was coming down off the headland and saw the farm and thought I'd like to check it out just in case. You never know, I might be able to persuade my wife to come down for a few days' holiday next summer.'

And Lynnford wondered to himself with amusement what Victoria, his informal fiancée, would have to say about that; probably more surprised by the idea of their marriage than the dismal prospect of being huddled in a seaside cabin.

'Well, we book up early. We had our last group this weekend. Or if you want you can also pitch your tent, but we don't encourage it.'

'It's certainly a peaceful spot here. I shouldn't wonder that it gets crowded with sailing boats in the summer.'

'You're right. It does a bit. But most of them go into the harbour at Westcliff, even with the mooring charges. Mind you, we've had our drama here this week with the sailor they fished out of the water on Monday morning. You must have heard about it? Westcliff's got nothing else to talk about. Some say he was bringing in contraband. I won't say it doesn't go on. People like to have things cheaply, duty-free imports, that sort of thing, especially with things as they are after the War. But he wasn't smuggling, and I should know. I can pick them out but there's nothing we can do, is there, Frank? Still, so long as it doesn't interfere with us. But this man, he was a foreigner. Foreigners don't smuggle. Locals smuggle, isn't that right? Fishermen bringing in something extra to help with the end of the month.'

'So what happened to the others?'

'Who?'

'The rest of the man's crew.'

'I haven't seen them since.'

'You saw them?'

'Of course I saw them. I see everything. Except, that's not quite true. This time I didn't see them. It was Sunday, wasn't it, Frank? Mist like All Souls' Day. I heard their voices. You see, young man, I still have my ears.'

'Men? How many?'

'Now, you're asking a little too much of an old lady.

But there was a woman and another man. They must have gone out in their dinghy. But where, I couldn't say. And the dinghy hasn't been found. Has it, Frank? Speak up!'

'He's walked off, Mrs Hope.' Lynnford explained her son's silence.

'He always does. He's not as polite as you to put up with me rambling on.'

Lynnford smiled. Like chalk and cheese, the mother and son. Under the avalanche of commentary, he had not been able to do much more than listen. But what she had told him seemed reliable enough. He thanked Mrs Hope and took his leave, walking back by himself to the gate where he had met her son. He turned round. She was still standing where he had left her, watching, one of the mottled cats in her arms. He waved goodbye.

He wandered back down to the beach where, a little further on, he came to the remains of a recent fire; a large circle of cold, black and charred sticks mixed up with piles of grey-white ashes. Probably made by the group Mrs Hope had mentioned, he guessed. One or two logs remained in the centre. Lynnford touched one with his shoe and it collapsed into ashes. He poked around with the aid of a stick that he had picked up, but found nothing of interest, not even an empty bottle. *They must have cleaned up after themselves*, he thought. He turned back and headed towards the spot where the road came down to the beach.

A short track continued from where the road stopped, passing through the low sand hills on either side. He paused, looking at the point where the track ran into the beach. A small, dark patch had caught his eye. Bending down, he touched it with his finger. It was heavy and sticky and, picking up some of the heavy grains of sand, he rolled them between his fingers, holding them close to his nose. Oil. Too far above the tidemark to have been brought in by the sea but, yes, a motor vehicle left here for maybe an hour or so considering the amount of oil, he mused. The weekenders? But they would not have driven down to the beach. It was only a couple of minutes' walk away. He scoured the track with his eyes, but there were no tell-tale tyre marks to help him. The car, or perhaps a lorry, must have driven down the track and overrun it slightly, he guessed. Then, lifting some of the sand with his foot he uncovered a pile of four or five cigarette ends. They looked recent. So, somebody had driven down into the cove and waited here. Waiting for what? And was it last Sunday? His mind began to race forward, setting out yet more questions that he could not answer. Had they, whoever they were, been waiting for the *Sea Breeze* before rowing out to meet it? But if so, how was it that the weekenders had not seen them? He decided to return to Westcliff.

*

Meanwhile as Lynnford left the beach in Sandy Cove, in The Blue Harp in Westcliff, in the privacy of one of the alcoves, two men were talking, hidden from the other customers.

'So they've taken the woman to the tower?'

The man in front of him assented with a slight nod of the head, 'This morning.'

'Good. Bait, so to speak, if I'm ever going to get my hands on it.'

'On what?'

'Just keep your mind on our business. Nobody has any concerns about you, have they?'

'Of course not! I've just sailed in the *Sea Bird* for them, haven't I? It's lying in Sandy Cove, waiting for them.'

'Never be too careful, Skinner. We're playing a dangerous game. Above all, keep clear of Pengal. He'd cut your throat than think twice if for one moment he had doubts about you.'

'I'm his match, Yeats.'

'Drink up, we've both got work to do.'

'And the shop?'

'You can drop it. No need to keep watch over it anymore. The busybody newsagent is locked up now in a police cell and won't be going anywhere for the moment.'

'And the reporter?'

'I'll deal with him if I have to. But I doubt that will be necessary. Not now that fool Tabby has burnt the body to cinders and my office to boot. Come on, drink up!'

ELEVEN

TOWER PORT

Back in Westcliff, Sam and Gwen's newsagents already in sight on the other side of the street, with the blue-coated form of a police constable standing outside, a hand clutched Lynnford's arm and pulled him into an alleyway.

'Robert!'

Gwen Mortimer released her hold.

'What's wrong?'

'Sergeant Evans.'

'What about him?'

'He's looking for you.'

'Has he found something?'

'No. About the fire.'

'What of it?'

'He's got it into his head that you had something to do with it.'

'Me! Isn't Sam enough?'

'Yeats, the harbour master, says he saw you hanging around the harbour before the fire. That's enough for him.'

'Several hours before, and it was in The Blue Harp. We spoke together. It was you he saw down on the quayside.'

'Still, I'd keep out of his way for a while.'

'Not so easy. Without Sam, I'm going to need to dig around. Any news about him?'

Gwen shook her head. 'They won't let him see anyone.'

'That can't go on much longer but in the meantime—'

'Listen, you might take a trip to Tower Port. That'll keep you out of the way for a few hours at least.'

'Why should I go there? Where is it?'

'The *Sea Breeze* put in there, I've been told. Last week, for repairs. For a couple of days or so.'

'So somebody might know something about the crew. It's worth a try. And with Sam safely in his cell, at least, the pressure's off a little.'

'It's just four or five miles along the coast.'

'Can I find a taxi?'

'A taxi? You're not in Oxford Street, Robert!'

Lynnford recalled the words of the station porter on his arrival.

'So, how can I get there?'

'Bus. There's a stop opposite the shop.'

'Bus?'

'It's the quickest way, unless you want to try hitching a lift. The next one goes at two-thirty.'

Lynnford looked at his watch, regretting not having driven down from London in his Morgan. Two-twenty, ten minutes to go. Gwen Mortimer indicated the constable.

'If you wait until it pulls up, you should be able to get on without him seeing you.'

Five or so minutes later the knot of waiting passengers was slowly unwinding its way into the bus. The driver, behind his wheel, wore a deadpan face.

'Take your time,' he called out, without any sense of irony. 'There're enough seats for everyone.'

'But some are better than others.'

'Come along, Mrs Walker, I won't leave without you.'

Lynnford took a seat behind the driver. He could feel the broken springs under its cover.

'Can you give this to Kendal? He'll be waiting for you at the other end.'

A grey-haired woman standing on the pavement had pushed up a large parcel onto the steps of the bus. The driver looked down at her with a familiar air.

'That's no bother, Dorothy. Put it on the seat behind me. Here, let me help you.'

Getting out of his seat, the driver took the parcel and placed it on the floor next to Lynnford.

'Do you mind, sir?'

'No, not at all,' Lynnford replied, co-operatively pulling in his legs and squeezing them in up against the back of the driver's seat in front of him.

The driver closed the door and started the engine. A few moments later they were driving along the high street. Lynnford glanced back at the police officer still waiting patiently in front of Sam and Gwen's shop.

Every so often the driver pulled in to let someone on or off. On one occasion, stopping outside a thatched cottage that stood directly on the roadside, the driver sounded his horn, whereupon an upper window of the cottage flew open, a voice crying out, 'Hold on, Will, he's coming.'

A few seconds later, a man appeared in the front door, pulling on a jacket. He jumped into the bus, waving back at the cottage as they drove off and taking the seat across the aisle from Lynnford. The driver looked back briefly.

'All right there, Derek?'

'Fine, Will. Just keep your eyes on the road.'

'And Sally?'

'She's fine. We'll see you on Sunday.'

The man took out a crumpled packet of cigarettes, selected one and replaced the packet in his jacket pocket.

'Got a light?' The man looked casually at Lynnford. Under his soft cap his hair was dark chestnut and his eyebrows thick and heavy. In his open mouth, his teeth showed yellow with nicotine. Lynnford shook his head.

'Sorry.'

The man shrugged his shoulders and turned round, repeating his question to the passenger behind him.

'Here.'

A young man in a sailor's uniform leant over and offered him the light from the cigarette that he was smoking. The two men fell into conversation, Lynnford half-listening as he looked out of the window.

'On leave?'

'Eight days. We put in at Portsmouth for a refit.'

'Portsmouth, isn't that where the naval armoury was broken into?'

'A couple of weeks ago. Before we put in.'

'Of course, but they got away with a bit, didn't they? Sten and Bren guns, rifles and explosives, so they say.'

'Don't forget the crates of corned beef,' joked a man sitting in the row behind.

'All the way from the Argentine!' chimed in another.

'And not for the first time!' added someone else amidst the hilarity.

Lynnford recalled the incident and several others reported in the press in the last month or so. Armed raids on military arsenals by groups of men dressed in British army uniforms.

'East End gangs, by all accounts.' Derek resumed the thread of their conversation.

'Newspapers! You can't believe too much what they say.'

'No, maybe for a sailor they're not much use,' replied Derek jokingly. 'Coming home?'

The sailor nodded.

'I haven't seen my folks for six months. That's a long time away from home.'

'It certainly is,' Lynnford's neighbour agreed.

'You must have seen the seven seas though. What luck! I haven't been much further than Exeter. Perhaps Bristol if I remember rightly.'

The young sailor laughed.

'Don't kid me. You look like you've seen the world right enough.'

Derek grinned.

'Perhaps I have, lad. Perhaps I have.'

He then turned and, leaning across the aisle, tapped Lynnford on the arm.

'Look ahead. There's the leaning tower of Pisa,' and he laughed out loud. 'Our very own leaning tower. What do you think of that?'

Lynnford looked over the driver's shoulder and out in front through the large windscreen of the bus. In the near distance he could see a squat, round tower, a bare flagpole poking up above the battlements. Short as it was, the tower nevertheless dominated the nearby countryside and, he guessed, the sea out to the horizon. It looked solid and in good repair. The bus was approaching it rapidly.

'It seems straight enough to me,' he remarked.

'Maybe it does and maybe it won't be for long.'

'What do you mean by that?'

The man looked at Lynnford, was silent for a moment and then burst into another loud guffaw, slipping the cap off his head and slapping his legs with it, full of hilarity.

'Just a joke, laddie. Just a joke. Like the beef just now.'

He replaced the cap on his head, straightening it with both hands.

'It was built at the time of the Spanish Armada,' another passenger chipped in. 'That's where Tower Port gets its name. Look we're going down now.'

The bus had turned sharply to the right, leaving behind the stone tower. The descent was very steep, making Lynnford feel as if they were plunging down like a seagull towards the rooftops of the small collection of buildings below, built one on top of the other, with the sea stretching out beyond. *A joke maybe*, Lynnford mused, *but might there not be something behind it? It had no sense, or did it?* The road wound its way down towards the town. As they got closer it levelled off, so that rather than almost falling into the town as one might have expected from the sharp descent, the town opened up gradually. And as they approached, it soon became clear that it was much larger than it had appeared from up near the tower.

'Tower Port,' announced Lynnford's neighbour. 'Your first time here?' Lynnford nodded.

'What are you doing?'

Lynnford's reply was non-committal.

'Oh, I work in London.'

The man laughed again.

'No, what're you down here for, fishing?'

'No.' Lynnford shook his head. 'Just looking up a friend.'

'Well, enjoy your visit. This is where we all get off.'

The bus lurched to a halt in a simple-looking bus station.

'Tower Port. Terminus,' the driver called out, almost unnecessarily.

A general commotion ensued as the passengers got up and stood in the aisle, collecting their bags together, putting on their coats and hats, and bringing down their possessions from the rack above the seats, some standing patiently, waiting their turn to move down the bus, others squeezing past. Lynnford was stuck in his seat by the parcel. Derek had slipped off his seat as soon as the bus had stopped and had disappeared with a wave of his hand.

'Don't forget the parcel,' Lynnford called out. The driver looked round.

'Oh yes. Dot would have had my guts for garters if I'd forgotten it.'

Getting off his seat and bending down, the driver put his hands around the box and with a jerk, pulled it out and up.

'Careful!'

But Lynnford's warning came too late. Caught against an exposed metal spring under the seat, the parcel ripped open as the driver carelessly brought it out.

'What's that?'

The bottom of the box had fallen out and with it had come tumbling its contents, scattering indiscriminately on the seat and floor as the driver continued to lift the box, unable to stop his movement. Cigarette cartons, forty or so. Lynnford picked one up, holding it in his hands: French, no duty.

'Couldn't she have packed it better!' the driver muttered to himself, ignoring Lynnford and throwing the cartons back into the box any which way. 'Where's Kendal when I need him?'

'A tidy saving for someone,' Lynnford commented, handing the carton to the driver and making as if to help him.

'Don't bother. I'll see to it myself.' A mixture of embarrassment and annoyance filled the driver's voice.

Lynnford stopped on his way down the steps.

'How do I get to the harbour from here?' he asked.

'Just follow the road.'

The driver pointed out the direction with his hand, glad to see him go.

'Thanks. By the way, what time's the next bus back?'

'On the half-hour, every two hours.'

Following the bus driver's directions, Lynnford was soon propelled out of the funnel-like streets onto the quayside where he headed directly for the harbour master's office. The door was open wide and led Lynnford directly into an internal office. A rectangular counter marked off the space open to the public. He approached the counter and pressed his palm over the brass bell stand. A man dressed in slacks and a navy-blue pullover appeared from behind a partition and came over to Lynnford. He was wiry and energetic. Thin strands of hair were combed back over his head. His skin was darkly tanned and showed signs of long years at sea.

'Yes, what can I do for you?'

His tone was blunt and to the point.

'Good afternoon. I've come to see the harbour master.'

'You're speaking to him. And you are?'

Lynnford skipped around the question.

'Some friends are expecting me. They should have arrived, but I can't see their boat in the harbour.'

'What's the name of their boat?'

'The *Sea Breeze*.'

'You're a bit late. She's already been and gone.'

'How's that?'

Lynnford faked a look of surprise.

'She was here last week for a few days then put out on Friday or Saturday.'

'Are you sure?'

'Take a look at the register yourself.'

The harbour master sounded annoyed.

'We don't get many boats like her at this time of year.'

He opened up a register and, thumbing through the entries, stopped at one.

'There you are. Sunday. My mistake.'

He swung the book around to face Lynnford, still pointing with his forefinger at the entry. The arrival of the *Sea Breeze* was neatly inscribed, together with its date of sailing, a few days later, and the settlement of its mooring charges. But there was no information about the crew.

'So they stayed for four days. Why couldn't they have waited?'

Lynnford spoke half to himself but sufficiently loud as to gain the harbour master's attention.

'Where have they gone?'

The harbour master shrugged his shoulders.

'So long as she's not up to anything illegal, it's her business not mine when and where she goes.'

He closed the book and replaced it.

'If I remember correctly, I think that she had put in for a refit.'

'Was she damaged?'

'She had hit some storms coming round Land's End. She'd taken a bit of a knocking. Nothing too serious. If you want to know anything more, ask around out there.'

The harbour master pointed out of the door to the quayside, and the groups of fishermen.

'One of them should be able to help you.'

Then his tone changed as if he was revising his first impression of Lynnford, and he looked gravely at him.

'Friends, did you say?'

Lynnford nodded.

'Then you haven't heard?'

Lynnford stared inquisitively at the harbour master.

'The *Sea Breeze*'s tied up in Westcliff. It was found empty around the headland from there with the body of a sailor floating in the sea alongside.'

'Are you sure?' and Lynnford allowed a look of horror to flash across his face.

'It's what I've heard.'

'Can you describe him?'

'I never saw him. Someone else came in to pay the mooring. He didn't match the description the sergeant from Westcliff gave me.'

'What about these?'

Lynnford took the photograph of the two cyclists out of his pocket.

'Yes,' the harbour master replied after some moments. 'That's him, at least. The man. He's the one I saw. Is he your friend? You'd better tell the police.'

'Yes, I'd better get over to Westcliff.' Lynnford covered his reply in a shroud of shock.

'Thank you very much.'

As he walked out of the office and onto the quayside, he sensed the harbour master behind him reaching for his telephone. Too bad, he reflected. He'd have to face Sergeant Evans again sooner or later.

TWELVE

OUTSIDE THE WATCH TOWER

A long the quayside, the fishing crews were preparing their boats.

'Good afternoon,' Lynnford addressed a group of fishermen collected around a boat tied up alongside the quay outside the harbour master's office. Nobody looked up but one replied whilst continuing to inspect the net spread across his knees.

'Afternoon.'

'Do any of you remember the *Sea Breeze*? A white yacht. It was moored up in the harbour for a few days last week.'

'When do you say that was?'

The same man spoke as if speaking on behalf of the others.

'Last week. She left on Sunday.'

'That's right. A Dutch boat. She fared badly in the storm. A smart little boat. Perhaps too smart for the likes of here.'

'Who was sailing her?'

'Ask in one of the stores. We've no time to talk with strangers.' The man squinted up at Lynnford. 'No offence meant of course. I mean we're too busy to interest ourselves over casual boats that come and go. See?'

'Any idea why it put in here for a refit? Wouldn't Westcliff have been a better bet?'

'No idea. There were three of them, two men and a woman.'

Lynnford nodded and thanked the man.

'Don't mention it.'

The man returned to his net, pulling another section over his knee, a wink, to the others.

An assistant in one of the ships' chandlers remembered a young, fair-haired sailor from the yacht, who spoke little English. He had bought canvas for a new sail and rope and had asked for a bill to be made out in the name of Chessington. A name at last! That was something. And the woman, the third member of the crew, could that have been his wife? Lynnford closed the door of the shop behind him, wondering what to do next whilst gazing across the harbour.

'A penny for your thoughts.'

Lynnford started.

'A penny for your thoughts.'

He looked round and recognised Derek. He already smelt of drink.

'A nice-looking harbour?'

Lynnford nodded but didn't say anything.

'Do you want to go fishing? I can get you a good captain who'll give you some real fishing.'

'No thanks. That's not my game.'

'You want to find sharks?'

'No.'

The man tugged his sleeve.

'Have you got some coppers for a thirsty sailor?'

Lynnford laughed. 'So that's what you want, is it? What's your name, again?'

'Jack, Jim. You name it.'

'I thought it was Derek.'

'As you like.' The man grinned. 'But I know this harbour like the back of my hand.'

He held up his hand in front of Lynnford's face. Lynnford brushed it away.

'I'm sure you do.' *And maybe you can tell me something about the Sea Breeze*, he added to himself. 'Come on, Derek! Let me buy you a drink.'

'That's a real gentleman. Harry in The Lord Nelson pulls a nice glass of Devonshire bitter.'

He pointed in the direction of a small public house behind them.

The barman smiled at them as they pulled up two stools at the bar.

'Who've you caught this time, Derek?'

'A friend of mine who's good enough to stand me a pint, isn't that right?'

'That's right, Harry,' Lynnford confirmed.

'Derek here tells me he has the thirst of an old sailor.'

Lynnford paid the barman and raised his glass to his new acquaintance. Derek put the glass to his lips and took a long drink that nearly emptied it. He lowered the glass and wiped his damp moustache with the back of his hand. Then, raising the glass again, he drank back what was left and placed the empty glass on the bar. Lynnford made a sign to Harry to refill the glass.

'Did you ever see the *Sea Breeze* that put in last week, Derek?'

'The *Sea Breeze*, eh? Is that what you're after?'

Derek grimaced and scratched his head.

'Can't say I did. What did she look like? There's no fishing boat of that name.'

'She's a pleasure boat. A white yacht. She put in for a few days.'

'Oh yes, that's right. I can see her now. She was moored up here, just outside.'

'What were they doing?'

'Repairs.'

'I suppose you got a drink out of them.'

The man gave a look of disgust.

'Not a penny. Right tight, the three of them.'

The barman joined the conversation. 'The young lad came in and drank a pint or two in the evenings. God rest his soul. They found him floating in Sandy Cove, a few miles down the coast. A nasty business.'

'Chessington, was that him?'

Derek gave a sly laugh and shook his head.

'Is this Chessington?'

Lynnford showed them the photograph. They both nodded and the barman replied, 'Yes, but twenty years ago.'

'And the woman?'

'That's his wife.'

'And you knew her?'

'Of course.'

'And were they on the boat?'

'On the *Sea Breeze*? I don't know. I only saw the Dutchman.'

'But he couldn't have been alone.'

'Why not? He was found alone.'

'But you just said there were three of them.'

'Did I? I only saw the sailor. I never saw Chessington. Probably wouldn't recognise him now if I had.'

'But what's happened to him, and his wife?'

'You asked me about the boat, and I told you. I don't know anything about Chessington. Maybe they had an argument with the sailor and pushed him overboard.'

'With two bullets in his back?'

'I wouldn't know.'

'But why abandon the boat?'

Derek and the barman looked blank. Lynnford prompted them. 'They must both be on land, somewhere.'

'No one's seen them. At least not here in Tower Port. Try in Westcliff.'

Lynnford sensed that he would not get anything more out of either Derek or Harry, careful the two of them about not saying too much about a local to a stranger. Still, he threw in another question.

'What was that you were saying, Derek, earlier on the bus about the tower up on the hill?'

He sensed the barman glance quickly at his companion and Derek gave another blank expression, shaking his head. He drained his glass.

'Here. Buy yourself another,' Lynnford offered, slipping off his stool.

'And you, barman.'

He'd learnt to recognise a brick wall and here was one, arousing as usual his curiosity, but he knew that neither the barman nor his friend would tell him anything more about it.

'I must be off now.'

'Much obliged to you, sir.'

And Derek lifted his cap to him in a mock salute, an ironic look in his eyes, but adding as if in payment for the extra drink, 'Maybe I did see him once. Bit of a shock after all this time.'

'Who?'

'Chessington.'

'With his wife?'

'No, with the harbour master.'

'From Tower Port?'

'No, with Yeats, the old codger from Westcliff.'

'Any idea what they were talking about?'

'I wasn't privy to their secrets.'

'Of course not! Well, thank you anyway.'

Once outside the public house, Lynnford looked up at the hill. The watch tower was hidden from view. *No harm in having a closer look*, he thought. *How long will it take to walk up there? Twenty minutes, maybe a little more. Time enough for me to catch the four-thirty bus back to Westcliff on its way past the tower.* He started to walk quickly back through the narrow streets, past the bus station, and up the road out of the town.

Walking up the steep road up the hill, bordered by high hedges on either side, was like climbing a spiral staircase within a tall church spire, punctured at every turn by large lancet windows open to the elements, openings with views of the sea, each time stretched out further and further away, and of the fishing town below; but whose roof tops were soon lost, leaving only the harbour in sight.

The road levelled off and the watch tower sprang into view, set back some distance from the road, its stone base hidden by scrubby undergrowth. The access to it was not clear, but he guessed that there should be some sort of entrance further along the road, possibly after the van which he had just spotted, pulled up off the road on a grassy patch. Two deep, muddy wheel tracks behind the van marked out its route off the road. It was painted in navy blue with, for emblem, a large loaf in a breadbasket. The bonnet had been lifted, and the man standing in front was lost to view, bent down as he was underneath it, busy fixing the engine.

'Need a hand?' Lynnford enquired.

A youthful, freckled face, crowned with short rusty-red curls turned towards Lynnford, still bent down under the bonnet.

'No, sir. Thanks a lot. Another turn and twist here and there and it's done.'

And indeed, a few seconds later he stepped back and straightened himself, wiping his hands on an oil-stained rag as he did so. He was wearing a blue delivery coat over a collarless shirt, his neck left exposed.

'She's always packing out on me. Especially after this hill. It's too much for her.'

And laughing, he walked round to the driver's door and tried the ignition. The engine leapt into life, chugging smoothly.

'See, as right as rain.'

Lynnford smiled.

'Your bread must have a good reputation for you to come all the way over to Tower Port.'

The delivery man's blue eyes looked back at Lynnford, not understanding.

'Sorry?'

Lynnford pointed at the address painted on the side of the van, underneath the picture of the loaf in the breadbasket.

'You've come over from Westcliff, haven't you?'

The young man laughed again.

'Oh, I see. Yeah, I suppose you're right. Word gets around.'

He moved as if to get back into the van, and then paused, looking round at Lynnford.

'Can I give you a lift? I'm going back to Westcliff right now, if that's where you're heading.'

'No, thank you. I've walked up the hill to have a look at the tower over there.'

As he spoke, he sensed the young man pull up short.

'The tower?'

'Yes, that's right. It looks impressive, don't you think? But you're local, so you probably don't see anything special in it.'

'No, that's right,' he replied hesitantly but with a hint of relief.

'What are you, a sightseer? You're a bit out of season.'

'History,' Lynnford replied, coming up with the first thing that came to mind.

'I teach sixth-formers and I'm always on the lookout for something new to show them, just like this tower. It must be full of local history. Do you know anything about it? What was it built for?'

The man cut out the engine with a sharp twist of his hand. Lynnford expected him to say something, but instead he shrugged his shoulders, and simply said, 'Sorry. It's just a stone tower to me. It's always been here.'

'Who are you?'

Another man had just appeared, walking along the grass verge towards the van. Older than the first, possibly in his thirties. He looked cold, like stone, and with a frame wasted from poor health. He had not stopped on seeing Lynnford and continued to approach him, his eyes challenging him.

'It's all right, Pengal. He's just a school teacher.'

The younger man brought down the bonnet, slamming it shut.

'Who says so? What do you want?' The man addressed Lynnford.

'Nothing, he's just come up to look at the tower,' continued the younger man.

'Just leave him to me, Kenny.'

And turning back to Lynnford, the man continued, 'It's all locked up. There isn't anything to see.'

He had stopped a short distance in front of Lynnford.

'That's perfectly fine. I didn't expect it to be open. Is it still used then?'

'It's just an old ruin.'

Pengal turned his attention to the van.

'Is it fixed now, Kenny?'

The younger man nodded.

'Then, let's go.'

'Well, good day to you.' Lynnford maintained a cheerful note.

But Pengal's suspicious mind couldn't resist a further question before leaving him:

'And so what do you teach?'

'History.'

'History!'

Pengal almost spat out the word with disgust before bending over double in a bout of raucous coughing.

'History,' he repeated. 'It's done nothing but screw us up.'

Seeing Lynnford walk off, the other two men made as if to get back into the van, and he expected to hear the engine break into life again. But it remained silent. He reached the entrance to the grounds around the tower, a half-broken gate, the wood worn heavily by the wind and rain; and still the van had not moved. Lynnford lifted the fallen gate strut off the ground and pushed it in front of him, letting the gate swing on its hinges. The track was furrowed deep with wheel tracks leading directly to the tower, dried hard by the wind. Lynnford picked his way over the ruts until he reached the edifice, still waiting to hear the van drive off.

It was a simple structure, wider at the base than at the top, its long age apparent from the roughly cut stone. Nothing suggested that it was about to collapse, or tilt to one side as Derek, the man on the bus, had implied. It was about forty feet high, and from its top, Lynnford could imagine its commanding view over the Channel; and from the arrangement of the narrow slits in the walls that made up for windows, he guessed that it must have four floors, possibly five.

Walking around the tower, he discovered only one entrance; a heavy door that was firmly locked. He banged on it with his fist, but there was no reply from within. Like the gate, the wood showed the signs of having endured for many years the bitter coastal elements, yet the timbers remained firm. *Nothing unusual*, he thought, and he was about to consider the possibility of forcing the lock when the sharp snap of a broken twig caught his attention. He turned round quickly but could not see anybody. And then the noise of the van's engine burst out. So they had been watching him, observing what he was up to. A stupid mistake if they hadn't wanted to arouse his curiosity, he reflected. They should have just driven off and relied on Lynnford losing interest and abandoning the site but clearly there was something about the tower that had prevented them from doing just that. They had had to make sure of something but what? And the fresh, still soft lorry tracks, that he now saw, caught in a large patch of mud in the middle of the small track leading up to the tower, what did these mean?

The noise of the motor engine had disappeared along the road to Westcliff. Lynnford turned back to the door, but soon realised that there was no way that he could open it. He looked at his watch. The bus back to Westcliff would be coming up the hill shortly. Wasting no more time, he left the old watch tower and walked back to the road, where he waited in front of the gate ready to wave down the bus.

*

On getting off the bus in Westcliff, Lynnford first went into the post office to check if there were any messages for him and then crossed the road, stepping into the newsagents to see Gwen. She'd still had no news of Sam.

'And Chessington, are you sure you don't know the name?' he asked her.

Gwen shook her head.

'It's not a name I've heard of.'

'What about the newspaper delivery book? You never know.'

Gwen shook her head before reaching under the counter and pulling out a hard-bound ledger. Placing it on top of the counter and, wetting her index finger against her tongue, she began flicking through the pages.

'No, just as I thought. No Chessington. Cheshire, Chester, Cheswick, Christiansen – Danish most likely – Creswall. But no Chessington.'

'The odd thing is that this man I met, Derek, recognised Chessington in the photograph and even said that he had seen him with Yeats in The Lord Nelson in Tower Port.'

'But didn't you say last night that you'd shown the photograph to Yeats? And that he'd said he didn't know who the two people in it were?'

'That's right, Gwen. Maybe this man Chessington looks very different now. That's what Derek implied. He said it was a shock seeing him. It is an old photograph.'

Gwen Mortimer closed the book and replaced it under the counter.

'So, what next?'

Lynnford waved a telegram that he had picked up in the post office.

'I've been summoned back to London by the editor.'

'What about Sam? You can't leave him.'

'Your husband needs a good lawyer but not just yet. He's safe enough where he is.'

'In a police cell!'

'Don't worry, he will be fine. I'll be back in a day or two, three at most. When does the next train to Exeter leave? I'll catch the night train back to London.'

*

Later that day in the evening, in Westcliff, several streets away from The Blue Harp, the late afternoon fading rapidly, Captain Jacobs banged his fist on the table. He was in the kitchen of a small, terraced house, together with Tabby, Kenny and a third man, Skinner. His anger was pouring out at Tabby, sitting in front of him, confused and surly.

'What's gone wrong in that head of yours? The gun, now this!'

'It's all one and the same, isn't it?'

'It's one more stupid prank. That it certainly is, Tabby.'

'It had to be done.'

'Are you mad?'

'Pengal—' began the unfortunate Tabby.

'Pengal again! Don't think Sergeant Evans is going to be able to stick the fire on Sam Mortimer for long. And what for?'

'To destroy the body.'

'What for? And you didn't, did you? The bones still tell a story. They're not daft. They've got eyes in their heads. They know he was shot in the back. What they don't need is a circus to bring everything out in the open!'

The captain glared at all three.

'And anyway who said you could let out Sam Mortimer?'

'He could have burnt to death!' Tabby objected.

'You blockhead! I realise that. That's if the fishing boat had caught fire, but it didn't, did it?' Jacobs replied angrily, before adding, 'Why not bring him here instead of dousing him with kerosene and leaving him on a beach for the police to find?'

'Pengal—'

'Again! At least Pengal will be out of my way for a day or so. But he'd better be back when we load up the boat. Just remember, the three of you, it's me who gives the orders around here!'

THIRTEEN
BACK IN FOUNTAIN STREET

It was raining heavily in London. With a sharp tug at the handle, Lynnford closed the cab door and settled down in the back seat, calling out to the driver, 'Fountain Street, offices of *The London Herald*.'

'Right you are, sir.'

The black cab moved off from the taxi rank outside Paddington railway station and joined the throng of London traffic. Horns blared, people cried out, the noise of engines was incessant and the rain beat down indiscriminately on all that moved. Westcliff seemed a long way off. Fresh sea air and picturesque houses rubbed out by the watery downpour as if they had been nothing more than one of the many pavement drawings of coloured chalk outside Hyde Park on a Sunday afternoon. Only the short wait outside the railway station for a taxi had been enough to leave him cold and wet; the wind ripping under the arcade roof and showering on him and his fellow passengers its sodden load of water.

Inside the taxi, he unbuttoned his coat and removed his hat. He swept off a cluster of raindrops from the rim of the hat and gave the damp bottoms of his trouser legs a shake. The rain pattered down on top of the metal roof above his head. The windows of the rear compartment had already steamed up again. He wiped a clear patch on the side window next to him and peered out through the glass. A red double-decker bus drove past in the opposite direction carrying an advertisement along its side for the Kensington Boat Show; its driver sitting high up above the traffic, ensconced and isolated in his cramped driving cabin. The bus was followed by a succession of other vehicles. Dreary, was the word he had most often heard applied to London weather and it came quickly to mind.

Still, the wait in the taxi rank outside the railway station had produced one surprise: the unpleasant man from outside the watch tower at Tower Port the day before crossing the station forecourt at a half-run, a damp newspaper held over his head. The rain had been doing nothing for the man's health, issuing from him a retching bout of coughing as he ran and so cementing Lynnford's recollection of him. Pengal, if he'd caught his name correctly. He wondered now briefly what had brought the man so suddenly to London.

The taxi passed along the northern side of Hyde Park, turning right at Marble Arch, passing the Grosvenor and Dorchester hotels, along Piccadilly, past the statue of Eros, along the Strand and finally into Fountain Street. Pulling up alongside the steps of *The London Herald*, Lynnford stepped out, settled his fare and strode through the front entrance. It was nine-thirty.

'Good morning, George.'

The senior clerk was already on duty. He looked up from the paper he was reading. Lynnford leant against the reception desk, looking through the glass panel.

'Any news?'

George slid open the panel.

'Mr Kombinski wants to know where you are. First thing this morning, he said.'

'Thanks. That's why I'm here. Post haste from the sea. Anything else?'

'No, except young Jack Worth's been at the Old Bailey all day Tuesday and Wednesday. And he was there on Monday. Says he's working for you again.'

'And I've asked him to go down to Somerset House this morning and look up some records there in the General Register Office of Births, Deaths and Marriages. If you don't mind, of course.'

'I thought he was supposed to be working for me. But that's the way with you gentlemen of the Press; undisciplined. No respect for order and the whole wide world at your beck and call. Let's hope Mr Churchill's back in Number 10 tomorrow.'

Lynnford left the clerk to his paper and took the stairs to his office. Maxwell was there, sitting at his typewriter, writing up the sporting tips and bits of gossip that he had collected the evening before; the ashtray next to his typewriter already beginning to fill up with ash and several cigarette butts. He stopped when Lynnford walked through the door.

'Nice to see you back.'

Lynnford nodded and placed his suitcase down on the floor near his desk, where he remained flicking casually through the papers that had accumulated in his absence. Maxwell continued, 'Jack's just called in and gone out. He said you had telephoned from Exeter late yesterday evening.'

'That's right, I told him to look up the name of someone in the register of births at Somerset House.'

'Also, Kombinski has been in and out like a figurine in a Swiss clock; as regular as clockwork. Each time with the same message; is he here yet? Where is he? What's he doing? He must want to do a piece on you. You know it's the election today?'

'Of course.'

'Turned up anything on your floating body?'

'Nothing much, except it was burnt to a cinder the other night, and almost me with it.'

Lynnford recounted what had happened, and the other information that he had been able to find out.

'An old family snapshot is not going to amuse old Kombinski.'

'No, I suppose not, Max. But a possible murder and a missing boat crew have got to have some mileage in them.'

'Maybe, but two days out of the office already and still no further than you were on Monday afternoon. I don't think he's going to think much of it.'

Before Lynnford could say anything else, someone pushed open the door slightly and a woman's head appeared, her body remaining hidden from view.

'Miss Wainwright!' Lynnford exclaimed, on recognising the editor's personal assistant.

'I see you're back, Mr Lynnford. Mr Kombinski would like to see you at once in his office, immediately.'

'And I see there's no way of getting out of it, if he's sent you down.'

Mabel Wainwright smiled and held open the door for Lynnford, waiting for him to accompany her. Max called out after him as he left.

'By the way, Lynnford, Victoria telephoned to say that she will meet you in the Savoy for lunch at one.'

*

'Enter.' The voice behind the oak-panelled door was loud.

'Careful!' Miss Wainwright warned. 'He's been expecting you for some time now. What for him must seem like a hundred years.'

Lynnford raised his eyes to the ceiling and pushed open the door. Mr Kombinski was seated behind an immense desk, organised to perfection, and occupying almost the full width of the office at the end furthest from the door. The editor of *The London Herald* was as heavily set as the desk before him. The two formed together an imposing presence in the room, a single mass of half-dormant energy, both direction and motor for the journalistic empire that emanated from the closeted confines of his sumptuous office.

Now in his early sixties, Mr Kombinski had been born amongst the dying embers of the nineteenth century, in a land of hope and glory; the son of Polish emigrants. He had since grown from a young boy through the different stages of manhood, bounding from strength to strength as he accompanied the frenzied and fearful events of the next fifty years; an era that had proclaimed aloud the virtues of modern civilisation whilst all around almost everyone had seemed driven to prove the contrary. A born observer and commentator, he followed these events as became his nature. Inspired by occasional flashes of insight, and pushed along by a love of risk, he flourished in his chosen world of newspapers, headlines, copy and printing presses. Mr Kombinski seemed to embody in one single person every facet of the newspaper that he ran. His only regret: an increasing awareness of his own mortality and the knowledge that he would not live long enough to see his century through to its end.

He was in his shirt sleeves, both forearms resting on the desk in front of him, his back bent forward, reading from a sheaf of papers that he held in his two hands, the top lifted slightly off the desk as if in an effort to bring the paper closer to his eyes. He pealed off the uppermost page and placed it face down on the pile next to him.

'Shut the door and tell me what you want.'

Mr Kombinski didn't take his eyes off the paper he was reading.

'You wanted to see me?'

The editor looked up and nodded. Lynnford closed the door and approached his desk. The editor let go of the papers, sat back and, waving a hand at what he had been reading, exclaimed in a manner full of pomp and ceremony, 'Do you know what this is?'

And, without waiting for a reply, continued, 'Copy for tomorrow's edition. Of course you know that, Lynnford. What day are we today?'

Lynnford stayed silent, a little confused by the editor's sudden change of tack.

'Thursday.'

The editor answered his own question and added, 'Morning.'

Lynnford still didn't say anything.

'The general election, but I know that doesn't mean anything to you other than a visit to the polling station. Still, Osborne? Does that mean anything to you?'

The editor was beginning to sound more than a little irritated and he looked hard at Lynnford.

'The Osborne case, damn it! Have you forgotten completely about it? Two days by the sea and everything's flown out of the window. I was there yesterday afternoon. Are you sure you're following it? It'll wrap up today. That's certain. Maybe the jury's already out and the verdict is expected any minute. Who knows? You certainly don't! Maybe he's already on his way to Princetown prison.'

'It's not yet ten,' Lynnford objected. 'The court won't even have begun to sit.'

'Just a manner of speaking, Lynnford. Don't quibble.'

'There's at least another day and a half. Jack Worth's following it and keeping me informed.'

'It's not his job. And there's no good in sending a young lad to do your work. How many times have I told you? Listen, I want this covered properly. It's an important case and I want it covered fully on tomorrow's front page. After all, damn it, you did all the work in bringing this fellow to court. You don't want to miss the grand finale, do you? We can't let Willy Tanner from *The Daily Chronicle* steal our thunder, can we? No. So get cracking!'

He carried on, half to himself, 'Time. Don't you know—'

And he returned to address Lynnford directly.

'Don't you know by now that time is what our business is all about? Yesterday's news is not today's. Getting copy out on time, that's our job: stories, deadlines, urgent business. Time, and the lack of it, it's what makes our business exciting and our pages interesting to read. If the Osborne verdict comes out this afternoon, as it surely will, and he's found guilty of killing his first wife, and attempting to kill his second, London and the rest of the country wants to read about it at the breakfast table tomorrow morning, not over a pint before Saturday's lunch. Do you understand?'

And without waiting for a reply, he continued, 'Sometimes, I get the impression that you're more interested in spending my money on chasing up fantastical stories rather than in putting pen to paper and telling the readers about them.'

'You don't have to worry. You know my story on Osborne covered the front page, and wiped the streets, when I brought it out early this year. The verdict will be in the paper. I've come back especially to do that.'

'Good! That's what I wanted to hear.'

The editor relaxed and was about to dismiss Lynnford with a wave of his hand when he stopped himself and asked with a brusque change of air, 'Anyway, what is this story I hear you're on? Something about missing sailors, down in the sticks somewhere?'

Lynnford gave a reassuring laugh and told him about the death of the sailor, the abandoned yacht and the fire. The editor sniffed, unconvinced.

'There doesn't sound much there, not for a national, but I suppose you know what you're doing. What else can I do?' And he waved Lynnford out of his office.

'But don't forget,' he shouted out after him as Lynnford walked towards the door, 'the Osborne verdict tonight without fail.'

Lynnford closed the door, smiled at Mabel Wainwright as he passed through her antechamber, and regained his own office, where he picked up his coat and notebook and headed off to the Old Bailey.

FOURTEEN
VICTORIA GIVES LYNNFORD A LEAD

There were some silly places to do business, and the lobby of the Old Bailey must surely be one of them. Some perverted sense of humour, perhaps? Pengal leant back against the stone wall and looked around. The huge hall was dragging in a crowd. He had been told to go to Court 6. Couldn't they have just met him at the railway station? A parcel in the left luggage and back home? Damn it! He cursed the bank notes in the holdall. Instead, they had him running across London and wet through into the bargain. Too much money to be carrying, and his life on it if he lost even a one-pound note. Wouldn't he be better off keeping it all? With what he'd collected on Sunday night delivering the necklace he could comfortably disappear. Not really. Too many people knew him. Too many people had a use for him, and he almost laughed. At least he would have, had he not felt his insides begin to burn again like acid, forcing him to retch forward in a spluttering cough that tore through his lungs. Christ! *The Spanish Inquisition could not have done better*, he thought. Looking up, in search of relief, his eyes crossed with those of someone still impressed on his memory. The busybody journalist he and Kenny had come across the day before outside the watch tower. Hadn't he pretended to be a school teacher or something like that? What was he doing back in London? Had he given up? Surely not now that he had spotted him. Damn! He should have just stuck to the job in Westcliff. Then he wouldn't have had to come to London, playing the post boy. But it had seemed like easy money at the time.

Lynnford carried on, softly pushing open the door to Court 2 and slipping into the empty place nearest to him on the back row, not a little surprised to have come across for the second time that morning in almost as many hours the man from the watch tower in Tower Port.

Since its opening on Monday, the Osborne case had now acquired the air of an established camp; an air of familiarity uniting its actors and followers. Even the prisoner seemed to have assumed a philosophical air of resignation. Papers and books littered the desks in front of the opposing counsel.

Lynnford could only see the defendant from behind, but he appeared little different from the day when he had first seen him leave his office in Whitehall and walk up towards Trafalgar Square. He had trailed him all that day, the civil servant completely unaware of his presence, much like today. After three days in the box, he must have got used to the eyes behind him, piercing into his back, trying to understand who he really was. Still, from the seeming lethargy of the courtroom, Lynnford could not see why the editor had got into such a flap. The case was not going to finish today. Not by a long chalk.

He felt a hand on his shoulder and turned round. It was Jack.

'No, don't sit down,' Lynnford whispered. 'I'll follow you out.'

In the corridor, Jack Worth sat down on the bench whilst Lynnford remained standing.

'So, tell me! What did you find out at Somerset House?'

Jack scratched his head.

'What's wrong?'

'Nothing, except, I had to go back a long way before finding a Chessington in Westcliff.'

'How far back are we talking about?'

'1860, or thereabouts.'

Lynnford gave a sigh.

'But I told you we're looking for the birth certificate of somebody who's still alive, or at least not coming up to his ninetieth birthday.'

'I know. But as I couldn't find anyone I just kept going back until I found one.'

'You probably did right but that's put paid to my idea of our Chessington being a local man.'

'Do you want me to keep looking?' Jack asked hopefully.

'No, but you can do that other job I mentioned yesterday.'

'And the Osborne case? Is it about to finish?'

'Maybe tomorrow, but then we'll have to wait for the verdict. The jury could well stay out until Monday. Anyway, off you go and find out what you can about any missing boat stories. But hold on!'

Jack stopped in his tracks.

'Yes, sir?'

'On your way through the lobby, just see if there's still a man there dressed in dark corduroys and looking like he's spent the night on a train. He's got a cough like a miner and looks a bit like one.'

'What about him?'

'See if you can find out what he's doing here. And then get on back to Fountain Street.'

Back inside the courtroom, the prosecution barrister and judge were still listening patiently, almost as observers, whilst the defence continued laboriously through its case. Occasionally one or other made a note. Lynnford listened, trying to immerse himself once again into the story that he had made. It seemed such a long time ago now. From time to time, he looked through Jack's notes. As he had predicted, the defence lawyer had spent most of Tuesday and Wednesday in attempting to discredit the witnesses that Lynnford had painstakingly uncovered, such as the hotel waiter who had seen the defendant slip away from his meeting in Coventry in time to return home and run his wife over in a stolen car. More worryingly, Osborne's second wife, whose suspicions had alerted Lynnford, had broken down in the witness box and seemed to have gone back on some of her story.

He began to feel hungry and suddenly remembered the telephone message from Victoria. He looked at his watch. Not yet twelve forty-five. He had just enough time to get to the Savoy without being too late for her. He got up quickly and let himself out. As he stepped into the corridor, an usher followed him, catching his attention.

'I was asked to give you this note at the adjournment.'

Distractedly, Lynnford thanked the usher and tucked the note in his pocket, continuing on his way quickly to the main hall where, before leaving the Old Bailey, he stopped in one of the telephone booths and put a call through to his office.

'Maxwell? Is that you? Sorry to bother you. Has Jack brought up anything from the library yet? He's been doing some research. No? And anything else?'

Maxwell's voice crackled back at him. 'About the man with the cough. Nothing specific. He found him in the public gallery in Court 6. Armed robbery. The prosecution case was on.'

'Interesting. What's that about, I wonder? By the way, would you do a favour and have my suitcase sent round to my apartment in a cab?'

'No problem, Lynnford. Enjoy your lunch.'

*

'You're late, Robert. Again.'

Victoria was sitting at a table set for two, with a view out onto the Thames. Lynnford gave her a polite kiss on the cheek and sat down in front of her. The dining room was full.

'I've already ordered. Dover sole for the two of us,' she announced. 'Really, Robert, you must improve your timing. I'm sure you don't keep anybody else waiting.'

'Kombinski,' Lynnford smiled, straightening himself in his seat.

'Robert! You shouldn't. You know I have the greatest respect for Paul Kombinski. He's somebody who knows how to work. Father and he were good friends. Treat him with respect. I don't want you losing your job. You would be unbearable.'

'No chance of that.'

The waiter appeared quietly alongside them and served bread. Victoria picked up the thread of her conversation.

'It's just that, it makes me feel so unimportant.'

'Oh, come on, Victoria. Stop teasing me. What have you been up to this morning?'

'I met Gloria. The Royal Academy. An excellent exhibition.'

'Gloria?'

Victoria sighed. 'Robert, you don't retain anything, do you? I simply don't understand how you can be a journalist. We were at the Sorbonne together.'

'Dover sole, madam?'

The waiter had reappeared.

During their meal, they carried on in similar vein, exchanging news on common friends and the humdrum of daily life in the capital until, by the time they had finished, both food and surroundings had conspired to give them a comfortable feeling of ease and satisfaction.

Lynnford let the waiter take away his plate.

'So, what's bothering you, Robert? I'm sure it must be something to do with your trip down to the West Country. Where was it, Eastbeach?'

Victoria is wonderful, he thought to himself. *She always knows how to keep business to the end.*

'Westcliff,' he corrected her, adding, 'Well, yes, I suppose it is to do with my investigation there.'

'Go on,' she prompted.

'Chessington.'

'Who?'

'Chessington. He's gone missing and a woman, probably his wife, as well as leaving a sailor floating dead in the sea alongside their yacht, the *Sea Breeze*.'

'Surely the police will find him soon enough, don't you think?'

'Possibly, but for the moment they seem happy enough to treat it as an accident.'

'But your old friend from the RAF tells you it's murder and that's enough to send you from pillar to post and back again, so to speak.'

Lynnford ignored the irony.

'Sam heard two shots. That doesn't sound like an accident. And before any real post-mortem could be carried out, the body's been reduced to ashes in a fire that everyone, or at least the local bobby, wants to pin on Sam, and possibly me.'

'Well, you have created one or two in your time.'

'It's suspicious, to say the least,' Lynnford continued, not taking the bait, 'and Sam's locked up in a police cell on a trumped-up charge of arson.'

'Still, it doesn't sound much more than a story of local smugglers falling out with each other. No wonder Paul's not interested.'

'There's much more to it.'

'Really?'

'Of course! There must be! Sam went missing before he was found half drunk on the beach and smelling of kerosene. Gwen, his wife, was threatened and told to keep away from me. Why should someone go to all that trouble for the sake of some crates of duty-free whisky?'

'Small minds, unable to think of anything else?'

'Listen, Chessington was not smuggling. The *Sea Breeze* was completely clean. All I found was this.'

Victoria took the photograph that Lynnford placed on the table and looked at it carefully.

'What a lovely couple. They're so happy together. Is this your Chessington?'

'It could be. I've been told it's him and his wife. It was taken some time ago. I found it on the *Sea Breeze*.'

'Well, it must be him, you fool!'

'That's all very well. But smugglers don't usually leave family snaps lying around for strangers to pick up.'

'Then he's not a smuggler. That's clear. Sometimes, Robert, you can be so slow.'

'But that's what I've been trying to tell you. It's not about smuggling.'

Victoria handed back the photograph.

'So, where do you think he might be, this Chessington?'

'I don't know. But I had been told he was a local man, which might have helped me find him. But now, I'm not so sure.'

'Why's that?'

The photograph seemed to have provoked Victoria's

interest, as if seeing the couple on their bicycles had suddenly made it all come real to her.

'Well, the photograph was taken in Westcliff in 1936. The date's written on the back. But I've just had young Jack Worth make a search of the birth register in Somerset House this morning and he's drawn a blank. Sam's wife also tells me that she doesn't know anybody of that name in Westcliff.'

'Perhaps it's someone who left a long time ago. He might not have been born there, but his family might have.' .

'Yes, that's possible. Come to think of it, Jack did say that he had found a Chessington born in Westcliff in the middle of the last century. So it could be his son, or more likely a grandchild.'

'Maybe he moved to Westcliff and married a local woman?'

'But then they would have been known in the town.'

'They probably were. What if Chessington adopted his wife's name?'

'Why would he have done that?' Lynnford asked, surprised.

'Oh, for any number of reasons.'

'Like what?'

'Well, for example, maybe Chessington wanted to hide a shady past behind the cloak of a respectable name. And didn't you say that the man you met on the bus knew the name — on a bus for heaven's sake, Robert — and in fact recognised him and his wife in the photograph? Or perhaps he had a modest background and wanted to better himself. Or—' Victoria smiled at Lynnford, 'could it simply have been out of love and marrying into an important family?'

Lynnford's eyes lit up, and he slapped the tabletop with his hand.

'Robert, really! Behave yourself.'

'But, Victoria, I believe you have it.'

He looked at his watch.

'Look, sorry, I must go now. There's something I must do straight away before the Osborne case resumes.'

Lynnford turned to look for the waiter.

'Can we have the bill, please?'

'But where are you going all of a sudden? What's got into you?' exclaimed Victoria, not a little put out. 'What about coffee?'

'Just down the road to Somerset House and the General Register Office of Births, Deaths and Marriages. I'm sure you're right. I'll telephone you this evening and let you know what I find.'

'No, you won't. I'm coming with you.'

FIFTEEN
SOMERSET HOUSE REVEALS A CLUE

Somerset House, opposite the Aldwych, was only a short distance away. Imperceptibly, Lynnford increased his stride, leaving Victoria one or two paces behind.

'Robert, slow down!'

He looked back apologetically.

'Sorry, Victoria.'

Victoria caught up and slid her hand through his arm.

'There's time enough, surely, for us not to make fools of ourselves, flapping about like the pigeons down the road in Trafalgar Square.'

'Of course, I'm sorry.'

'You weren't trying to lose me by any chance, were you, Robert?'

Crossing Lancaster Place, they were soon at the entrance to Somerset House. The sombre archway was quiet. A solemn guardian of the nation's past, present and future.

They walked into the cobbled courtyard and cut straight across to the public entrance to the General Register Office of Births, Deaths and Marriages on the other side. Inside, time seemed more sacred than the sun-bleached remains of faraway antiquity. The reading room was impregnated with an air of respectful silence. Although not empty, everyone, clerks, doormen, ushers, and visitors moved quietly about their business. Victoria disentangled her hand from under Lynnford's arm. A hall clock struck the quarter hour and without stopping, the slow, rhythmic swing of the pendulum continued its mechanical tick-tock.

Lynnford handed the clerk a chit of paper on which he had scribbled details of the marriage registers in which he was interested.

'We'll bring them to you, sir. What desk are you at?'

Lynnford pointed to the table where Victoria was sitting and then joined her. For some minutes, whilst they waited, they observed in silence the coming and going of the two clerks charged with distributing and collecting the registers within the reading room; a service that was conducted simply and effortlessly as if the clerks were no more than figurines attached to some complex mechanism, repeating itself every so often, and the reading room no more than a stage for their display. Eventually, one of the clerks stopped at their table with three large volumes containing records of the marriages celebrated in the Parish of Westcliff for the years 1915 to 1929. He reappeared with another three volumes covering the years 1930 to 1944.

'So many marriages just in one small fishing town!' Victoria exclaimed quietly under her breath.

'Why so far back?'

'Let's just get on with it.'

Lynnford pulled over the first volume.

'Here. You work back from 1944. I'll start with 1915.'

The pages moved steadily from right to left, from one volume to the next, plunging Lynnford and Victoria into Westcliff's past. Two ceiling lights above their desk reinforced the feeble daylight from outside. Victoria picked up another volume. Upside down, she turned it around and as she did, it opened up on the table and her eye glimpsed the first entry at the top of the page.

'Lynnford! I've got it.'

'Shush!' someone, somewhere in the reading room, hissed.

Lynnford pulled over the book and read the entry to himself: *Certificate of Marriage solemnized at St Mary's Church in the Parish of Westcliff in the County of Devonshire. Married 21st October 1931, Alfred Chessington, 26 years and Jennifer Stewart, 18 years.*

'Twenty-six years old,' he commented, almost to himself, adding, 'That would make him forty-six. He could well be our man.'

'Of course he is!'

'Shouldn't we go through the rest, just to make sure?'

'Lynnford!'

Irritation flashed across Victoria's face. She could hardly see the point, and half suspected a certain measure of damaged pride.

'Fine, Victoria, I agree with you.'

'Good!'

'But there's something missing.'

'What?'

'Shush!' someone again interjected from across the room.

'Look! Don't you see?'

Victoria took back the book and examined the entry again.

'No, I don't see. What is it?' she whispered back.

'The address, it hasn't been recorded.'

'But of course it has.'

Lynnford shook his head.

'No, not fully, only the name of the town.'

Looking again at the record, Victoria realised that he was right.

'That's odd. Isn't it a requirement? They could have been living anywhere in Westcliff.'

'That's just the point. The address, if we had it, would have told us where he lives, or at least where he had lived.'

'So, what now?'

'Let's go outside and have a think in the fresh air.'

On their way out, Lynnford handed in a request for an extract of the marriage certificate.

'You never know, it might still be useful.'

Outside, the courtyard was empty, and the grey sky hanging low over head gave the square space a desolate, lonely air. Several cars were drawn up along the sides. The rough cobbles sank slightly towards the centre. A quiet autumn's afternoon, Lynnford mused, half to himself. Victoria gave him a sharp nudge with her elbow, her hands tucked firmly in the pockets of her coat.

'Keep your mind on the job, Robert. I want to get home as soon as possible. There's a reception at six o'clock, and I have to get ready.'

'You're free to go,' he quipped.

'Yes, of course I am. But I put you on to the idea of looking for the marriage certificate and I want to know before the end of the day how far my idea's got you.'

'Your idea? Fine, let's see.'

Lynnford sat down on a stone seat outside the windows of the reading room. Victoria remained standing in front of him, her hands still in her pockets, staring down at the toes of her feet.

'The marriage certificate at least ties Chessington to Westcliff and more so than the photograph. But both take us back quite a long time, almost twenty years in the case of the marriage.'

'Twenty years exactly. Last Sunday was their anniversary.'

'Indeed. And another thing is the yacht, the *Sea Breeze*. It doesn't come from Westcliff, possibly from Holland. In which case, I guess that's where he's living now. If he was trying to smuggle something into the country, why not choose a place you know? Somewhere like Sandy Cove, a safe harbour, free from prying eyes?'

'I thought we'd discarded the idea of smuggling, Robert? But let's not waste time now on guessing his motive for coming back. It's fairly clear that he knows Westcliff. We're here trying to find an address for where he might have lived.'

'Indeed.'

'So, say Chessington first came to Westcliff to marry.'

'Fine, and?'

'Don't you see? His wife, what's her name?'

'Jennifer Stewart.'

'That's right, Jennifer. Then she was probably from a local family.'

'And she could well have been born in Westcliff.'

'Exactly, Robert.'

'And the birth certificate may give her address, or at least that of her mother. That's why I got Jack to search for Chessington's birth certificate.'

'Yes, it does. I know, because I needed mine the other day. Here, I still have it in my handbag.'

Victoria snapped open the bag and produced a piece of paper, carefully folded in four. Lynnford took the paper in his hands, unfolded it and spread it out on his lap. As Victoria had said, the document gave her mother's address in Westminster. He nodded, 'Just so.'

But before he could read anything else, Victoria snatched back the paper.

'That's enough! You don't need to see anything else.'

'Such as?' he laughed.

She ignored him. 'Come on. Let's give it a try. As I said, I want to be home for six.'

Once back inside the reading room, they quickly found the entry in the register of births. Lynnford read it out.

'Jennifer Stewart, 2nd September 1913, North View House, Westcliff. Father, Rupert Stewart, colonel (retired). Mother, Charlotte Stewart, born Weston.'

'North View House must be the family home. It's also given as the mother's address,' Victoria commented.

'Pity there's no number or street name.'

'Still, for only the house name to be recorded must mean that it was sufficiently well known. Otherwise, the registrar at the time would have written in the road.'

'Let's hope so, Victoria. We just need to find it.'

Walking under the arch that led out of Somerset House onto the Strand, and with extracts of Jennifer Stewart's birth and marriage certificates in his hand, Victoria turned towards Lynnford and, raising herself on her heels, kissed him lightly on the cheek in mock triumph.

'There you go. Didn't I tell you?' she teased.

Wounded pride would have forced a riposte had not Lynnford, unconsciously putting his hand in his coat pocket, felt with the touch of his fingers the note handed to him earlier in the day by the court usher in the Old Bailey as he had left the courtroom. He'd forgotten all about it! He stopped and took out the note.

'What is it, Robert?' Victoria asked, a little disconcerted at his lack of attention.

Lynnford unfolded the note and read out its contents, 'Don't go back to Westcliff. Not if you want to live!'

'A death threat! Somewhat amateurish, don't you think?'

'Possibly,' Lynnford replied hesitantly as suddenly, for the third time that day, he caught sight of the man from the watch tower in Tower Port, Pengal.

There he was! Pressed against the window on the upper deck of a bus heading towards Fleet Street and the City beyond, and seemingly part of another advertisement for the Kensington Boat Show stretched out below him on the outside of the bus. Their regards crossed by chance for a fleeting moment, a glance that seemed to repeat the written warning as surely as if Pengal had shouted it out through an open window on the bus.

SIXTEEN
THE BOAT SHOW

Pengal turned away from the window. Angry with himself for having let the newspaper man see him again. Angry with himself for having agreed to deliver and collect the money for the necklace because otherwise he would not have had to come back to London. Angry with the person who had stolen the necklace making him criss-cross London in pursuit of a trail of secret messages just so that the money could be delivered to him without Pengal ever knowing who he might be. And above all angry with himself for having had the stupid idea of writing that note. What had he been thinking of? *Now I'll have him on my tail all the way back to Westcliff!* Pengal banged the side of the bus with his fist in mad frustration.

*

'I must catch that bus!'

'Robert!'

Victoria's call fell on deaf ears as Lynnford sprinted off. Hurtling into the Strand, he almost collided with Jack Worth hurrying back to Fountain Street, surprise crossing their faces.

'Quick, Jack! He's on the bus.'

Jack looked round, momentarily bewildered.

'That one!' Lynnford cried out. 'Quick, whilst it's stopped.'

'But George?' Jack objected. 'He wants me back at *The London Herald*.'

'Don't worry about him now. Get on the bus. The man with the cough. See where he goes. I'll be in the Old Bailey.'

Lynnford gave him a final push and turned to Victoria who had caught him up.

'What's all that about, Robert?'

'The man who wrote the note,' Lynnford explained, pointing towards the bus. 'He's on that bus.'

'Was it wise to send a young boy after him? If you think the warning's serious.'

'He's seventeen. Old enough to look after himself.'

*

Standing up in the central pit of the courtroom after a long afternoon, the defence barrister was addressing the jury with an air of openness, frankness and sincerity reinforced by a tone that remained throughout solemn, never flippant, and always respectful of the traditions of impartiality that surrounded him. *That's as maybe*, thought Lynnford, *but the judge will still leave his summing-up to tomorrow*, as indeed the judge announced several minutes later. Whereupon the usher, detaching himself from the wall, lizard-like, took a step forward and cried, 'Court rise!'

'Mr Lynnford.'

'Yes, Jack?'

Jack Worth had managed to squeeze into the courtroom moments before it began to empty.

'So where did he take you?'

'Here.'

'Here! Where?'

'Where he was this morning.'

'Court 6?'

Jack nodded.

'He spent the whole time there?'

'More or less. He left ten minutes ago.'

'Why didn't you follow him?'

'I tried, but he was too quick for me.'

Lynnford sighed.

'Are you sure he left the building?'

'I thought he had. But I'm not so sure now.'

'Why? Did he meet anyone, talk to anyone?'

'No one.'

'What can he be up to? Whatever it is, he's not going to stop me going back to Westcliff. Threat or no threat.'

'When?'

'Tonight. On the night train if I can finish what I need to get done. First of all, Kensington, and for that we need a taxi, otherwise we'll never make it in time. Are you coming?'

The courtrooms and corridors were emptying as Lynnford and Jack headed towards the main entrance, giving the Old Bailey all the air of an office closing down for the day. Here and there stood clusters of black-gowned figures, clutching untidy bundles of papers; their horsehair wigs still in place, or occasionally held casually in a free hand. Depending on the fortunes of the day, the debriefings were optimistic, short and upbeat, or melancholy, long and resigned.

Only once they were in the cab did Jack have time to discover where they were going.

'The Boat Show, to see some real boats,' Lynnford informed him, adding, 'background research, if you like, whilst I've got an hour or so to kill. Now, tell me what you found out this morning.'

'About the missing boat stories?'

'What else?'

Jack's face lit up before taking a deep breath.

'A forty-five-foot cruising yacht, a white Zephyr, that's the model, disappeared from its moorings in Whitehaven harbour a month ago without trace. The local police are treating it as theft. But they've nothing to go on. They think that it's probably been taken over to the continent.'

'Or possibly down to Westcliff. Good work, Jack. Any others?'

Jack shook his head.

*

Several minutes earlier, Pengal, after having observed the journalist appear on the steps of the Old Bailey, had slipped out from his concealment under a pillared porch and, flagging down a passing cab, had instructed the driver to follow the taxi that Lynnford and Jack had taken. Some ten to fifteen minutes later the cab driver called out, 'Do you want to get out here? They're stopping.'

'Where are we?'

'Earls Court. The Boat Show.'

Pengal shut the door and paid the fare. The news reporter and his companion were already disappearing up the steps.

*

The Earls Court exhibition hall was full of people, visitors threading their way in amongst the exhibits in all directions. It was as if the harbour in Westcliff had dried up and the passers-by, instead of looking down upon the boats floating prettily in the water, had climbed down onto the muddy beach and were now looking up in wonder at their exposed hulls – their necks held back in astonishment.

Two wide alleyways spread out on either side of the hall, forming a rectangle as they ran down the sides, with the boat displays in the middle. Information stands lined the alleyways, some more elaborate than others, some popular, others deserted with their owners left occupying themselves in rearranging piles of brochures, looking for distraction in their technical booklets or simply gazing upon the throngs of visitors passing them by. Others had left their stands and were exchanging notes with colleagues, assuming an air of casual nonchalance; one or two smoking a cigarette.

Halfway down and Lynnford was held up with a strong sense of *déjà vu*. Given pride of place, a gleaming new yacht reflected a spitting image of the *Sea Breeze*. About to step over towards the boat he suddenly felt Jack tugging at his sleeve.

'Mr Lynnford. Have you seen him?'

'Who?'

'He's about two stands behind us, wearing a blue raincoat.'

Lynnford turned round, but his view was blocked by a throng of people that seemed suddenly to have entered the hall, as if released by a sluice gate.

'Who? I can't see anyone.'

'The man from the Old Bailey. The man you told me to follow. I'm sure it's him.'

'What's he doing here? I don't want him to see you with me, Jack. See what he's up to. I'll be over here.'

Lynnford indicated to Jack the stand with the boat resembling the *Sea Breeze*. Jack nodded his agreement and melted into the crowd around them.

'A very popular model, sir,' the salesman commented, responding to Lynnford's interest.

'Really?'

'Yes. It's a relatively robust craft and easy to handle even for the occasional sailor.'

'What is it?'

'A Zephyr 300; forty-five-foot, two-berth cabin cruiser, galley kitchen and saloon, mahogany finish, equipped with a hundred and ten horsepower marine engine, single mast.'

'A Zephyr, you say?'

Exactly the model that Jack had discovered stolen and which he guessed was now floating in Sandy Cove, most likely with a new name. It was helpful to see it close up. To his untrained eye, it looked very much like the *Sea Breeze*, just like the boat he'd seen in Sandy Cove on Wednesday, although perhaps a different model. Was there anything in their similarity?

'What sort of crew does it need?'

'You can handle it yourself quite easily, provided you've done some sailing before.'

'She could cope with a channel crossing then?'

'Lord, yes! I see you're new to the sea. Yes, perfectly, without any difficulty.'

'What kind of speed can it get up to?'

The salesman looked at Lynnford critically.

'Ten knots. Just over. If you want to cross the channel, you could do a return trip during the day if you have a fair wind and an experienced sailor. Depends of course where you sail from.'

'Of course.'

'And what does it cost? You haven't mentioned the price yet.'

The salesman laughed.

'We always leave that to last. A boat like this will cost you over a thousand pounds. One thousand two hundred to be exact.'

'It's not everybody who can afford that sort of money. Anyway, thank you for your help. I'll think it over.'

Lynnford took some brochures from the salesman and looked around for Jack. He spotted him almost immediately.

'So where is he?'

Jack shook his head, embarrassed.

'You lost him again?'

'He just disappeared. He must have gone and left.'

'And leave us here?'

'Maybe it was just a coincidence.'

'Possibly, but I doubt it.'

*

The foyer was empty as Pengal passed through it, worrying about the journalist's interest in the Zephyr. He couldn't trust anyone. Why had Skinner, the skipper of the *Sea Bird* at anchor in Sandy Cove, been so clumsy? Suddenly, the electric light in the foyer failed, leaving the pale luminosity of the evening dusk outside to filter through. He walked out onto the steps and looked down. No one, except for the occasional visitor in the forecourt, strolling home. He resolved his thoughts in an instant. Voices approached him from behind. He stepped aside and watched the couple, a man and woman, descend. Waiting in the dark, the wall concealed him from the inside.

Some more visitors leaving the exhibition appeared on the concrete apron before walking down the steps, their footfalls clicking loudly against the hard surface. One, two, three. Pengal continued waiting. A sailor's patience. Finally, the reporter came striding through, alone, a foot on the step below. Nothing more than a push and he'd lose his balance. Pengal reached out, a knife in his hand to make sure.

Left behind, having stopped to tie his loose shoelaces, Jack hurried through the unlit foyer in time to catch the scene. The raised arm about to let fall a mortal blow. Time only to let out a warning cry.

'Mr Lynnford! Behind you!'

Lynnford stepped aside and slipped. The knife fell down through the empty air, the body of Lynnford's assailant staggering behind it, cursing loudly before fetching himself up and bounding down the steps, not bothering to waste time for a second glance. Jack ran out.

'There he is!'

Jack stretched out his hand in the direction of the man in the raincoat and shabby corduroys, running across the forecourt towards the exit. He was already within reach of the gate.

'Quick!' cried out Lynnford, back on his feet and bounding down the steps with Jack on his heels. But even as he spoke, they saw that it was too late. Pengal had run through the gates and jumped onto the open platform of a passing bus. Lynnford pulled up short.

'Forget it. We've missed him.'

'Who is he? Why have I been following him all day?'

Lynnford shook his head.

'I don't know, Jack. Pengal's his name. Unpleasant and most likely dangerous. At any rate, a nasty piece of work. Somehow he's mixed up in Sam Mortimer's story but don't ask me how.'

'What's he doing in London?'

'What, indeed? At least it seems he's had time to get himself a raincoat. Listen, Jack. Tomorrow morning, first thing, go back to the Old Bailey. Make sure you're the first in.'

'What do you want me to do?'

'Check everywhere he went, especially the places where you saw him sitting. Court 6. But don't forget the main hall. See if he didn't leave something there. Something for somebody to pick up.'

'This is great!'

'Let's hope they haven't already been and gone. By the way, the Whitehaven boat. Did the newspaper article give its name?'

'*The Dolphin*. Why?'

'Oh, nothing. Just an idea. Leave a message for me with Maxwell.'

As he waved goodbye to his young colleague a bus pulled up in front of him, slowed down by the traffic, a Number 74 heading towards Knightsbridge. Never mind what Victoria might think about catching buses! And he jumped quickly onto the platform, just as it began to move off again.

'Hold tight there!' the conductor shouted from within the lower deck of the bus.

*

Park Mansions was quiet. The porter, Mr Cobley, greeted Lynnford as he pushed open the double doors that led into the lobby.

'What's the news, Mr Lynnford?'

'You probably know better than me, Cobley.'

'How's that?'

Lynnford laughed. 'Come on, Mr Cobley. You and your

dear wife know everything there is to know about what goes on.'

'You're pulling my leg! It's a big world out there and you've come fresh in from Fountain Street.'

'The Osborne affair, you remember that?'

'One of your scoops. A year or so ago if I remember right.'

'That's it. But not so long ago.'

'So what's the news? Has he been hanged?'

'It could go either way, I'm afraid.'

'But if it hadn't been for you, he wouldn't even be on trial.'

'True enough but the Press and the Law have different rules to play by.'

'That's true, indeed!'

Mr Cobley turned to go back into his flat.

'Before you go, Cobley. I'm leaving London tonight.'

'Again! You've only just come back.'

'I'll leave an envelope with you on my way out. Could you make sure it goes over to *The London Herald*? It's very important.'

'Certainly, Mr Lynnford. You can rely on me. By the way, sir, have you had a chance to vote yet? The polling booths will be closing soon.'

'Not yet, Cobley. I'll see if I have time.'

Lynnford closed the door of his apartment behind him and took off his shoes. He was tired but there was no question of him lying down. He would fall asleep and miss his train. A light meal had been left in the kitchen on a tray by his housekeeper. But he was not hungry. Instead, he poured himself a Scotch, mixed it with some ice and water and sat down at his desk and began typing steadily, without hesitation or the mechanical failures that had plagued him earlier in the week, on the day that the telegram from Sam had arrived. An hour later a pile of typed sheets lay to one side, next to the machine. After completing two more, he sat back and reviewed the several pages of copy, made a correction here and there, expressed a sigh of satisfaction and placed them in an envelope. Taking out a thick black pen, he scribbled across it, "*Guilty*".

He then took up a fresh sheet of paper, rolled it into the typewriter and recommenced. Roughly another hour went by until he finally stopped. Once he was satisfied with this second text he placed it in another envelope, on the outside of which he wrote the words, "*Not guilty*". Just in case, he said to himself. Like this Kombinski will get what he wants, whatever happens. Slipping the two envelopes into a larger envelope which he had addressed to *The London Herald*, he set about repacking his case and after a quick telephone call for a taxi went downstairs, leaving the envelope with the porter. It was almost eleven o'clock. Time enough to get the train back to Westcliff. But it was too late to vote. Still, his vote or not, Churchill's fate was already sealed. He'd find out in the morning.

SEVENTEEN

A TURN UP FOR THE BOOKS

'So, it's true?'

'What's that, dear?'

'Your loose tongue told everyone about Sam Mortimer's friend.'

'What of it?'

Mrs Knight and her husband were standing in the hall to their guest house. Mr Knight had returned with the daily newspaper only a few moments earlier, leaving as usual the front door ajar.

'You know full well. Why else would those two louts have given him such a beating the other day only hours after he'd arrived?'

'But anybody could have told them.'

Joyce Knight bit her lip, wrapping her hands nervously in her apron before continuing, 'Mrs Parry from the post office must have told the whole of Westcliff about Sam's telegram.'

'But Joyce, he's our guest!'

'Maybe, but he's a snoop. And what business had he coming down here and poking his nose around? Tell me that. She should never have married Sam. Look what a mess he's got himself into.'

'Sam never did that. He's been set up. Everyone knows that.'

'Well, he's fair turned everyone against poor Gwen. Bringing strangers down here. He'll never be one of us.'

'He's God-fearing, just like us. And murder's a sin. They've gone too far, Jacobs and his ilk.'

'There's only Sam that says that. And it wasn't him as fished the Dutchman out of the water. If they say it was an accident, we can't say otherwise.'

'Can't or won't, Joyce?'

A knock on the open front door made them turn round.

'Good morning. Sorry, I hope I'm not interrupting.'

Lynnford stood in the entrance, suitcase in hand.

Embarrassment flashed across their faces. Mrs Knight lowered her eyes.

'Mr Lynnford! Back already?' Mr Knight paused before adding, holding up the newspaper, and pointing to the headline, 'The Tories are back in, then.'

'Yes, indeed. Just like me! Would my room still be available?'

'Of course,' Mrs Knight replied, recovering her wits. 'Peter, show him upstairs.'

'No bother, please don't trouble yourselves. I know the way. Thank you.'

A quarter of an hour later, after putting away his clothes and freshening up, Lynnford looked into the kitchen. Mrs Knight was standing behind an ironing board whilst her husband was sitting at the kitchen table reading through the election results in the newspaper.

'So what happened here? Any change?'

Mr Knight shook his head.

'No, we held on to Exeter.'

'Tell me, have either of you heard of North View House?'

Mr Knight looked up from his paper, relieved slightly at the innocence of the question.

'North View House? No.' He shook his head. 'Not in Westcliff.'

'I was told it was.'

'In Westcliff? I've never heard of it. Joyce?'

Mrs Knight stood up the iron and shook her head.

'Whereabouts? Have you an idea?' continued her husband.

'None whatsoever,' Lynnford replied. 'That's the problem.'

'Well, you could try at the police station.'

'Better still at the town hall,' suggested Mrs Knight.

'Good idea. I'll do that. When's it open?'

'It's gone nine-thirty already. You could also try the post office.'

'Thank you.'

Lynnford made to leave but stopped as something else crossed his mind.

'By the way, maybe you can help me. Would you know who this is? A man in his thirties, straight black hair, medium height, strong face but the rest of his body looks as if it's wasting away with consumption. Frightening cough.'

The Knights exchanged what Lynnford thought to be a worried look. But it was gone before he had time to properly register it. They shook their heads.

'Where have you seen him?'

'With the red-haired lad that delivers bread. He seems nice enough. Offered me a lift the other day when I was in Tower Port.'

'Oh, that's young Kenny. He's harmless,' Mr Knight replied. 'In that case, the other man must be Pengal. A Cornishman. They're often together since he came back.'

'I didn't know he'd come back,' commented Mrs Knight.

'Has he been away?'

'At sea.'

'London, Joyce.'

'As good as,' sniffed Mrs Knight, picking up her iron.

*

Lynnford had no luck in the post office. No one had either heard of the house or recalled receiving any mail to be delivered to such an address. Before leaving, he put a call through to his office and told Maxwell about the two envelopes that he'd asked Mr Cobley to have sent over with the alternative verdicts for the Osborne case, telling him to make sure that Kombinski got the right one at the end of the day. Gwen Mortimer, across the road, informed him that her husband had been taken to nearby Overcombe, apparently at the request of the chief constable. He was still being refused visits. She had not heard of North View House either.

The receptionist in the town hall had never heard of North View House. She had suggested the planning office, located in the depths of the building, but it also had not been particularly helpful; the two gentlemen there not much over twenty, enjoying their quiet Friday morning and celebrating the election victory, making it quite clear to Lynnford that he was wasting their time. Still, he had extracted from them a detailed street plan of the town, which he had rolled up and taken out with him.

Outside the town hall, he looked at the street plan. Where might a house like North View House be found? The name suggested that it had a view, most likely over the sea, in a northerly direction. The problem was that almost the whole town was north-facing, and being built on the hillside, looked out towards the sea. So for the best part of an hour Lynnford tramped up, along, and down the streets of the town, finding many houses with names that for the most part evoked the sea and all that was connected with it, but not North View House. He also canvassed the length of the high street, calling in on estate agents, solicitors, and shops he guessed that made deliveries but to no avail.

It was almost eleven o'clock when he found himself back in the high street, outside Sam and Gwen's newsagents. The shop was empty, much as it had been earlier that morning, indeed all week.

'They're no longer watching over the shop,' Gwen remarked. 'Maybe they've given up. But with all the trouble

Sam's got himself mixed up in we seem to be on the wrong side of the whole town.'

'It'll turn around, Gwen.'

'As dead as a crypt. I may as well close up. I don't know why I don't. My last customer was on Tuesday, when you came in. Although Peter Knight was in this morning as usual to pick up the newspaper.'

'Once Sam's cleared, they'll come back.'

'Maybe. Anyway, you look deadbeat. Turned up anything?'

Lynnford shook his head.

'You know, Gwen, why are they covering up for this man Chessington?'

'How's that?'

'Sergeant Evans, Yeats the harbour master. Why are they so keen to ignore the obvious? Chessington was on the yacht. He's disappeared. Who else could have killed the sailor? Why persist in the idea of an accident?'

'And the harbour master set fire to his own office?'

'Why not? It wasn't Sam, was it? And I've seen odder things. Insurance.'

'Was Chessington on the boat?'

'The chandlers in Tower Port wrote him out an invoice. He was seen with Yeats. So he's definitely come back from wherever he's been.'

'Still.'

The bell tinkled again and an elderly woman, smartly dressed, her grey hair sleek and tied back, entered the shop. A customer!

'Good morning, Mrs Henderson. I have your paper for you.'

'Thank you, Mrs Mortimer. I'll take it in a minute. Finish with the gentleman. I want to choose something for my grandson. I'll look around if you don't mind.'

'Very good. Take your time. Let me know just as soon as you're ready.'

Gwen smiled at Lynnford, a look of relief on her face. A customer!

Mrs Henderson began looking at the games and toys. Gwen and Lynnford continued with their conversation, returning to the subject of North View House.

'I can only think that its name has been changed.'

'It's possible.'

'What I find surprising is that no one in a small town like this has heard of either the Stewarts or the Chessingtons. The Stewarts, at least, were here for two generations or so.'

'People come and go. I can't recall either name.'

'But still. North View House must be here somewhere. It can't have just disappeared. You know, I still haven't tried down by the harbour. I'll go there now. The Blue Harp will soon be full of people.'

Lynnford was about to turn round when he felt a gentle prod in his side. The elderly woman was standing close to him. He'd forgotten all about her. She clasped her hand around his arm, just below the elbow.

'Excuse me, sir. Did I hear you mention North View House?'

'Yes, I did. Do you know it?'

'Yes, of course.'

'At last! I've spent the entire morning looking all over Westcliff.'

'But, young man,' the woman replied, smiling, 'it's not in Westcliff; at least not in the town properly speaking.'

'Where is it then, Mrs Henderson?' Gwen interjected on Lynnford's behalf.

'Where? North View House?'

The old woman seemed pleased with the interest she had aroused and could not resist the temptation to play out the suspense.

'Yes.'

'Well, it's in Sandy Cove, of course.'

'Sandy Cove!' exclaimed Lynnford and Gwen almost in unison.

'But of course! That explains a lot.'

And the reason why Chessington and the *Sea Breeze* had sailed into the cove was now clear to Lynnford.

'But there are no houses there. Except the Hopes' farm and their holiday chalets and cottages,' objected Gwen.

'That's right,' agreed Lynnford. 'Is it one of those cottages? That would surprise me.'

'You can't see the house from the cove itself,' the woman explained, still enjoying the mystery. 'The house doesn't look onto the cove at all. It's built on the cliff, on the other side. It looks out directly to the open sea, although it's set back a little. The trees hide it completely from the cove.'

'That's North View House?' exclaimed Gwen, surprised.

'I had heard that there was an old, abandoned house up there. But I've never heard it called North View House. Nobody's lived there for years as far as I know.'

'No, that's right,' confirmed the woman.

'Except during the War when it was requisitioned by the government and used as a rest home for convalescing airmen. Since then, the house has been empty and boarded up. I doubt if there are many people in Westcliff who know or remember anything about it, let alone whether it exists. Or if they did, they've probably forgotten about it. It's in the past, do you understand? Like me, I'm afraid. Possibly they might have spotted it from the sea, but they wouldn't know the name or anything about who used to live there.'

'And the Chessingtons and Stewarts? Did you know them?'

'No, I can't say that I knew them very well. I don't think that anybody did, at least not in Westcliff. Catholic and Protestant rivalries, you understand. They were Catholic and the town's largely Protestant.'

'And if the house doesn't look on to the cove, how do you reach it?'

'There's a turning on the road to Sandy Cove, just before the road starts to go down to the sea. Follow the signpost to Cliff Point.'

Lynnford smiled to himself at his luck. The woman took her paper, informed Gwen that she hadn't quite made up her mind about what to buy her grandson, and would come back another day, and left the shop. The bell tinkled again as she went out.

'That's a turn up for the books and no mistake, Gwen.'

'What do you plan to do now?'

'Get over there straight away. What do you think?'

'Is it wise? If Chessington has come back and if he did kill the sailor then he may well be hiding there.'

'It's a risk. I'll be careful.'

Gwen looked doubtful.

'And Sam in all that?'

'Don't worry, Gwen. Sam's innocent. We'll get him back. The police can't stop his visits much longer. Now, how can I get there? The path to Sandy Cove?'

'You're best taking the road. It's a pity you've just missed the Tower Port bus.'

*

It was a lonely road, curving gently and often; a road-builder's compromise. The unmarked road was laid with macadam. On either side, thick hedges rose up almost to head height, still leafy-green and wooden-grey; the fields behind them empty of crop. The pale sky around him was full of light grey cloud, brought down almost to within his reach, or so it seemed.

A motor engine broke the silence and suddenly a car appeared from around the bend, approaching Lynnford. The horn blared and the car shot past, a light blue and green Rover; the driver at the wheel with his attention fixed on the road ahead. The engine noise faded, and silence soon enveloped him once again.

He must have walked about another mile when he heard the sound of a second motor engine. The noise got louder and louder. It was coming from Westcliff. When he guessed that he was in sight of the driver, he turned around and stuck out his thumb, hoping for a lift and looking all the time straight ahead at the driver.

It was an old van. It drove past and stopped, some fifty feet or so ahead. Lynnford ran up and opened the side door. To his surprise, he recognised the face of Mrs Hope, the owner of the farm and holiday cottages in Sandy Cove.

'Hop in!' she said, her hands remaining on the wheel and gear stick, ready to drive off again. She smiled at him.

'Are you still looking for a holiday chalet?'

Lynnford returned her smile and shook his head.

'Where are you off to then?'

'Cliff Point.'

'Get in then! I'm going some of the way.'

The van rattled off.

'It's a nice spot,' she continued. 'There's also an old house up that way. North View House. Although not many people in Westcliff know about it. Boarded up and abandoned for years. What a waste!'

'Really?'

Lynnford quickly changed the subject, not wanting to arouse her curiosity. 'Have you been into town?'

'The weekly supply run.'

Mrs Hope jerked her thumb behind her.

Lynnford glanced backwards and saw that the back of the van was full of groceries, several loaves of bread poking out of the carton nearest to him. He had half-suspected to see crates of contraband.

'Have you always lived in the cove, Mrs Hope?'

'I was born there. Fifty-five years ago.'

Lynnford itched to ask her whether she knew the Stewarts. Given her age, she must have done. And even Chessington. He wondered whether there was a link between them all, the Stewarts, Chessington and the Hopes. Yet he knew it would be foolhardy to so openly declare his hand to someone he did not fully trust.

'And your husband?' he asked instead.

'My old man died in the War. Or rather he came back from it a dying man and died here. God rest his soul.'

'I'm sorry.'

'It's the way it is.'

'Was he a local man as well?'

'Oh, no! The parents wouldn't have heard of it. Percy was a salesman. He used to pass by every so often trying to sell us machinery for the farm and the like. One visit he got held up by the bad weather and stayed the night. We got married almost straight away afterwards. The holiday chalets, they were our idea, Percy's and mine.'

The van lurched to a halt.

'Well, here you are. Cliff Point.'

Lynnford climbed out of the van, thanked Mrs Hope and waved as she drove off, the road soon plunging her down into the cove. He, on the other hand, was quickly hemmed in by tall trees, towering above him on either side of the narrow road, the light cut out as if he were at the bottom of a mineshaft, leaving the road sombre and menacing. High above, a solitary seagull screeched out loud. A few seconds later, the sound was repeated and then the bird was gone, leaving Lynnford in front of a set of wrought-iron gates. Thick iron bars rose up in the form of an arch with wild grass covering the bottom rails. On either side, two moss-covered stone pillars supported the gates and held back the holly bushes that pressed in against them. The name of the house was chiselled into the right-hand pillar.

'North View House,' Lynnford read out loud.

Through the iron bars, Lynnford could see the house beyond, a solid Georgian villa full of symmetry across its façade. A stone wall held back the surrounding wood from the house and its grounds, allowing the abandoned residence to still bathe in the midday autumnal daylight. The gates were padlocked together with a heavy chain. Lynnford rattled the gates, but the chain held firm. The only way through was to climb over. He pulled himself up and swung over the gate, letting himself fall down on the other side. No dogs barked. No one cried out after him. He picked himself up, brushing off the gravel from his clothes. Panting a little from the exertion, he listened. But nothing had changed. There was the same silence as before. The place was deserted. Or was Chessington watching him from one of the windows in the house, alerted by the rattling of the gates? He would have to take the risk.

He walked straight up to the house. As Mrs Hope had said, it was boarded up. Planks of wood were nailed up against the frames of the lower windows. Beaten by the changing fortunes of the weather, although discoloured they still held strong. The paint was showing signs of age and the plaster around the two entrance pillars was cracked in several places. There was little point in ringing the doorbell. He did, however, try pushing open the door. It didn't budge. It had been built to withstand both force and time. He followed the house round to the back. It bore the same external appearance throughout: boarded-up windows, unattended plasterwork and weather-worn timber. As much an altar, the terrace at the back of the house looked out over a wild abandon of rhododendrons, yews and ivy to the limitless horizon formed by the sea and sky.

Completing a circuit of the building, he passed along the border of a meadow in which a herd of cows was grazing before noticing a small chapel, a little to one side of the house, and half-hidden from view by the bushes. Well, if anything, the Stewart family must have been affluent to maintain their own chapel, he reflected. Why the house had been left abandoned he could not begin to guess. An overgrown cemetery surrounded the chapel, with some of the roughly hewn gravestones, clearly much older than the house, leaning to one side and sinking slowly into the earth. He bent down in front of a more recent white marble plinth. The inscription was dedicated to Rupert Stewart, 1872–1930. Jennifer Stewart's father, he guessed. At any rate, here was the family. An old Catholic family. Possibly Royalists at odds with the local community. But where was Chessington? And his wife? Lynnford turned again towards the villa.

EIGHTEEN
NORTH VIEW HOUSE

The dry basin of the fountain in the lawn to the back of the villa was surrounded by three large swimming fish, their mouths open, ready to spout out water that had probably not passed their stony lips for many a decade. Staring into their large, lifeless eyes it suddenly came to him. If Chessington had sailed into the cove, and wanted to visit the house, there had to be a path off the beach leading directly up to the house. And so Lynnford set off, skirting the wall to the grounds; the brambles amongst the ivy and rhododendrons sticking into his clothes and cutting across his hands and wrists as he tried to keep them away from his face. Still, he soon found what he had been hoping for: a hole in the wall, no more than a simple break in the stonework, on the other side of which there was a path that appeared to descend steeply.

He passed through the gap and followed the path down. Low-hanging branches, bushes and undergrowth hemmed him in on both sides. The early afternoon daylight was lost and in one place he nearly lost his footing when the path turned sharply without warning. Eventually, the path brought him out of the trees and to the water's edge. Across the water, on the far side of the cove, he could see the boat that he now guessed, from Jack's research, had been stolen from Whitehaven; the Zephyr, with its smart white hull and single mast, floating gently at anchor.

Retracing his steps, something in the undergrowth, around about where he had almost lost his footing on the way down, caught his eye. Lightly parting a clump of nettles on the side of the path with his foot he revealed to his surprise the sole of a plimsoll lying amongst the undergrowth, its toe stuck in the ground. Pushing aside the overhanging bush, he gave a start. The body of a man lay plunged headlong down the steep bank. Lynnford almost expected the man to jump up and berate him for having made him fall, getting in his way and tripping him up, as if his accident had only just happened; but the body remained still and silent.

Lynnford eased himself down the bank and alongside the body until he was in a position to examine it. The head had hit a stone stuck firmly in the ground. The body was cold and lifeless. Carefully, he raised and slightly turned the head just off the ground and looked at the face. Chessington! The man in the photograph, he was sure, although much older now. From the body's condition, it looked as though it had been lying there for several days. What had happened? Had he been running away from somebody? Or had he heard the gun shots on the *Sea Breeze*? And where was his wife?

He would have liked to have moved the body up onto the path where it could rest in a more decent position, but he knew he had to leave it as it was, lying pathetically and undignified, almost on its head. The police would not thank him if they found it otherwise. Still, he could not resist the temptation to search the man's clothes to see if he could learn anything about the man's death before Sergeant Evans got his hands on the body.

Chessington was lying flat on his chest, hampering Lynnford's efforts and forcing him to lift, first one side and then the other. He was wearing flannel trousers and an overcoat, under which he seemed to have a thick woollen jumper. Inside the plimsolls, his feet were bare. The coat was unbuttoned and had spread out on the man's fall. A small velvet bag was tightly held in the grasp of a hand caught under the weight of the man's body, but Lynnford knew he couldn't take the risk of prising open the fingers. Hopefully, he'd learn later from the police what the bag contained. In the man's trouser and coat pockets there were no papers or anything else that might confirm his identity or explain his presence except for a largish key; a door key. And Lynnford's thoughts immediately leapt up the path to the house he'd just left.

He had to go past the house anyway to get help, he reasoned. He remembered having seen a telephone box at the turning where Mrs Hope had dropped him off. So what would be lost by him first checking out the house, should the key let him inside?

Some minutes later, Lynnford stood on the terrace gazing at the rear of the house, the gardens stretching out behind him to the sea and sky beyond, the boarded windows of the house barring his way, the door key nestling uselessly in his hand. He'd been around the house once already, unsuccessfully trying all the doors; firstly, the large front door, then a door at the side of the house and, finally, a kitchen door on the other side. Maybe, after all, the key had nothing to do with the house? Then, with a start, he realised there was a set of French windows looking onto the terrace. Of course, the French windows! The key slipped into the keyhole in the door and, turning the key gently to the right, he heard the soft click, releasing the lock.

The open door cast a short path of daylight into a drawing room. The parquet tiles were bare, but their dull polish still reflected a little light. Higher up, some more daylight squeezed in from around the boarded windows. Not a table, chair, or other piece of furniture. He cast his eyes around the room. It seemed to extend for the full width of the house, or at least for a good part of it.

Looking rapidly into the other rooms on the ground floor and then upstairs, Lynnford found nothing more than confirmation that the house had been vacated, with the few contents that had been left all under dust sheets. The walls were mostly bare, and the carpets had all been taken up. Clean and orderly, as it must have been left at the end of the War after the last convalescing patients had been sent home.

Returning into the large drawing room, a sudden movement caught his attention. A swift patter of feet and it was gone. Lynnford rushed outside and onto the terrace. Nothing. Standing still, he listened; nothing, only the muffled sound of the sea. A cat maybe, or a fox? It must have crept inside through the open door. Or was there somebody out there, hiding in the garden? That man Pengal again? He couldn't seem to get rid of him. *No*, he thought, *that's unlikely*. Taking another pace forward, his shoe scraped against something small but hard on the terrace paving stone. Bending down, he picked up a button: a coat button. Who'd lost that, he wondered. Chessington? Lynnford dropped it in his coat pocket. It might be useful. One never knew.

He stepped back inside the drawing room for one last look and for the first time he noticed the painting above the empty fireplace, one of the few left hung on the wall. An oil portrait of a woman framed in gilt; he felt he knew her but could not immediately place her until, smiling, he pulled out the photograph of the two cyclists, and held it up to the portrait. Yes, it was definitely her, Jennifer Stewart. Chessington's wife. She was the woman in the photograph. Now he had the names of both cyclists: Alfred Chessington and Jennifer Stewart.

Chessington and Jennifer Stewart. Some of the pieces of the puzzle were coming together, if not exactly falling into place. Lynnford closed the French windows, locked them with the key, and headed towards the wrought-iron gates and the telephone box at the end of the road. What he had to do now was inform the police about the body.

*

The bright-red telephone box, with its low-domed top, was cut into the hedge. Lynnford pulled open the heavy glass-panelled door and stepped inside. Lifting the receiver, he spoke to the operator and asked to be put through to the police station at Westcliff.

'Good afternoon, may I speak to Sergeant Evans? Tell him it's Robert Lynnford.'

He heard the receiver being put down and the call for the sergeant to come to the telephone. A door banged and the receiver scraped the desk as it was picked up.

'Yes, who is it?'

'Robert Lynnford. We spoke on Tuesday. About the *Sea Breeze* and the murdered sailor.'

'Oh, you! Aren't you in London?'

'No, I came back this morning, on the night train.'

'So, what can I do for you?'

No mention of the fire.

'I believe I've found another member of the crew.'

'What crew?'

'The *Sea Breeze*. He's dead.'

'You're reporting a dead body? Where?'

'North View House. It's the—' Lynnford began, before being cut short.

'I know where it is. Dead, you said?'

'It looks like he had an accident some days ago.'

'In the house?'

'No, in the woods, leading down to the cove.'

'Don't move. I'm coming over straight away.'

'You can pick me up at the turning off the road down to the cove. I'm in the telephone box.'

'Don't move from there.'

Lynnford cut off the line and checked the time on his watch; just gone one o'clock. He called the operator again.

'London, Chelsea 3381 and reverse the charges, please.'

The telephone rang for several moments before a woman's voice answered at the other end.

'Victoria. It's Robert.'

'Robert darling. Where are you? Let me guess. Land's End or John O'Groats?'

'Westcliff!'

'Oh yes, that's right. Well, I'm about to go out, but I've got a few minutes. So where are you up to? Have you found the house? What's it like?'

'You'd like it. Antique, abandoned and full of mystery.'

'And, so where's Chessington and his wife?'

'Well, his wife, I don't know. But I believe I've just found him, or rather his dead body, in the woods outside the house.'

'How dreadful!'

'Yes, it is. I'll tell you about it later, I'm expecting the police any minute. Where are you off to now?'

'I've a meeting of the British & French Orphans' Trust. Why?'

'Could you give it a miss, just this once? I know it's asking a lot.'

Victoria sighed. 'What is it you want me to do for you?'

'Go back to Somerset House. But this time, look up the register of deaths.'

'Who for?'

'Jennifer Stewart.'

'Robert, you don't think?'

'It's just an idea. Can you do it?'

'Well, I suppose I can. But why you call on me to help

you when you have an entire newspaper at your disposal I can never work out. I'll go after the meeting.'

Lynnford would have preferred that she did it straight away, but he had to accept that it was something that could wait, and he knew that there was no way of getting Victoria to give second place to her charity work.

'If you must. But keep an eye on the time. It's Friday afternoon, and they may close early.'

'Leave it with me.'

'Thanks Victoria. Can you telephone Sam's wife or phone me at the Harbour View Guest House if you find anything, but don't leave a message. Better still, call the shop directly.'

Victoria noted down the number.

'I'll be in touch.'

Lynnford replaced the receiver and looked at his watch again. Time enough for two more calls.

'Operator, could you get me London, City 4022 and reverse the charges.'

He waited a few moments whilst the woman on the other end of the line put him through.

'Hello, *The London Herald*, Sports desk, Maxwell speaking.'

'Max, it's me, Lynnford.'

'Oh! It's you.'

Max sounded disappointed.

'What's wrong?'

'Nothing. I'm just expecting a hot tip on the afternoon race at Chepstow. That's all.'

'Tell me, what's the news on Osborne?'

'Guilty. Pleased?'

'Well, it's what he deserved. A majority verdict?'

'No, unanimous.'

'And when's the sentence?'

'Monday. Anyway, I put your prepared piece in and added some slight changes. It's on tomorrow's front page.'

'Good work. Thanks, Max.'

Lynnford breathed a sigh of relief.

'Well, that's something out of the way.'

'How about you, any news?'

'Some. Listen! Is Jack there?'

'Not with me but he must be somewhere in the building. Do want to speak to him?'

'If you don't mind. Could you go and find him? I'll ring you back in a couple of minutes.'

He could see the police car approaching when Jack finally picked up the receiver.

'Quickly, Jack. Tell me! What did you find? Nothing?'

'An envelope under the bench in Court 6.'

'Still there! And?'

'Just a key.'

'Nothing else?'

'No, but it has a number. It looks like a safe deposit key.'

'Interesting.'

'Mr Lynnford.'

'Yes?'

'I took the key and left your telephone number. Was that the right thing to do?'

'Not bad, young man, for an apprentice. What happens if they call now, whilst I'm here in Westcliff?'

'Mr Maxwell said he would take care of it.'

'Good.'

A car horn sounded behind him.

'I must go now. Well done, Jack.'

He replaced the handset and stepped out of the cabin, wondering how he was going to explain to the sergeant his presence in a wood whose only access was through the private grounds of a long-abandoned house.

NINETEEN
CONSTABLE SMITH MAKES A FIND

'So this is how you found him?'

Bent down, the sergeant raised with one hand the branches of the tree that were covering Chessington's body, steadying himself with the other as he looked back at Lynnford, enquiringly. Lynnford nodded in reply.

'You didn't move him then?'

'No, Sergeant. Why should I have done that?'

'We'll see. You'll give me a full statement later on back at the station. For the moment—'

The police officer paused as he concentrated on progressing down the bank without slipping. The branches of the tree fell back immediately as he let go. Lynnford lifted them, following the police officer's movements.

'Did you pick up anything? Or see anything?'

'No.'

'Well, it looks to me like his fall killed him, just as you

said. But he could still have been pushed from behind or tripped up. I'm keeping an open mind. We'll see what the doctor has to say when he turns up.'

Level with the man's head, the sergeant bent down and raised the shoulder off the ground, trying to get a good look at the face, letting go once he had satisfied himself. He shook his head, almost to himself.

'Don't you recognise him, Sergeant?'

'No.'

'Try a bit harder.'

'Don't play games with me. I still want to talk to you about the fire down at the harbour on Tuesday.'

The sergeant scrambled up the bank, puffing a little from the effort.

'So, Mr Lynnford, you're going to tell me who it is?'

'There's a good chance it's Chessington.'

'Who?'

'Come on, Sergeant. You know who I mean.'

'Do I, Mr Lynnford?'

'The *Sea Breeze* was Chessington's boat. Look at the way he's dressed, he must have just come off it.'

'There was nothing on the boat to indicate who owned it.'

The sounds of several voices coming down the path from the direction of the house interrupted them.

'Come on down,' the sergeant shouted up.

A few moments later the bend in the path where they were standing was filled by four more men and then a fifth, slipping down the path almost one on top of the other, like children piling up at the bottom of a water slide.

'Good afternoon, Doctor.'

The sergeant greeted the first of the new arrivals with a handshake and then, noticing the fifth man, added with surprise, 'Yeats?'

'Yes, you don't mind, do you?'

The harbour master looked at the company around him and with a slight look of annoyance at the sight of Lynnford.

'I heard you'd found another body. The doctor was kind enough to give me a lift.'

Sergeant Evans gave a curt nod by way of reply and addressed the doctor once more.

'Could you take a look before we move the body? It's a bit difficult. He's face down headlong under that.'

The sergeant pointed at the branches and undergrowth.

'He seems to be holding something in his hand, if you can let me have it,' Sergeant Evans called after the doctor.

As the doctor started to make his way under the tree and down the bank, the sergeant beckoned over Smith, the young constable who had just arrived with the others, having met them outside the house. But before he could say anything to him the sergeant's attention was caught by the sight of the harbour master about to follow in the doctor's footsteps, a hand held high, raising a branch in order to give himself passage.

'Where are you going, Yeats?'

'I thought I'd just help the doctor.'

'Just stay up here on the path, if you don't mind.'

The sergeant turned back to the constable.

'Smith, lad, give me a hand. See what you can find. A weapon. Anything. Start over there. I'll take this side. And, Yeats, stay where you are. You too, Mr Lynnford.'

'Of course, of course,' the harbour master replied, smiling apologetically. And for Lynnford's benefit, added, 'I was just at a loose end, you know.'

The two other men, two ambulance men, one holding a stretcher up on its end, had not moved since their arrival. One took out a packet of cigarettes and, after offering one to his colleague, took one for himself. He struck a match, cupped his hands around the flame, and lit his cigarette, dropping the match on the earth around his feet.

'Hey! Mind what you're doing,' the sergeant's voice barked out. 'Don't go dropping things around here. You'll mess up our clues. Clot head.'

The ambulance man made a face to his colleague. Lynnford smiled.

'Do you need any help, Sergeant?' he asked.

'Just stay where you are.'

A few minutes later the doctor's voice interrupted the silence.

'Fine, Sergeant, I've done as much as I can with the body as it is. Can you get them to take it up onto the path and place it on the stretcher?'

'Right you are, Doctor.'

The sergeant's face reappeared out of the undergrowth, pushing back the branches to make a way down for the two ambulance men.

'Easy does it. No need to tramp through like a herd of elephants.'

The two men brushed past him, holding onto the branches to steady their balance. One of them bent down, grabbing hold of the legs and started to tug at the body.

'Clot head! Take a care!' screamed out the sergeant slipping back down the slope and, taking his place, helped the other ambulance man to raise the body properly off the ground by each taking hold of a shoulder, but the corpse proved to be heavier than any of them had expected and it took the three of them to lift the body up onto the path, staggering as they laid the body onto the stretcher that Lynnford had unfolded in readiness.

'Sergeant Evans!'

The constable's voice came ringing through the green wall that separated him from the rest of the party on the path. The sergeant looked away from the face of the corpse that he had just begun to examine with the doctor.

'What is it, Smithy, lad?'

'Sergeant, look at this!'

'What is it? Don't touch it!'

As Sergeant Evans uttered his warning, the constable reappeared on the path alongside him, a triumphant grin on his face as he spoke.

'Look at this, Sergeant,' he repeated as he held up, stretched out between the fingers of his two hands, a dazzling necklace. Its fine craftwork was like lace, falling softly between his fingers, a fine clasp linking strings of diamonds.

The stones sparkled in the partial afternoon light. Everyone looked at the constable in astonishment except, Lynnford noticed, the harbour master who, biting his lip, seemed only just able to restrain a flash of anger; a cold stare containing his emotion. And more surprising still for Lynnford was the absence of two buttons from his jacket; the remaining buttons being identical to the one in his pocket, which his fingers now caressed lightly as he pondered the discovery.

'That's a find if ever there was one,' the doctor remarked, feigning casualness. 'It must have come out of this.'

The doctor held out a small, black velvet pouch.

'It's the bag he was holding in his hand, Sergeant.'

Nobody else spoke for a while. The corpse on the stretcher lay forgotten. The sergeant took possession of the necklace and bag and asked the constable to show him where he had found the necklace. Whilst the two police officers went back down the bank, the doctor resumed his examination of the body. Once they were back up on the path, the sergeant looked enquiringly at Lynnford.

'Well, what do you think? You seem to know so much about him.'

'What on earth can he know about him?' the harbour master interjected.

'He says his name is Chessington. And from here, apparently. What do you say, Mr Lynnford?'

'If you need identification, there's a woman in Westcliff who may be able to recognise him. Gwen Mortimer should be able to give you her name. She's a customer, but don't you recognise him, Mr Yeats?'

'Me? Why should I?'

'I was told you met him in Tower Port last week.'

Mr Yeats shook his head.

'Not him. Never seen him in my life before.'

Sergeant Evans stared doubtfully at the harbour master before turning to Lynnford again.

'And the necklace, any ideas? It's not from here at any rate. At least no one's reported the theft of a necklace.'

'If I'm not mistaken, Sergeant, it is very much from around here or at least from this part of the country. It looks very much like the Exmoor Jubilee necklace. How Chessington had it and what he was doing with it, I've no idea but it was stolen from a flat in Mayfair in the summer.'

'By Chessington?'

'Maybe.'

'And where was he going with it?' asked the doctor, closing his medical bag as he spoke. 'This path doesn't lead anywhere.'

'Is there anything to say whether he was alone and tripped by accident or whether someone was chasing him, or even hiding here and waiting for him to pass by?'

'Well, that's more your field, Sergeant, but what killed him was the blow to the head as he hit the stone when he fell,' the doctor replied. 'You'll have my report in the morning.'

'And when did he die?'

'He's been here a few days at least, judging from the condition of the body.'

'Last week?'

'No, not so long ago.'

'Sunday?'

The doctor turned towards Lynnford. 'Yes, certainly not any longer.'

'Any idea of the time?'

'I'll be able to be more precise when I've had a chance to examine the body more closely.'

'And, Doctor—' Lynnford detained him lightly with his hand.

'Yes?'

'What did kill the sailor from the *Sea Breeze*? You must have seen the body.'

'What's that to do with you? No, in fact I didn't.'

The doctor hesitated, looking quickly at Sergeant Evans but allowing Lynnford sufficient time to detect some impatience tinged with contempt.

'The body was destroyed in the fire on Tuesday. I thought you knew that.'

'Still, not completely.'

'No, indeed. Sergeant Evans has my report.'

The afternoon sunshine was beginning to pale, leaving the air cool as they emerged out of the woods and passed through the hole in the wall, walking around the house towards the front gates. Sergeant Evans, in conversation with the doctor, led the party, followed by the two men carrying the stretcher and Constable Smith. Lynnford and the harbour master brought up the rear.

'A pity a house like this should be left empty,' the doctor remarked. 'Houses should be lived in, and it looks solid enough.'

'Better for the neighbourhood as well,' added the sergeant. 'You never know what mischief an empty house like this attracts.'

The gates to North View House now stood wide open. An ambulance was parked alongside the sergeant's car. The driver was resting against the bonnet of his vehicle, smoking a cigarette, waiting for them to return. He looked up on hearing them approach.

He opened the back of the ambulance and stood to one side, allowing the two men who were carrying the stretcher to lift it into the back and step in after it. The driver closed the doors, and strolled round to the front, his hands in his pockets.

'Right, thank you, lads.'

The sergeant made a sign to the driver.

'Take it along to the morgue. We'll see if we can find someone to formally identify the body.'

Turning to the doctor, the sergeant asked him if he wanted to come along with him rather than ride back to town in the ambulance.

'No, thanks all the same. I'll leave my place for Yeats.'

'You too, Mr Lynnford?'

'Thank you very much, Sergeant,' Lynnford replied, not that he thought he was being given much of a choice.

'Smith, close the gates and put this around them.'

The sergeant reached into his car and pulled out a heavy iron chain.

'And give me the key once you've locked it,' he added.

The two vehicles drove through the gates, the sergeant slowing down to let the constable climb in after padlocking the gates. At the turn-off to Sandy Cove, Lynnford asked the sergeant to drop him off. The sergeant cocked his head, looking back through the rear-view mirror.

'Eh, what's that?'

'If you don't mind, Sergeant, could you let me out here? I'd like to walk down to the cove and return to Westcliff across the headland. I fancy the walk.'

The sergeant stopped the car. He turned round to face Lynnford.

'If you must, but I shall need a full statement from you. So drop in at the station as soon as you get back.'

Lynnford nodded his agreement and opened the door. Unfortunately, the sergeant had pulled up too close to the hedge and Lynnford could only open the door a couple of inches.

'Here, I'll let you out this side.'

And so saying, the harbour master opened his side door and stepped onto the road. Lynnford pushed himself across the back seat and got out, allowing the harbour master to slip back in.

'You know you've got a couple of buttons missing, Mr Yeats?'

'Eh! What's that?'

The harbour master looked back at Lynnford.

'Your coat. There're two buttons missing. I just thought I'd tell you.'

'Oh yes, of course! Came off just before in the hurry to come out. Damn fool thing. Hanging on by a whisker,' the harbour master replied with a smile, tugging at the door that Lynnford still held, trying to pull it to.

Teasing him for a few seconds, Lynnford released his clasp and the door banged shut. Suddenly he remembered the key. Taking it out of his pocket and bending down, he tapped on the glass side window to attract the sergeant's attention.

'Hold on there. I forgot to give you something.'

'What's this then?'

The sergeant wound down the window, turning to look up at Lynnford, his fleshy neck folding over his shirt collar as he bent his head round.

'An old key. I knelt on it when I found the body. I forgot all about it.'

Lynnford looked apologetic.

'But you picked it up, anyway?'

The sergeant's tone was ironic.

'Maybe it was there before he fell. But I suppose it could have fallen out of his pocket,' Lynnford admitted as he dropped the key into the sergeant's open palm.

The sergeant inspected the key with a silent crease across his face, before taking out a white handkerchief that he folded around the key to make a small parcel which he then pushed into his trouser pocket.

'It doesn't look very dirty,' he commented dryly.

'It's probably rubbed off in my pocket. Anyway, I thought it best in your hands.'

'Make sure you come over to the station as soon as you get back to Westcliff.'

The sergeant wound up the window without further comment and Lynnford watched them as they drove off, leaving him alone in the road.

TWENTY
FRANK HOPE AND THE MAN IN THE BOAT

The sergeant's car was quickly out of sight and Lynnford started walking down the road to Sandy Cove. He wanted to pay another visit to the Hopes' farm. One of them could have come across the body in the woods; Frank Hope's dog sniffing it out? And Chessington's wife, the third crew member on the *Sea Breeze*, could well be there, hiding in one of the chalets. Certainly, he couldn't trust Sergeant Evans to find out. There was nothing for it but for Lynnford to do the legwork himself.

The close of the afternoon was not far away. Fresh sea air rolled up from the cove as the tide flowed and ebbed along the beach down below; each successive wave breaking yet higher up on the sands and with its fall releasing a heavy perfume that rose up the cove like a mist, mingling on its way with the scents of cedar trees and damp grassy fields. The light autumnal whistles of birds hidden in the trees and hedgerows seemed to herald Lynnford's approach.

The night train and his arrival in Westcliff early that morning were a distant memory. He had had no lunch, and now he almost regretted having let the others abandon him in the lane. He had embarked on another adventure that was unlikely to bring anything to eat for several hours yet. Coming round a bend in the road, and a break in the wall of hedges, the long sweep of open road gave him a full view of the farm at the bottom of the cove.

He was soon on the beach and striking out on a path that ran along the farm, looking for an access that would lead him, unobserved from the farmhouse, directly to the chalets and cottages. Here the sand was mounted up in soft dunes, spiked through by clutches of hard grass. Past one such sand dune, Lynnford was met by the excited yapping of a dog, and he recognised Frank Hope's golden Labrador, raised forward on all four legs and firmly holding its ground. There was no mistaking it. The animal made no attempt to move.

'What's the matter, honey boy?' Lynnford spoke half to himself. 'What's bothering you? What's your name, hey?'

He looked around but there was no sign of the owner. Curious, Lynnford approached the dog. It still did not move, but it continued to bark.

'What do you want then?' He spoke softly to the animal. 'What can I do for you?'

The barking became less intense, and the dog looked up at Lynnford as he came nearer, and as he crouched down, let him rub its neck, slowly relaxing under his caresses. The animal ended up by sitting down on the sand, its forelegs spread out in front and its tongue hanging out of its mouth as it quietly panted.

'Maybe you're just lonely, my friend. Who has Frank left you for, eh?'

Lynnford continued patting the dog along its sides whilst he looked over the sand dunes towards the farm and along the beach. But there was still no sign of Frank Hope.

'Strange. I wouldn't have expected him to have left you on your own like this. Where could he be?'

Lynnford stood up. The dog got to its feet as well.

'Oh, so you want to play? Let's take a run across the beach and see if he turns up.'

So saying, he gave the dog a tug at its collar and started to jog towards the line of low-breaking waves that marked the water's edge. The dog followed at his heel.

Halfway across the beach, Lynnford stooped and picked up a small piece of dry and gnarled driftwood. Waving it in front of the Labrador's face, he stretched out and threw it as far as he could, so that, curling through the air, it landed with a splash in the shallow ebb of the sea. Straight away, the dog had started racing after it, barking with delight. It splashed through the water, grabbed up the stick in between its teeth, furiously shaking off the water and, triumphant, scampered back to Lynnford, dropping it at his feet, panting and wagging its tail.

'Hey, hold on there!' he cried out, laughing and jumping away from the spray of sea water.

'Toby! Toby, come here! At once do you hear?'

The command needed no repeating. The dog pricked up its head and dashed back in the direction of the sand dunes without a sound. Lynnford turned round and there was Frank Hope, standing just outside the line of the sand dunes, leaning against his walking stick. The dog ran up to him, walked round behind him, brushing its wet coat against his legs as it did so, and lay down beside him on its stomach so that the two of them were now facing Lynnford.

Lynnford walked up to them. Although he'd drawn out the man, he regretted his bad luck. For a second time Frank Hope had spoilt his chance of approaching the camp unobserved. Still, there was probably very little chance of getting anywhere near the chalets without being intercepted by one or other of the Hopes.

'Good afternoon.'

Frank Hope did not reply.

'That's a fine animal you have.'

Still no reaction from the man standing in front of him. He stood staring at Lynnford. He was dressed much the same as before: corduroys, a frayed jumper over a collarless shirt. There was, however, something different. His aspect was different; less certain of himself, and bleary-eyed. His hair was a little dishevelled. The dog had covered the lower part of his trousers below the knee with wet sand that clung to the material in little lumps. But there were also grains of dry sand on his jumper, giving Lynnford the impression that he had been dozing behind one of the sand dunes.

Changing tack, Lynnford addressed the dog.

'Toby. That's your name is it, then?'

The animal whimpered by way of a reply.

'Here Toby, take this!'

Lynnford made as if to throw the piece of driftwood

again, but the dog remained at Frank Hope's feet, quietly watching and waiting. Reaching into his trouser pocket, Frank Hope pulled out a biscuit.

'What about this?' he asked the dog, holding the biscuit under its nose.

The dog opened its mouth and he slipped the biscuit into the dog's mouth and stood up. Frank Hope looked up at Lynnford.

'A dog, that's a friend for life. Did you know that?'

'So they say.'

'Do you have one?'

Lynnford shook his head. Frank Hope acted as if they had not met before.

'Well, you seem to have a way with Toby. Toby wouldn't play with you unless he was sure of you.'

His voice was slightly slurred. Had he been drinking?

'I don't know, we just seem to have hit it off. We met the other day. Do you remember?'

The man nodded.

'So, you've found Chessington, then?'

He lifted his stick up in the air, pointing towards the woods that hid the house on the hill.

'There's not much that goes on here without us knowing about it sooner or later, even up at the big house. Is there, Toby?' he added, grinning at the dog, his yellow teeth showing, full of decay.

'What do you know about it? Did you know his body was there?'

Frank Hope looked at Lynnford without saying anything for a few seconds.

'No, but if you've got time, I'll show you something.'

'What?'

'Follow me.'

He turned his back on Lynnford, heading off through the sand dunes. Toby followed alongside him. Lynnford shrugged his shoulders and followed suit, wondering what had made the man open up. Friendly, he was not. But he was certainly more expansive than on the last occasion. Only a few yards on, Lynnford's foot stumbled on an empty beer bottle, half-hidden in the sand. Several other bottles lay close by, around a flattened patch in the sand. Frank Hope! He must have spent the morning out here drinking, maybe even the night. The dog had been here waiting for him to wake up.

Frank Hope took him along the fence separating the farm from the beach and, past a wicket gate that led up to the chalets, Lynnford found himself being taken into the woods at the far end of the beach and onto a path that began to climb through the trees up the side of the cove towards North View House. From time to time, as he walked up the path, he glimpsed the water in the cove below filling the gaps in the leaves. And on one such occasion, on turning round, he saw far over on the other side, the white Zephyr yacht, still in the same place, bobbing gently unattended at her anchor.

'Come on!'

Frank Hope's voice was rough, sensing Lynnford's distraction. But something else had now caught Lynnford's eye. Beyond the yacht, out towards the open sea, he could see a man in a boat, bending energetically backwards and forwards from the waist, rowing with two long oars extended out on either side of him. From the line that it had taken it seemed fairly clear that the rowing boat was pulling away from the yacht, already some hundred yards or so distant from it. Rowing with his back to the open sea, the man seemed to have his eyes fixed on the yacht and the beach beyond. He was heading out of the cove.

Was this why Frank Hope was leading him out of the cove, to not be a witness and ask questions? But to what? And why? Lynnford cupped his hand over his eyes, but he was, however, too high up and too far away from the rowing boat to be able to distinguish the man clearly. He was wearing a flat black sailor's cap on his head. Possibly bearded and certainly strongly built from the manner he was working the oars. An outboard motor, attached to the stern of the boat, was raised out of the water. What was he up to? The little boat was now almost level with the headland. He must be heading for Westcliff or perhaps a sailing boat waiting for him around the tip of the headland. A sharp prod in his back made him turn round.

'Are coming up or not?'

Frank Hope withdrew his stick, and they resumed their walk, the golden Labrador trotting alongside them. At the next opportunity he looked again, casting his eyes out across the expanse of grey sea, crested with broken white lines of rolling waves. The little boat was turning around the headland, keeping close to it.

Shortly, the path brought them to the stone wall that enclosed the grounds. Here the path ended. Pushing back the brambles, Frank Hope led Lynnford along the wall until a few minutes or so later they arrived at the gap with which he was now quite familiar.

'Where are we going?' he asked.

But the man leading him said nothing, passing through the gap, taking Lynnford across the lawns and directly to the small cemetery. He stopped in front of a grave, much more recent than the others; a low, black-chained rectangle of white stones lying before a rose granite headstone and marked in each corner by a marble angel. Lynnford was surprised that he had not noticed it before. Strewn weeds and clumps of grass on the ground around it showed that someone had very recently made an effort to tidy it up. Some white lilies hung limply in a pot at the base of the headstone. He read the inscription, *Jennifer Stewart, 1913–1938*. Chessington's wife!

'Did you know her?' Lynnford asked. The question seemed unnecessary.

'I haven't been up here for years.'

'Chessington's wife?'

'We grew up together. She was a bit older than me. Two years, but it didn't matter. We used to play down on the beach when we were kiddies. She was beautiful even then: auburn locks and deep green eyes. A real mermaid. They didn't like it. She used to come out through the gap in the wall when her mother thought she was playing in the garden. She would run down the path and meet me at the bottom. Sometimes I would wait for her behind the wall.'

'Were you at school together?'

He shook his head.

'No, they were too good for us. When she was twelve,

they sent her away to a boarding school. Catholic. She forgot about me. I never saw her again. When she came back, she married.'

'Did you know her husband?'

He shook his head. 'Not to speak to.'

'What happened when she died?'

'He closed up the house.'

'And the children?'

'There weren't any.'

'When was this?'

'Thirty-nine. A year after she died.'

'What did she die of?'

'Something to do with her blood. I don't know what exactly. It happened very quickly.'

'So Chessington came back to visit the grave? And you knew the *Sea Breeze* was his?'

Frank Hope fell silent and would say no more. His head dropped, and he turned away. He moved away from the grave and started walking back towards the house and out of the grounds. Lynnford followed him until they were back down on the beach in front of the wicket gate. There, he called Toby, waved his walking stick as a sign of departure and left Lynnford standing alone. He wasn't going to tell Lynnford anything more. If Mrs Chessington was dead, who then had been the woman with Chessington on the yacht and where had she gone? A hunger pain shot through his stomach, interrupting his thoughts. Time to get back to Westcliff! And he set off across the beach, heading for the coastal path.

Up on the headland, a long straight section of the empty

path now stretched ahead of him, and he was about to burst into a light run to make short of the return to Westcliff when, amidst a loud rustle of leaves and branches, a man sprang out onto the path, some thirty yards ahead of him, heading off in the direction of the town. Thickly set, with a jacket, trousers tucked into a pair of sea boots, his socks rolled up over the tops of the boots, and a black sea captain's cap on his head, it was unmistakably the same man that he had seen in the rowing boat, an hour or so earlier. But where had he come from, and what had he done with his boat?

Letting the man disappear ahead of him, Lynnford stepped into the undergrowth and found a path that seemed to fall down the cliff. He could hear the waves hitting the rocks below. With steps built into the rock face, the path took him right down to the sea and into a cleft in the cliff. A rowing boat had been pulled out of the water and left, its keel caught in the rocks and two oars lying inside, their ends resting on the edge of the boat. Two other dinghies had been left leaning against the rock wall, one carrying the name of the *Sea Breeze*! So this was where it was but how had it got here? And why store three dinghies here?

Stepping around the boats and taking a few paces further in, a wall, some ten feet in length, blocked his way. Plastered over roughly to dissemble its appearance, it was clearly false. A door had been worked in the middle of the wall. It was unlocked.

Pushing it open revealed nothing but pitch darkness. He pushed it open a little further but could still see no better. His shoe hit against a metal can and looking down, he saw that it was an oil lamp, placed carefully next to the door frame. A flattened box of matches lay on the ground next to it.

Lifting up the lamp in his hand, it still felt warm. He struck a match and lit the lamp. The shaded light cast a yellow glow around him. Holding the lamp high up in his hand, he examined the rocky chamber. Wooden crates and cardboard boxes filled most of the space from floor to ceiling, leaving room only for a low camp bed. Looking inside some of the boxes, Lynnford found them full of bottles of spirits, boxes of cigars and packets of cigarettes. A smuggler's dump!

He put out the lamp, replacing it carefully as he had found it. Leaving the cave, he quickly climbed the path up the cliff side and was soon within sight of Westcliff across the fields and the stile that led to the high street.

TWENTY-ONE
OUTSIDE A KITCHEN WINDOW

It had gone five-thirty and the light outside The Blue Harp was fading fast. After his walk back from Sandy Cove, Lynnford sat huddled around the table at the window. In a few days, The Blue Harp had become a regular haunt. The young lad behind the bar had nodded to him as he had approached the bar, more perhaps in recognition than familiarity. Perhaps he should try another pub, one of those up in the high street? He preferred it here, where he could keep an eye on the *Sea Breeze*, still tied up next to the burnt-out remains of the harbour master's office, and so keep in mind the centre of the affair – clearing Sam and getting to the root of what had inspired him to bring Lynnford down from London.

'There you go. Two rounds of cheese and pickle.'

A white plate clattered on the scratched wooden table. He sat up, startled by the noise, his train of thought broken.

Sweeping up two empty glasses from the table, the barman retired behind the bar leaving Lynnford to pick up one of the sandwiches. At last, something to eat! It had been a long day without food. Two half slices of thickly cut bread, wedged with a piece of strong cheddar and squeezed against a spread of pickle that slipped out at the sides with every bite. He took a mouthful of beer from the pint glass that he had brought over from the bar. A radio behind the bar sparked into life and the quiet strains of a band began to stray across the room.

Staring out from his table, the fading view of the harbour was framed by four tall panes of glass, the brown paint peeling in places. One or two people passed by outside. The boats, only loose shapes now, bobbed up and down in the harbour on the rising tide, the yellow lights of their lanterns pinpricking the dusk. Inside, the tables around him were empty. Several regulars were gathered around the bar; leaning against the counter, standing or sitting propped up on stools. Their conversation drifted over to him. A quiet murmur, fusing with the smoke that hung suspended around the lamp in the middle of the ceiling. Lynnford's mind was, however, locked onto the world outside.

Smuggling: he came back to it again with the dump he'd just discovered. Control of the local trade, was that what it was all about? Had Chessington and his crew been trying to muscle in on someone else's patch? If so, the crew of the *Sea Breeze* had come off second best. Chessington's death may have been an accident, but the sailor's certainly wasn't. And the woman? Frank Hope had just shown him Jennifer Stewart's grave, so it wasn't her. What had happened to the third sailor aboard the *Sea Breeze*, then? Was she dead too? Lynnford shook his head. There had to be more to Sam's telegram than a fight over a few crates of whisky; certainly, if he was to keep Kombinski, his editor, happy. Even with two dead sailors.

A cold draught drew his attention momentarily away from the window and to a newcomer who had just entered, the door shutting behind him. Lynnford let his eyes idly follow the man. His movements were strong and agile. He took a stool at the bar and ordered a whisky.

And the Exmoor Jubilee necklace! Lynnford's thoughts drifted back to the events of the afternoon. He still couldn't get over his surprise. How had that ended up here, on the north Devonshire coast? How had Chessington got hold of it? Was Chessington the Mayfair burglar whom Detective Chief Inspector Sheffield and he had been searching for since the summer? But if Chessington had just sailed into Sandy Cove on the *Sea Breeze*, had he come to deliver or collect the necklace? He had dropped it in his fatal fall, so it looked as if he had been taking it back to the boat. So, had it been stashed away in North View House since the burglary?

He should call Sheffield and let him know straight away that the necklace had been found, and he was about to get up and go over to the public telephone when a knock on the window drew his attention. Peter Knight's face was pressed against the glass pane. And at the same time, in the doorway, another familiar face appeared: Mr Yeats, the harbour master. Seconds later, Peter Knight had joined Lynnford inside, apologising for his wife in the morning before going to the bar and returning to the table with a drink in his hand.

Meanwhile, Mr Yeats had gone straight to the bar, joining the stranger and taking him to a quiet table, out of earshot of the crowd. The two men spoke casually, almost as if they were not in conversation with each other, exchanging words but not looks.

'He'll be here shortly.'

'I'll be gone before then,' the harbour master replied. 'Is there a problem?'

'He's going to sail her with me.'

'Jacobs?'

The man nodded.

'He doesn't trust you?'

'Obviously not.'

'What does he know?'

'Nothing.'

'So why the change of plan?'

'I don't know.'

'It'll be hard dealing with him out at sea.'

'Then you'll need to stop him getting aboard.'

'I'll think of something. Until then don't contact me again. Go back to the bar.'

Lynnford witnessed the harbour master's departure out of the corner of his eye. Shortly afterwards the door opened again, and this time Lynnford gave a start. It was the man in the boat. The man he had seen on the path from Sandy Cove. He went up to the bar and spoke to the man who had just been speaking to the harbour master.

'Who's that?' Lynnford whispered, tugging hold of Peter Knight's sleeve and adding by way of description, 'The man with the captain's hat, standing next to the man on the stool.'

'The fellow standing up?' Peter Knight clarified.

'Yes.'

'Jacobs. Salt of the sea as they say. A descendant of the shipwreckers that worked this coastline if ever there was one. Except he's harmless enough. A cousin of Evans.'

'Sergeant Evans?'

Peter Knight nodded.

'Not that half the town's not related in some way. But Jacobs is a sort of an outsider. Cornish like Pengal who you asked about this morning, on his mother's side. She married a Westcliff man. They brought him up there before coming back to Westcliff. The other man, I don't know. But he's not local, and you know what? He just fits the description of the man Gwen Mortimer had keeping watch on her shop. That is until Sam turned up.'

'Yes, that's right. I recognise him now. He was there on Tuesday morning when I arrived, and Gwen wouldn't open up. Hold on! They're going.'

The first man at the bar slipped off his stool and followed Captain Jacobs who was already heading for the door.

'Sorry, Peter. I must go. I'll catch up with you later.'

So saying, Lynnford got up, as if heading for the bar. But as soon as the door had closed behind the two men he darted out after them, just in time to see them walking up the hill. Not looking behind, they carried straight on, not suspecting that they were being followed. Lynnford, the excitement beginning to make his pulse beat a little faster, wondered where they might lead him.

In the increasing darkness he could not afford to stay too far behind for risk of losing sight of them. They were walking at quite a brisk pace, notwithstanding the hill. Yet he could not get too close for fear they would hear his footsteps and turn around. About a quarter of the way up the hill, they crossed over and turned into a road running parallel to the harbour below, glancing casually back down the road beforehand but not sufficiently to remark Lynnford on the pavement behind them. Further along, a street light at the corner of a side road illuminated them, briefly. Gaining the street corner in his turn, Lynnford found himself looking down upon the dark shadows of the large boatsheds that lined the promenade at the far end of the old harbour. On either side of the narrow street, small, terraced houses led down towards a high wall that backed on to the boatsheds. He crossed over, following the shapes ahead of him and staying parallel to the promenade below.

Keeping close to the house fronts, he eventually moved too close, stumbling against the protruding concrete doorstep of one of them.

'Damn!'

And he gripped his face muscles tight to avoid crying out. Still, straightening up as quickly as he could the two men had already disappeared. If his toe had not been still smarting, he might have kicked the doorstep again. Where had they gone? He quickened his pace, almost running. Several yards further on he came to a side street, another *cul-de-sac* leading down to the back of the boatsheds. And, almost at the bottom, he spotted the two men. He stopped and watched. They went up to the very last house on the left. One of them took a key from his pocket. A light shone out briefly from the hallway as the door opened.

Lynnford looked at the black and white nameplate fixed against the dark brick wall – Tenby Street. He walked down the road, keeping to the pavement on his side. At the bottom he crossed over and approached the house. Number 31. No sound came from within it, the front half of which appeared to be empty. They must have gone through to the back. How could he get round there? The wall backing onto the boatsheds was too high to climb. Anyway, he might attract attention. Then he had an idea; the alleyway at the back of the houses.

He ran back up to the top of the street and down the alleyway on the other side. It was roughly cobbled with large stones sloping into a central channel that ran all the way down to the bottom. Two brick walls ran down its length on either side, punctured at regular intervals by wooden gates; the one or two that he tried being unlocked. Either nobody considered it worthwhile to bolt them or they had simply forgotten. However, when he arrived at the last gate and pressed down the iron handle it did not budge. The gate had been securely bolted on the other side. He looked up at the top of the wall. It was only a foot or so above his shoulders. He reached up and tapped gingerly along the top, checking for broken glass. Nothing.

Pulling himself up so that his head was clear of the wall, he peeped into the backyard. There was a small outhouse next to the gate. The back of the house was built in an "L" shape that was mirrored by the house next door. A light shone in the ground-floor kitchen window. The window was open slightly, releasing the muffled sounds of several voices.

Pulling himself up further, he scrambled over the wall, landing on the roof of the outhouse. Slowly, he let himself down to the ground on the other side of the gate, quickly looking into the outhouse to check that nobody was inside, and then slipping stealthily up to the back of the house, where he stood to one side of the window with his back flat against the brick wall, listening. The voices of at least two men could be clearly heard now.

'How much longer do I have to hang about? I've been here since Monday. I don't like leaving the yacht too long in one place.'

'Don't fret, Skinner. It's safe enough where it is,' an older voice replied and in a tone that was more dismissive than reassuring.

'Nobody's going to recognise it. She's got a new name. It's the *Sea Bird* now, not *The Dolphin*, isn't that right?'

'But it shouldn't be taking so long.'

'You know we missed our chance the other day.'

'But you didn't get the supply until the next day.'

'We delayed when you didn't show up.'

'That blasted mist put me a day out. And the cove, I thought that it was supposed to be closed for the season. Stranded out off the headland waiting for the weekenders to pack up wasn't my idea of fun.'

'It is. Closed, that is. I don't know what Frank Hope was playing at. They decided to open up. Anyway, there's no point us sailing until we get the go-ahead again on the other side. You don't want to run the risk of being caught with all that stuff aboard.'

'Who's it for anyway?'

'Nobody you need to know.'

'South Americans?'

'I told you, it's none of your business. Best you know nothing, in case you're caught.'

'But you're sailing with me now, aren't you?'

'That's right. You're just crew this time, Skinner.'

'Fine, you're the skipper, Jacobs.'

'So he thinks.'

A third voice spoke up and Lynnford recognised the man with consumption. Pengal. The man who'd tried to put a knife in him outside the Kensington Boat Show. Had he caught the night train like him? Someone else spoke.

'I don't know why we're even doing it. Why change?'

'The money. Much more than we can make bringing in booze and fags.'

'Still, I don't like it. Why risk our necks?'

'They're our boys.'

'Whose boys?'

'Never you mind, Skinner.'

'It ain't just smuggling, Pengal. It's treason!'

'Listen to Tabby,' Pengal replied with scorn. 'This is the modern world. Didn't you know?'

'It's still against King and country.'

A dry laugh interrupted the conversation.

'They don't have a king, not for many a century.'

'You're not going back to that again. It's all dead and buried, Pengal.'

A heavy fist crashed on the table.

'By God, it's not!'

'The Irish, Pengal! Let them sort out their own problems.'

'They're Celts like us Cornish, Jacobs.'

'Like you, Pengal, not me. We're Protestants not Catholics. Look now, it's a job and better paid. And we're in it. There's no getting out of it for any of us. So, let's not mess it up, lads, otherwise we'll surely all lose our heads.'

'You won't regret it,' the few words ending in a dry, rasping cough.

'Anyway, the *Sea Bird*'s sailing on Sunday, first thing. We're loading her tomorrow night.'

There was a short silence.

'You could have told us earlier.'

'You do what and when I tell you. I've told you often enough. Tomorrow, you load up the baker's van. We'll take the two crates from the cave out in the boat.'

'Why didn't you just leave them with the others in the tower? It would have been easier.'

'Just a question of not having all our eggs in one basket, Pengal. In case we lost them. Or someone found them.'

And then the speaker's tone changed. 'Now, put that down, Tabby. You're drinking too much.'

'So what if I am?' The reply was petulant.

'And what about the woman? What do we do with her? It makes no sense keeping her.'

'She's safe enough where she is, Pengal.'

'She knows too much.'

'I tell you she doesn't know a thing. She's been out to the world.'

'She saw what happened on the boat. You should have done away with her at the same time as the sailor.'

'And the body in the woods at Sandy Cove?'

'That's got nothing to do with me.'

'You're lying, Pengal.'

'He fell over and hit his head on a stone. The stupid sod.'

'That's what Evans says.'

'You don't believe your own cousin?'

'Don't give me that, Pengal. You were up there on Sunday night. Frank Hope saw you.'

'The fool! But I didn't kill him. What for?'

'Who knows what you're up to, Pengal. But I don't see anyone queuing up to finish her off. Still, never mind that now. The important thing is that she hasn't seen anything. She's been well-drugged for most of the time and with a blindfold for the rest.'

'She saw Tabby shoot him.'

Lynnford recognised the voice of the driver of the baker's van, the young man with the wild rusty-red hair. A silence followed.

'And the newspaper man? What about him?'

'Yes, Pengal, why did you let him come back? You should have dealt with him in London.'

'I did.'

'You did? Like hell! I just saw him down in The Blue Harp having a quiet drink with Peter Knight.'

Lynnford did not hear the reply. A chair was scraped back across the tiled floor. Someone got up and walked towards the window. A hand reached out and pulled it shut, and Lynnford could hear no more. He decided to leave. Nothing more would be gained by hanging about. *I'll let myself out through the gate. Let them think that one of them forgot to bolt it and that'll get them at each other's throats if they're not already,* he mused as he quietly opened the gate and then carefully retraced his steps back up the alleyway.

So, one of Jacobs' crew had shot the sailor and they had kidnapped the woman. No wonder Sergeant Evans was being so difficult, if he was Jacobs' cousin. Had he also set up Sam? A light rain began to fall as he turned out of the alleyway and walked past the entrance to Tenby Street. He lifted his jacket collar and hid his hands deep in his pockets. Hearsay was not going to be enough to force the police officer's hand. He needed to catch Jacobs red-handed for that. In the meantime, first thing in the morning he needed his help to get back into North View House.

TWENTY-TWO
THE KEY AND THE NECKLACE

'Good morning, Sergeant.'

'So, you've come to make your statement? You've taken your time, Mr Lynnford.'

Sergeant Evans half rose to his feet.

Lynnford closed the door to the sergeant's office, the parrot's screech mocking their exchange. Apologising for the parrot with a wry smile, the police officer waved at Lynnford to take the seat in front of him. Lynnford pulled the chair away from the desk a little and sat down.

'So, what about the fire on Tuesday?'

'Sam Mortimer didn't do it, Sergeant.'

The police officer tilted his head to one side. Lynnford thought of the parrot.

'And who did, then?'

'I seem to remember having got out of bed in the middle of the night to help put it out.'

'That's as maybe, but the fire still succeeded in gutting the harbour master's office. The body of the sailor from the *Sea Breeze* was burnt to a cinder, and almost the yacht with it. All the evidence in one bang. Well, almost.'

'Wasn't it careless not to have taken the body to the morgue straight away? The doctor seemed to be unhappy about it.'

'Be careful, sir. Arson is still a crime, and you were seen down on the harbour just before it.'

'Not just before, some hours.'

'Well then, let's have your story.'

The sergeant pulled open one of the drawers to his desk, but before he could take out the statement form as he intended, Lynnford interrupted him with a gesture of his hand.

'Time enough for that, Sergeant. I need to tell you about the key and the necklace.'

The sergeant raised an eyebrow.

'Fables, is it now?'

'I think I can tell you why Chessington had the necklace.'

'Can you indeed?' The sergeant's tone changed despite himself. 'How's that?'

'First of all, the key. I found it on Chessington. It's the key to North View House. At least, a key to the house.'

A moment's silence followed. The sergeant repeated Lynnford's words, slowly. 'You found it on Chessington.'

He let out a soft whistle between his teeth.

'No, I didn't think much of your story about finding it on the ground, just by chance alongside the body.'

Lynnford said nothing.

'And so, for a good story, you decided to see if you could find the door that matched the key before reporting the matter to the police. And for good measure, from what you say, I imagine you didn't deprive yourself of the pleasure of poking around inside first, did you? What the devil do you think you're playing at, Mr Lynnford? I don't care who you are, this is my patch and my job. I could have you locked up for withholding evidence and obstructing a criminal investigation.'

The sergeant was now angry.

'What investigation?'

'I've a good mind to put you under arrest.'

'You appear to have only been waiting for a reason, Sergeant.'

'You don't cut any ice with me, Mr Lynnford.'

He paused for a few seconds, and then, sitting back in his chair, added in a more conciliatory tone, 'Go on. Get on with your story. I'll overlook the key for now.'

'And Sam Mortimer?'

'Don't push me. What about the necklace?'

'The necklace was Chessington's, or at least his wife's.'

'So what was he doing with it in the dead of night, in the middle of nowhere?'

'North View House. It belonged to his wife's family.'

'The Stewarts? How do you know about the necklace?'

'Take me to the house and I'll show you.'

'Can't you just tell me here and now?'

'You need to see it with your own eyes.'

'Don't think I've got time for a wild goose chase like you.'

'Sergeant. Ten minutes there and back in your car.'

'Fine. I didn't know I was such a walk-over! Smith!' the sergeant called out to the young officer at the reception desk.

'I'm taking Mr Lynnford over to the house in Sandy Cove. Pass me the key to the padlock that we put around the front gates, will you?'

'Could you bring the necklace along as well?'

The sergeant looked at Lynnford with a mixture of suspicion and astonishment.

'Don't worry, Sergeant, you can trust me!'

'Fine. Wait for me outside.'

*

Once out of the high street and onto the open road, the sergeant drove quickly. He didn't ask Lynnford any more questions. But he appeared preoccupied. It had taken him some ten minutes or so before finally joining Lynnford outside the police station, grave and extremely ill-at-ease. The two men sat silently next to each other, looking out through the windscreen and along the bonnet of the car to the rolling road ahead. Coming round a bend, a tractor blocked their way, the driver perched high up above the road between the two large rear wheels, smoke billowing out from the little chimney pipe at the front of the tractor, and the engine chugging noisily. The farmer seemed unaware of the police car behind him. Round another bend, the tractor moved over to let a van heading in the direction of Westcliff go by. As the van drove past them Lynnford recognised Mrs Hope behind the wheel. *Off to Westcliff, no doubt*, he thought to himself.

'Damn!' The sergeant let out a curse. The tractor had moved back into the middle of the road. 'Hasn't he got ears?'

The sergeant sounded his horn sharply. The driver turned round slowly, nodded at them, and edged the tractor up close to the hedge, waving them on.

'At last!'

The sergeant pulled out from behind the tractor and raced ahead.

'Some people seem to have all day. You'd think he worked for a newspaper!' he exclaimed sarcastically as he pressed down the accelerator, his horn blaring loudly.

The tractor was soon lost behind them and a few minutes later they stopped in front of the gates to North View House, the sergeant pulling the handbrake up sharply.

'Now, let's see what you've got to show me. And it'd better be worth it!'

'This way.'

And Lynnford led him around the back of the villa and to the French windows. Taking the key from the policeman, he pushed them open.

'After you.'

The sergeant stepped inside.

'So this is North View House.'

'This is what we've come to see.'

'What, exactly?'

'The painting above the fireplace.'

The portrait of the woman smiled down on them.

'Quite a beauty!' the sergeant exclaimed.

'This is Jennifer Stewart,' Lynnford explained. 'And,

before her death, the owner of North View House, along with her husband, Alfred Chessington. At least, that's my guess.'

'So?'

'Look at the necklace she's wearing. It's a perfect match to the one we found yesterday, alongside Chessington's body. The Exmoor Jubilee.'

The sergeant stared at the necklace in the portrait.

'Why not compare them, if you don't believe me? That's why I suggested you bring it along with you.'

The policeman did not move, continuing to stare at the portrait.

'Evans!'

The sergeant's regard remained fixed, his lips tightly drawn.

'What is it, man? Where is it?'

After a short silence, the policeman shook his head, hunching his shoulders.

'I don't know.'

Lynnford's reaction was an expression of incredulity.

'I don't know,' repeated the sergeant.

'You don't know? It's not possible. What have you done with it?'

'I haven't done anything with it. It was in the safe, and now it's gone.'

'Someone's taken it?'

'It appears so.'

'From a police safe! When did you discover this?'

'Just now, before we left. That's what tied me up.'

'Good God, man, have you any idea what it's worth?'

'I know my job.'

'Do you? Why didn't you mention it before we left? Now we are wasting our time. Why aren't you out looking for it? You should be raising high heaven. Every police officer in Devon should be out there.'

Lynnford paused, an idea coming to his mind. 'You know who's taken it, don't you?'

Sergeant Evans stared angrily back at Lynnford, without saying anything.

'Well, at least you can't blame this one on Sam or me,' Lynnford added with scorn.

'I've no intention of accusing innocent people. An investigation is already underway.'

'For your sake, don't bungle it.' Lynnford turned as if to leave. 'Well, there's no point staying here any longer.'

'Anyway, Mr Lynnford, coming back to the reason why you brought me here, I agree it is the same necklace.'

'Now we are making some progress!'

'So the necklace was here in the house and Chessington came back for it?'

'Possibly, Sergeant. I'm only demonstrating the link between Chessington and the necklace. It belonged to his wife, but it doesn't explain how it got here.'

'So he didn't steal it, then?'

'He may not have but, remember, it was stolen from a London banker this summer, so it wasn't his any longer. You really need to be out there looking for it.'

'I informed the superintendent before we left. It's a matter for the plain-clothes detectives at Overcombe, now.'

'Well then, what about Chessington? Have you had

him identified? Have you found the woman I mentioned yesterday?'

'Not yet. Without a name, it's not that easy.'

'I told you to speak to Gwen Mortimer. She knows the woman.'

Impatience filled Lynnford's voice as he added, 'Come on, Sergeant! Get a move on! Let's go and speak to her now.'

*

Back in Westcliff, Sergeant Evans pulled up outside Gwen and Sam's shop in the high street.

'If you stay here, I'll just be a few seconds,' Lynnford offered as he made to open the side door.

'No. I'll come with you.'

The sergeant had already climbed out of the car and was straightening his jacket, folding out the creases that had collected around his stomach.

'Better not,' advised Lynnford. 'I doubt you'd be welcome.'

The sergeant stopped beside the car and Lynnford entered the newsagents.

'Hello, Robert,' Gwen smiled nervously. 'Is that Sergeant Evans out there?'

Lynnford nodded. 'Don't worry, he's not coming in. Listen, Gwen, do you remember yesterday, the lady who told us about North View House? You remember, about the family and how to get there. Who is she? I didn't catch her name.'

'Oh, that's Mrs Henderson. I can't believe she's in any trouble. What's she done wrong?'

'Nothing, just that she might be able to help us a little further. Can you tell us where she lives?'

'Opposite St Mary's Church. The one down the hill. The Catholic Church. Number 18, Acacia Road. By the way, a Mrs Beaumont telephoned and left a message for you. Here, I wrote it down for you. Is that Victoria?'

Lynnford nodded as Gwen Mortimer handed him a piece of paper.

'They're the dates of someone who died, Jennifer Stewart. Does that help?'

'Thanks Gwen. I asked her to call here, I hope you don't mind.'

He didn't want to say that he'd already found Jennifer Stewart's grave.

'Not at all.'

'Mrs Henderson, Acacia Road, Sergeant.'

'Yes, I know where it is. We'll be there in a jiffy. We can leave the car here and walk down.'

TWENTY-THREE
ANOTHER COAT BUTTON

Number 18, Acacia Road was a terraced, grey-brick, slated-roof house with white lace curtains hanging in the ground and upper floor windows. Sergeant Evans lifted the latch and swung open the gate to the small, enclosed garden. Before even knocking on the door, one of the curtains had been lifted to one side and Lynnford recognised in the corner of the window the face of the lady he had met in the newsagents. The sergeant made a sign that he wanted to speak with her. The lace curtain fell back into place and Mrs Henderson disappeared from view.

Wrapped up in her coat, the other day, Mrs Henderson had seemed to Lynnford a fairly ordinary-looking woman. The woman who opened the door to them was very different. She had a graceful air and a youthful appearance despite her years that surprised him. She was wearing fine gold-framed glasses that fitted well with the sharp features of her face and her pale skin.

'Well, two visitors at once. What a pleasure! And to what do I owe this honour?'

The sergeant took the lead.

'Mrs Henderson?'

'Why of course, Sergeant Evans. Who else do you expect to live here?'

'Indeed. This is Mr Lynnford, he's visiting Westcliff. You met him yesterday, I believe?'

'Yes of course, in Sam and Gwen's newsagents up in the high street. What can I do for you? Oh! But where are my manners. Please come in, won't you?'

'Thank you.'

The hallway led into a spacious but rather gloomy sitting room. To the lace curtains were added tall columns of heavy curtains from ceiling to floor, tied by thick cords. The whole gave the room a sombre air. Two armchairs were positioned on either side of the fireplace, the chimney piece of which was covered with small memorabilia and surmounted by a mirror. No doubt it was the mirror that gave the room its sense of space.

The mirror reflected the two visitors as they entered the room: the sergeant in his blue uniform, clean white shirt, collar and tie. Lynnford, however, was showing the signs of his travels, short nights and a lack of fresh clothing. Both men had removed their hats on walking through the front door. Mrs Henderson followed them in and closed the sitting room door behind them.

'Well gentlemen, how can I help you?'

Lynnford took over this time.

'You remember telling me about the Stewarts of North View House?'

'Yes, of course.'

'Well, without being melodramatic, a body has been found in the woods just outside the grounds of the house.'

The old lady opened her eyes wide in surprise and put her hand to her mouth. Lynnford continued, 'I should say that I found the body yesterday after speaking to you.'

'Oh dear, how dreadful.'

'Yes, of course,' the sergeant interrupted.

'Mr Lynnford here has an idea that perhaps you would be able to help us with the identification of the body. We need someone to formally identify it.'

'I'm not sure about that. How could I possibly know who it is?'

'It's possible that it's Jennifer Stewart's husband.'

'Alfred Chessington? But that's simply dreadful! It's been so long.'

'Quite possibly, you're one of the few of us who knew them. Is that right?'

Mrs Henderson nodded.

'Well, it probably is so. There's not many of us left now. Mr Yeats, but I can't think of anyone else. They didn't come into town very often, but for important occasions they used to all come down to St Mary's.'

As she spoke she pointed out through the window towards the other side of the road.

'I could see them all go by from here. My maid used to work for them. But that was a long time ago.'

'Would you mind then accompanying us to the morgue, Mrs Henderson? It won't take more than a few minutes.'

Mrs Henderson made a face and shuddered.

'Do I have to?'

'Well, it would be a great help to us.'

She sighed and gave a little nod in agreement.

'Fine.'

The sergeant's tone was businesslike. 'I'll nip up and bring the car round. Mr Lynnford will wait here with you.'

The sergeant glanced across at Lynnford for his approval.

'Take a seat, Mr Lynnford, whilst I show the sergeant out.'

Once Mrs Henderson had closed the front door on Sergeant Evans she returned to the sitting room and sat down opposite Lynnford, her back straight and her hands in her lap.

'Young Frank Hope and his mother of course.'

'I beg your pardon?'

'The Hopes and the harbour master, Yeats. We're probably all that's left who knew them.'

'Yes, I see. I met somebody on the bus to Tower Port the other day who knew them, at least Chessington. A fellow called Derek.'

'Derek Tring. Yes. A most unsavoury man and I doubt he's reformed.'

A few minutes later she asked, 'Would you like a humbug?'

'I'm sorry?' Lynnford's mind had been miles away.

'A boiled sweet?'

'Oh yes, of course. No, thank you.'

'I will if you don't mind.'

And she stretched out her hand to a glass jar on the side of the fireplace, lifted the top and took out a sweet.

'I buy them from Mortimer's you know.' Mrs Henderson paused a moment before adding, 'His poor wife. They've all turned against her now of course. Sheep, the lot of them!'

She didn't say anything more. Her fingers twisted and untwisted the empty cellophane wrapper, smoothing it out and twisting it up again and again whilst she sucked hard on the sweet in her mouth.

'Here!' Lynnford interrupted the silence and pulled out the photograph of the smiling couple on their bicycles. 'I found this. Do you recognise them?'

Glad of the distraction, the old lady took the photograph from Lynnford and examined it, holding it close to her eyes.

'Why, of course. It seems like only yesterday. It's the two of them, indeed.'

She continued holding the photograph, as if she were looking, fascinated, through a peephole onto the Westcliff as she remembered it.

'And why did he leave when she died?'

'Broken heart. He was devastated by her death. Well, that's what I was told, because I never saw him again, and I can well believe it. He must have left before the War broke out. Anyway, as I think I told you yesterday, the government requisitioned the house during the War and since then no-one has lived in it.'

'You've not heard of him coming back since then?'

Mrs Henderson shook her head.

'Tell me, do you know anything about her necklace? There's a portrait in the house with Mrs Chessington wearing it.'

'Why, yes. It was her wedding present.'

'From him?'

Mrs Henderson shook her head again. 'Where could he have got the money from? No, it was a present from her parents. It had been in the family. It's very famous, you know, the Exmoor Jubilee necklace. And worth a fortune!'

A few moments later, they heard the sound of a car pulling up outside the house.

'Perhaps you should get ready to go,' Lynnford suggested gently.

As she got up the car horn sounded.

'I'll get my coat and we'll be ready to go straight away.'

*

The morgue in Westcliff was situated just off the high street, in a small side road. The premises were owned by a firm of family funeral directors whose office fronted the building. The sergeant parked outside and led Lynnford and Mrs Henderson around the back of the office to an open entrance that led into a roughly cobbled courtyard.

'It's this way.'

Sergeant Evans introduced them into the building and asked them to wait in the lobby. He disappeared for a few moments and then returned, beckoning them to follow him into another room. The dead man lay on a trolley in the middle of the room, a white sheet covering the body up to the neck. At the sergeant's invitation, Mrs Henderson cautiously approached the trolley. She looked down at the man's face. A clock on the wall counted the seconds that passed.

'Mrs Henderson, can you identify the man as Mr Alfred Chessington, formally of North View House?'

Mrs Henderson nodded, made the sign of the cross, turned and walked out of the room. The swing door closed after her.

'Anything new, Doctor?' the sergeant asked.

'Death was caused by the impact of the skull hitting the heavy stone in the ground when he fell. His blood is on the stone. Almost certainly an accident. Although, there is some minor bruising and broken skin to the hands consistent with a fight, additional to what he suffered from the fall.'

'Time of death?'

'Five or six days ago.'

'So, almost as soon as he arrived.'

'And that would coincide more or less with the shooting, Sergeant,' Lynnford commented.

'Oh, there is one other thing.'

The doctor picked up a button from the nearby work top and showed it to them. Lynnford recognised another of the buttons from Yeats' coat.

'What's that?'

'A coat button, Sergeant.'

'I can see that. Where was it?'

'In the turn-ups to his trousers. Right leg. Somehow it must have fallen in there. It doesn't belong to his overcoat.'

'You should ask Mr Yeats about the missing buttons to his coat, Sergeant.'

'What's that?'

Lynnford continued, 'His coat is missing two buttons. I picked one up from the terrace outside the villa and this is the second. Chessington must have had some form of altercation there with Yeats before running down the path to Sandy Cove and killing himself. You can see the body shows signs of a fight, and Yeats' face as well, if you care to look. What could that have been about, Sergeant? The necklace, by any chance?'

'Leave the investigating to me, if you don't mind. Anything else, Doctor?'

'Just this.'

The doctor held out a small label of silver paper. The sergeant took it from him and read out aloud the inscription.

'Spring's Florists, Tower Port.'

He shrugged his shoulders and directed Lynnford towards the exit.

'I'll take Mrs Henderson back home, Mr Lynnford.'

'Very well, Sergeant. You can check the florists, but almost certainly Chessington bought a bunch of white lilies from them last Saturday before sailing round to Sandy Cove the next day.'

'And why would he have done that?'

'To place them on his wife's grave. Last Sunday was their wedding anniversary. They were married on 21st October 1931.'

'I see.'

'Tell me, Sergeant, why was the sailor's body left in the harbour master's office and not brought up here straight away?'

'It was Yeats' idea.'

'Really?'

'Hindsight's a fine thing, especially for you newspaper men.'

Mrs Henderson was waiting for them in the vestibule, on a chair. She stood up on seeing them.

'I'm so sorry, Mrs Henderson,' Lynnford sympathised. 'That must have been unpleasant for you.'

'Not at all.'

Her reply was short and distracted.

'Sergeant Evans is offering to take you home.'

TWENTY-FOUR
A NARROW ESCAPE

Skimming away from Westcliff harbour, the sea spray blowing in his face, Lynnford guided the small boat that Peter Knight had lent him for the afternoon out towards the open sea. He wanted to search the yacht moored in Sandy Cove, before it set sail the next day. The chugging outboard motor rendered all else about him silent; and his thoughts returned to what he'd overheard Jacobs, Pengal and their friends talking about in the house in Tenby Street on Friday evening.

From what he'd overheard, the *Sea Bird* had to be the boat moored in Sandy Cove and it was going to be loaded that evening in order that it might sail first thing on Sunday morning, the next day. What was it that it was going to carry? Nothing had been said about that except that some of the load was to be taken from a cave. If that was the place he'd found on Friday, he'd only seen spirits, tobacco and the like, nothing to warrant the angry exchanges that had flared up. Something much more serious had to be afoot; but what? And what was the connection with Chessington and the crew of the *Sea Breeze*?

Glancing back for a moment, the railings of Westcliff promenade and the buildings behind them were now no more than the size of a thumbnail. Some minutes later, as he rounded the headland, a fishing boat came into view, lying motionless and directly in his course. Concerned that it might have its nets out, he cut the motor and let himself drift towards the boat. A man's face peered down at him. Underneath a woollen hat, the dry face was lined and taut, the chin bone strong. His bloodshot eyes were large, and a broad grin revealed a set of yellowing teeth. Looking back up at him leaning over the side of the boat with his arms spread out along the wooden rail, Lynnford had the impression of a fisherman inspecting the catch in his net. He squirmed, almost instinctively, within himself. The sailor looked a little drunk.

'Have you got your nets out?' Lynnford shouted up.

'Don't worry about that, young man.'

Lynnford nodded, indicating he understood.

'But you're a long way out for messing about in a little boat like that.'

'I didn't realise how far I'd come.'

'Mind the sea doesn't carry you further out.' The sailor's mouth opened in another large grin. 'You're not the first out after lunch, though.'

'Oh?'

'Ferrying about in and out of Sandy Cove.'

The sailor pointed with his arm across the stretch of water. 'Somebody you know?'

'I wouldn't say that.' The sailor winked at Lynnford who said nothing, hoping that the old sailor would continue, which he did after a few moments.

'But I don't mind telling you a secret.'

Lynnford's ears pricked up.

'I was out here last Tuesday night.'

'Here?'

'No, just outside the harbour. Just before the fire.'

'Really?'

'Two men in a boat just like yours rowed up to the beach below the railings. They got out and dumped someone on the sand, just above the water. What do you make of that?'

'I don't know. Any idea who they might have been?'

'Ah that, I couldn't say. It was too dark. But they'd only just come from the harbour wall. That much, I know. Outside the harbour, not inside. They'd carried whoever it was down the steps, just where the harbour master's office is. There was somebody else with them who stayed on the harbour steps.'

'And then the harbour master's office went up in flames?'

The sailor smiled down at him and before Lynnford could say anything else he had invited him aboard.

'Come on up!' the sailor called down. 'I'm having a little party here all by myself.'

He paused then added, 'To celebrate my birthday you see. Some company would suit me. Nothing but this boat and me for miles around.'

A deep pang of sadness fleeted across the man's face. But

it was gone in a flash as he reached down to give Lynnford a hand up.

'No, no,' Lynnford objected. 'That's very kind of you. But I really must carry on.'

'Must?' The sailor's tone suddenly changed, sounding surly. 'I don't see anyone forcing you.'

But his tone changed back again. 'Have it your way.'

And he disappeared from sight. Lynnford shrugged his shoulders. He had been in two minds, as the sailor clearly had information that could help absolve Sam, but the *Sea Bird* was more pressing. He ripped out the motor cord and, with the engine throbbing once more, began to manoeuvre around the fishing boat. He had still not cleared its bow when the sailor reappeared.

'Here!' he shouted. 'Take this and drink my health. Catch!'

And so saying, he lobbed a small bottle overboard.

Lynnford reached out an arm and caught the bottle, bringing it quickly into the safety of the boat. It was a bottle of Scotch, three-quarters empty. He held it up in the air to acknowledge his acceptance.

'Many happy returns,' he shouted out and waved goodbye.

The sailor, grinning, returned Lynnford's salute.

Bending forward, Lynnford tucked the bottle inside his knapsack and continued on his way, pleased with the information that the fisherman had given him. It would help Sam's case. Sandy Cove now opened up before him. The *Sea Bird* was still there, at anchor, close by the rocks below the coastal path. She was pulling lightly at her anchor, with the bow pointing towards the beach. Lynnford took his boat around the yacht's stern so that he was alongside the port side; hidden both from the open sea and from anyone in the cove, in particular from the Hopes' farm.

He let the dinghy drift alongside the white hull of the yacht. Reaching up with his right arm, he caught hold of the railing and passed a rope around it to secure his boat. Then, slipping off his shoes and dropping them into the knapsack, he stood up. Taking hold of the edge of the yacht, he pulled himself up and tumbled sideways onto the deck.

Satisfied that he was alone but staying low down in case he might be seen, he peered over the side towards both the beach and the open sea. There was nobody in sight. A padlock secured the hatch. He swung the knapsack off his back and, placing it on the wooden deck, lifted the flap of one of the side pockets and took out the two fine metal picks he'd already used on the *Sea Breeze*, the night of the fire. In a few seconds he had released the lock and was down inside the cabin. He left the hatch open behind him, just in case he needed to get out quickly.

Below deck, the yacht was empty. At least the woman from the *Sea Breeze* was not there, but in the galley he found fresh provisions. Water biscuits, tinned food, fresh milk and bacon which he guessed must have only just been brought aboard by the man the old sailor had spotted in the rowing boat. *She's ready to sail*, he thought, closing shut the two tiny cupboard doors above the sink. What he had overheard the previous evening seemed to be confirmed. The loading would have to take place that night. But the loading of what exactly and with what destination? He still had no idea.

He did another tour of the boat. He found some charts rolled up in the galley, but nothing on them showed the course that the boat might be taking. Then an orange lifebelt hanging from the cabin wall caught his eye. Across the flat edge was written in white letters, *The Dolphin*. He smiled. Jack's *Dolphin*, the boat from Whitehaven that had been reported missing. So he had been right! At this rate, it seemed to him that, in the wake of his search to resolve Sam's mystery shooting on Sunday night, he was on the way to clearing up crimes more quickly than Scotland Yard. He mounted the steps and climbed back up on deck.

Emerging onto the deck he could see right out across the expanse of water separating the yacht from the entrance to the cove. The blue water sparkled under the cold early afternoon sunshine. But with a start, he now saw a rowing boat rounding the headland and heading directly towards him. The squat form of Captain Jacobs sitting in the bow of the boat was clearly recognisable, the two oars splashing regularly in and out of the water on either side of him. It was lucky for Lynnford that, for some reason, he wasn't using the outboard motor, as it meant that he had his back to the *Sea Bird*. Otherwise he would surely have spotted Lynnford.

Ducking down, he scrambled out of the gangway and, turning round, quickly closed the hatch and put the lock back in place. He then sat down on the deck with his back against the hatch door, thinking quickly what to do. He had to leave the yacht. The problem was the dinghy. It would surely be spotted, even if he abandoned it and swam back. He calculated that he had about another five minutes.

Really, he only had one option. With the knapsack

around his chest, he slipped over the edge of the yacht and into the water alongside the dinghy. The water was cold and soaked through his clothes immediately. But he didn't have time to worry about his discomfort. Taking the boat's rope in his hand, he pulled the dinghy a short distance away from the hull of the yacht and then let go, letting the receding tide take it as far away as it could before being spotted by Jacobs. *Better he finds an empty boat and makes of it whatever he can,* thought Lynnford, *than a boat with me in it.* Meanwhile, he swam softly back to the yacht, slipping around the hull so that he was hidden from sight. He could hear the splash of oars in the water now. Jacobs was approaching the yacht. Then, as Lynnford expected, the rowing stopped. *He's spotted the dinghy and he's wondering what it means.* Lynnford heard the oars hit the water again and their sounds moving away. He strained his ears trying to work out what Jacobs was doing. He couldn't risk looking as he would be in the sailor's line of vision. But he couldn't stay where he was much longer. The cold was getting into his bones. He looked towards the shore. The yacht lay between the shore and Jacobs, effectively blocking his vision. Lynnford calculated that it could not be more than twenty yards. Could he swim it quickly enough? He needed to be safely hidden on shore before Jacobs finally got aboard the *Sea Bird* and from where he would certainly spot him in the water. He had no choice. The cold water was getting the better of him. He couldn't waste another second and immediately struck out towards the shore, swimming strongly and surely, although hampered by the knapsack hanging from his chest and from the weight of his sodden clothes.

Lying flat in the water, as he was, the cliff towards which

he was swimming seemed to tower up above him. Ahead of him, he could see the water breaking in white foam around the rocks that lined the cliff base. There was no beach, and he guessed that the rocks would surely be wet and slippery. The sea was now pushing him towards them and this, together with the drag of the underwater current as it washed back, was making it difficult for him to control his movements. A large block of rock suddenly loomed up on his left as the water was sucked away in a deep swell, before rushing back and pushing him almost over the rocks in front of him. He reached out to break his fall. His hands struck the rock and he slipped down as the water receded once again. The brownish-grey rock in front of him was punctured with little white shells and covered in places by thin green strands of seaweed. There was nothing to take hold of. He waited for the sea to rise again and lift him above the rock. The water came back with a rush, and he had to be careful that its force did not make him break a leg or an arm as he hit the rock again.

He landed safely and, getting up, picked his way as quickly as he could across the rocks, dropping down behind the clumps of bushes that marked the bottom of the cliff. He leant back against the cliff wall, letting out a sigh of relief mixed with exhaustion.

His clothes were heavy with the weight of the water. He began to feel the cold creep back into his bones as he rested. His teeth started to chatter. 'I must get back to Westcliff as quickly as possible,' he muttered. 'Where are my shoes?' He released the knapsack from its uncomfortable position on his chest and as he rummaged inside for his shoes, his hands touched on the hard glass of a bottle.

The whisky bottle! He could almost feel the joy and surprise running through his blood as he silently thanked again the old sailor for his parting gift. Never had he needed a tipple as now and he unscrewed the metal cap, fumbling with his wet hands. He took a large mouthful, gulping down the whisky and letting the liquid rush down his throat. The alcohol made him splutter. Yet a warm sensation rebounded through his body, making him forget temporarily the discomfort of his wet clothes.

Taking more long draughts of whisky, he stared across the water. There was no way of knowing whether he'd been spotted by Jacobs. He could see Peter Knight's dinghy now tied in tow of Jacobs' own boat but there was no sign of him. He must be below deck. How long he'd be there Lynnford had no idea, but he could only hope that it would be long enough to let him scramble up the cliff face unseen and onto the coastal path. Fortunately, it didn't look as steep as it had appeared from the water. Again, he had no choice. He had to get back to Westcliff without delay.

TWENTY-FIVE
WHAT THE TOWN ALREADY KNEW

Breathing hard, having run the last fifty yards or so and most of the way, Lynnford pushed open the door to the newsagents, concerned for Gwen's safety. Seconds earlier and already within sight of the shop, he had recognised the young barman from The Blue Harp leaving. A furtive air about him had made Lynnford fear the worst. Yet, one step inside, Gwen's reaction was the quicker.

Seeing Lynnford standing in the shop, his clothes soiled and dripping with water, her face dropped.

'Good heavens, Robert! What have you been up to?'

Lynnford brushed back his wet hair and grimaced.

'I had a forced dip in the cove.'

'If only you could see yourself.'

'I can feel it.'

'You'd better get changed straight away, before you die of pneumonia. Come on upstairs. I'll get you some dry clothes.'

Lynnford followed Gwen up the bare wood stairs.

'I've just got back from Overcombe.'

'You spoke to Sam?'

'Yes. I got a call this morning telling me he was allowed visits now, but he didn't have much to say. I don't think he wanted to say anything in case he was overheard. Not about Sunday night anyway.'

'And what about what had happened to him?'

'Nothing. All he knew was that he had been kept in the hold of a fishing boat in Westcliff harbour.'

'Westcliff harbour! And who kidnapped him?'

'He doesn't know. He never saw them.'

'And what did he want?'

'Who?'

'The lad from The Blue Harp.'

'He brought up a box of fresh fish.'

'Is that all? He looked like he didn't want to be seen.'

'I don't think he did.'

Gwen shook her head, carrying on up the stairs. 'Poor Sam! What have I done to him?'

'Don't worry yourself, Gwen. We'll find out who did this to him and why, soon enough.'

'Well, don't waste your time thinking too much. Here's the bathroom. I'll fetch some of his clothes whilst you take a bath. They should fit you.'

'There's really no need.'

'Before you die on me. I'm serious.'

She reached over and opened the taps. 'The water should still be hot.'

The hot water began to steam out of the tap. Gwen closed

the door behind her, and he began to undress, throwing his clothes into a pile on the floor. A few minutes later she knocked on the door and called out, 'There's a jumper and a pair of trousers. They should fit you. You don't look like you've changed much since you had to squeeze into a Spitfire. By the way, there's a towel in the cupboard behind the tub.'

'Thanks Gwen, I won't be a minute.'

'I'd better go back down to the shop. Not that there's much business. They're still keeping away as though I'm a leper.'

Soaking in the hot water, Lynnford's mind wandered back to the yacht floating at anchor in Sandy Cove. Another knock on the door interrupted his thoughts.

'Lynnford?'

Peter Knight!

'Gwen Mortimer says you're all right. I saw you pelting down the road.'

'I'm fine. Wait there. I'll be out in a minute.'

'I'll put on some tea. Gwen will be closing the shop shortly.'

Lynnford quickly dried himself off, pulled on the pair of trousers that Gwen had left outside the bathroom and slipped the cotton jumper over his head. When he entered the sitting room Gwen was just placing a tea tray on a low table in the middle of a group of armchairs, into one of which Peter Knight had folded himself. They looked up on hearing Lynnford come into the room.

'So soon? I hope we didn't make you hurry.'

Lynnford laughed. 'If Peter hadn't knocked on the door I'd have fallen asleep and that wouldn't do. I feel I'm abusing my welcome as it is.'

'Don't be silly. Sam would do anything to help you out. He's told me how you saved his life by flying him out of France on the last plane before the airfield was overrun.'

Lynnford smiled. 'That was sometime ago now. I'm sure the slate's been rubbed clean, if ever there was one.'

'Sam's clothes suit you. How do they feel?'

'Fine. We're about the same height.'

'But I haven't given you a shirt! What was I thinking of?'

'Don't worry, Gwen. This will do fine until I get back to my digs.'

Gwen sat down and lit a cigarette.

'If you can give me a bag for my wet clothes that would help. I'm afraid there's a pool of water in the bathroom.'

Gwen dismissed his concern with a wave of her hand.

'Don't worry about that. Here, have a cup of tea.'

'What happened then?' Peter Knight asked.

'To the boat?'

'What else? You looked like a fish out of water, flapping along the high street.'

'Jacobs has got it. I had to leave it. Sorry.'

'Don't worry, I'll get it back from him soon enough. When all this is over. In the meantime, Joyce will give me hell. Putting myself out for strangers.'

Lynnford described the afternoon's events.

'What do you expect? It's not news. It's in his blood, smuggling for generations. You'll never change Jacobs. Whatever it is, he'll take it so long as it's tax free and he can carry it in his boat.'

'But I think it must be something special this time. Something that Sam had got wind of but didn't want to tell me on the telephone or to Gwen when she saw him this morning.'

'And you didn't find anything on the boat, you said?'

Lynnford shook his head. Peter Knight seemed to have come to a decision, pushing up the sleeves of his sweater as he spoke, looking a little to one side.

'Well, it is something special this time.'

'What, you know, Peter?'

'Guns, Gwen. Guns, that's what it is. Now I've told you.'

'Guns! Is he mad? And you knew?'

'Everyone knows. The whole town, Gwen. They've agreed to smuggle them across to the Republic.'

'Ireland? And what are they going to do with them there? Have they gone mad?'

'Take them across the border, to the north, no doubt,' Lynnford answered.

'But where have they got them from?'

'The break-in at the naval stores in Portsmouth,' Lynnford replied, thinking aloud and beginning to put together some more pieces of the puzzle.

'Westcliff's own gun runners. What shame! And for the Irish Republican Army! Really, we're at rock bottom. The town has lost its soul! And you knew about this, Peter? You and your wife, and the whole town? I don't believe it. And what about Sam? He didn't say anything this morning. They could have killed him, Peter.'

'Come on, Gwen. Everyone knows.'

'And Sergeant Evans? Why doesn't he arrest Jacobs?'

'They're family. You know that. And anyway, he needs evidence. You didn't find anything on the boat or in the cave, did you, Lynnford?'

'No, that's right. And what Sergeant Evans doesn't look for, he won't find, will he?'

'That's about right!'

'So you say this is general knowledge?'

'Well, perhaps not everyone. I got it through Joyce. The harbour folk, they're a tightly knit community.'

'Too right. As close as pilchards in a tin!'

'But they're as much Westcliff as you and me, Gwen. They probably don't agree with it either but they're not going to put out their necks. Some extra shillings coming their way. Who's going to say no to that?'

'Shillings! Gold sovereigns more like!'

'They're used to turning a blind eye and not asking too many questions.'

'I guess reporters aren't their cup of tea.'

'Sam shouldn't have brought you down. That's how they see it. And now Gwen's paying the price.'

'I don't need them.'

'Your shop won't survive without their custom. But they'll be back, once it's all blown over. When Sam gets out. You know that.'

'Don't think I'll forgive and forget so quickly! Poor Sam!'

'I meant to tell you, Gwen, that we may have a witness to Sam being dumped on the beach after the fire.'

'Who, Robert?'

'A fisherman.'

'Well, that's something, at least.'

'Don't worry, Gwen, we'll get him out.'

'I know, Robert. You keep saying. I'm just tired of all this.'

'So, the town's sympathetic to the Irish Catholics?'

'Not especially, Lynnford. Not since the War. We thought them too fond of the Germans. But you might find someone.'

'Anyone in particular, Peter?'

'Pengal.'

'The man with the rasping cough?'

'That's him. You were asking about him yesterday. Sounds like he's bringing up a Cornish tin mine every time he coughs.'

'Hasn't he been up to London?'

'That's right, Gwen. They say he brought the guns business down with him.'

'There's the other stranger. The man outside Gwen's shop. Who's he?' Lynnford enquired. 'He was in The Blue Harp last night with Jacobs. You remember, Peter?'

'I don't know him, but they say he sailed in with the *Sea Bird*. That's the boat they're going to use.'

'I know that now. You could have told me earlier.'

'Do you think Frank Hope and his mother are involved?'

'I'm not sure, Peter. Maybe they just keep an eye on what comes in and goes out of Sandy Cove. Sort of unofficial harbour masters.'

Gwen gave a weak, nervous laugh, momentarily breaking the tightening look in her eyes.

'If they had anything heavy to bring in or take out it would have to go by the road that leads onto the beach,' Lynnford continued. 'And that sort of traffic can't go unnoticed by the Hopes.'

'And what about the other boat, the *Sea Breeze*?'

'Alfred Chessington sailed into Sandy Cove to visit his wife's grave and to collect or deliver a diamond necklace that had once been in the family and which, this summer, had been stolen from its current owner in London. The necklace is worth a fortune, as you can imagine. I'm not sure the *Sea Breeze* had anything to do with Jacobs and his smuggling.'

'Unless they wanted to get their hands on the necklace themselves. You say it's worth a fortune.'

'You could be right, Gwen. Someone might kill for it, but it would mean that somehow they knew Chessington had the necklace aboard the *Sea Breeze*.'

'Or that he'd come to pick it up from the old house, as you suggested.'

'But how could they have known? Chessington was hardly known in Westcliff. Only a handful of people knew him. The Hopes, possibly. Mrs Henderson, Derek Tring, and Mr Yeats, the harbour master. Now, he's a possibility.'

'Mr Yeats?'

'Yes, Gwen. He was seen talking to Chessington in Tower Port last week and the two of them met up outside North View House on Sunday evening or whatever day it was that Chessington died.'

'How do you know, Robert?'

'Both of them showed signs of having been in a brawl of some sort and Mr Yeats is missing two coat buttons. One of which I found on the terrace at the back of the house and the other was in the turn-up of Chessington's trousers.'

'Yeats tried to steal the necklace from him, is that what you're saying, Lynnford?'

'Possibly, Peter.'

'And so did Chessington steal the necklace from the Mayfair flat?'

'It's possible, otherwise how could he have it on him? But the evidence of the burglary seemed to point to a professional. Maybe Chessington was a professional burglar but if it was him then he did it for personal reasons.'

'But if he had the necklace, what was he doing with it down here? Why bring it back to Westcliff if he was no longer living here?'

'Exactly, Gwen. That's why I believe it more likely that he came here to collect it but that would mean money, and a lot of it if he was going to buy it. Even stolen, the necklace must be worth a small fortune. Could Chessington have had that sort of money? I don't know.'

'And where had he been all this time, Chessington?'

'Rotterdam, quite likely. At least that's where the *Sea Breeze* sailed from. You know, maybe the crew of the *Sea Breeze* simply fell out with each other over the necklace. The third sailor, the woman, is still missing.'

'But she didn't run off with the necklace, did she?'

'No, Gwen, she didn't. So where is she?'

'She's safe enough, it seems.' Peter Knight gave an embarrassed look. 'They've got her stowed away somewhere.'

Gwen Mortimer stared at him, shocked.

'So, you know that as well, Peter? What on earth is this town coming to?'

'Stop playing the innocent, Gwen!'

'But I am, totally innocent!'

'Who's stowed her away, Peter?' Lynnford asked, trying to diffuse Gwen's anger.

'Jacobs and his gang. It seems there was a stupid mix-up on Sunday. Jacobs mistook the *Sea Breeze* for the *Sea Bird*.'

'So that explains it! Couldn't you have told us this sooner?'

'It's only what I've just picked up and put together, listening to you now, Lynnford. Little phrases let slip here and there. As I told you, it's a tight-knit community. They don't share information easily.'

'And any idea where they're holding the woman?'

Peter Knight shook his head.

'And what has all this got to do with gun running in Westcliff? That was Sam's story, I suppose. That must have been why he brought you down, Robert.'

'True, Gwen. They'll be loading the *Sea Bird* this evening. We need to catch them red-handed. Without hard evidence, Sergeant Evans, I suspect, won't lift a finger, not when it involves his family and Westcliff people. And we have to get the evidence ourselves. Where do you stand, Peter?'

'I'm with you. We want the best for this town.'

'And your wife, Mrs Knight?'

'Joyce as well.'

But Peter Knight didn't appear too sure of his last reply.

The clock on the mantelpiece chimed the half hour.

'What time is it? It can't be five-thirty already.'

'Six-thirty,' Gwen corrected.

'I'd no idea. We must get going.'

'What have you got in mind?'

'If we wait on the beach for them, they may not even come that way.'

'It's the most likely, however. It's the nearest point to the boat. And if you row out into the cove you won't see a thing, not in the dark. Anyway, I'm not sure where we can get another boat this evening.'

Peter Knight got up and went to the window. Lifting back the curtain he looked up at the sky.

'There's a lot of cloud about. I reckon it'll be a dark night.'

'You need to be on the yacht. That's what you're saying, isn't it?'

'That's right, Gwen. But to go down below deck would mean un-padlocking the hatch, which anyone coming aboard would notice straight away.'

'I've got an idea.'

Gwen stubbed out her cigarette and stood up, standing in front of Lynnford with her back to the fireplace.

'Why don't the two of us go aboard? Once you're down below I can close up the hatch, put the lock back in place and then leave the yacht. Nobody will be any the wiser.'

'But how will you get back?'

'The same way as we'll have to go as we don't have another boat.'

'Swimming?'

'Gwen, you can't!'

'It's my idea. Stop me!'

'But the water will be freezing.'

'Listen, Peter Knight, I'm too mad at you and all the people of this town to care. Selfish, small minds. My blood is boiling!'

Peter Knight paused for thought, his face colouring.

'Let's see, I reckon I might just be able to get hold of two wetsuits. Just give me a couple of minutes. I'll give Ted Harrison at the boatyard a call. Can I use your telephone?'

He crossed the room to the hall table next to the door and picked up the telephone. His call was answered almost immediately.

'Okay, Lynnford, we've got two suits. I can go down and pick them up in an hour. Ted doesn't live far away.'

'An hour? It's too long.'

Lynnford looked at the clock.

'We should be getting there as soon as possible.'

'Don't worry. You've got plenty of time. Anyway, we can't do it any quicker. You need the wetsuits otherwise you'll freeze waiting in the boat for Jacobs to arrive.'

'You're right,' Lynnford agreed reluctantly.

Gwen nodded, her lips drawn.

'Fine, I'll meet you and Gwen at nine at the end of the high street. I'll bring everything you need.'

TWENTY-SIX
BACK ON BOARD THE *SEA BIRD*

Lynnford and Gwen were at the stile at the end of the high street at least ten minutes before nine. It was dark and standing there Lynnford already began to feel the chill of the sea air blow through his clothes. He pushed his hands deeper into his coat pockets and stamped the ground, impatiently; pushing the prospect of being submerged a second time in the cold sea water to the back of his mind. Looking back down the high street he almost felt they were at the edge of two worlds. Sporadic street lights lit up the pavement and buildings, and beyond them house lights flickered on and off as those inside passed the evening together or prepared for bed. Turning his back on the town, the fields and woods of the headland stretched before him, shrouded in a semi-darkness that revealed only their dull shapes. Strands of whitish clouds blew across the low night sky.

Life seemed to have been extinguished but for the distant hoot of an owl and the headlights of a car approaching Westcliff along the winding road from Tower Port, flashing from time to time as it rounded a bend or passed a break in the hedge. A cyclist went past them, taking the road out of town. Lynnford looked at his watch. Two minutes to nine. Someone was approaching along the high street.

'Here he is.'

Gwen had recognised the figure of Peter Knight, walking quickly towards them.

'So you're here already.'

'Have you got everything?'

Peter Knight swung off his shoulder one of the two knapsacks that he was carrying and handed it to Lynnford.

'Here, take this.'

'And for me?'

Gwen held out her hand.

'It's all right. I'm coming with you.'

Gwen shook her head.

'You've done enough already, Peter.'

'Are you sure?'

He sounded relieved. Lynnford replied, 'Of course, Peter.'

Lynnford took hold of the knapsack, swinging it on his back, adjusting the straps slightly. Gwen took the other one.

'Come on, Gwen, let's get going.'

Lynnford and Gwen climbed over the stile, leaving Peter Knight behind, watching them until they were out of sight. They set off at a brisk pace across the fields until the path brought them out along the cliff. The tall gorse bushes smelt strong and sweet in the evening air and, although the moon was severed by the wreaths of cloud strung across the sky, the path was still clearly visible; a light-grey ribbon disappearing in the darkness some twenty yards or so ahead of them. Peter Knight's prediction of a dark night appeared to be turning out not to be good. Neither of them spoke, keeping their thoughts to themselves.

Lynnford led the way, his arms swinging purposely back and forward. Gwen followed closely behind. The sea breeze rustled gently through the trees and bushes that lined the path, making the tops of the trees sway very slightly from side to side.

'All right, Gwen?'

Gwen whistled a tune by way of reply.

They were almost at the point where the hidden path led down to Jacobs' cave when suddenly Gwen whispered behind him.

'Listen! Somebody's coming along the path behind us.'

They stopped and listened. The sound of hurried movement was quite distinct, quickly catching them up; two persons at least. As one, Gwen and Lynnford stepped off the path and into the gorse, crouching down behind the bushes, waiting. Quiet and alert, almost like prowling foxes, two men suddenly appeared before them. Lynnford recognised Jacobs but not the other man. He and Gwen held their breath, letting them walk past. And almost as quickly, they saw them duck down into the broken hedgerow on the other side of the path, melting away as if by magic with only the rustling undergrowth betraying their progress.

Gwen was the first to speak, whispering, 'Where are they going?'

'Sandy Cove. We need to hurry,' Lynnford replied, carefully pushing himself out of the gorse bush.

'Down there?'

'Their storeroom is in a cave with access to the sea. They'll have gone to pick up a dinghy to help them with the transport from the beach. We need to get to the *Sea Bird* before them. Come on, run!'

Gwen nodded, adding, 'That was Tabby with Jacobs.'

Very quickly they had rounded the headland and could see the cove, and its black pool of water stretched out before them.

'It's here, Gwen. Look, the yacht's down there.'

'I see it, right down onto the deck. There's no sign of Jacobs or Tabby.'

Lynnford looked out to sea and then across the cove and cast his eyes along the pale strip of beach. Nobody, yet.

'Still, they could turn up any minute. There's no path. We'll have to scramble down. Come on!'

Lynnford slipped through the bushes in front of him, keeping hold of the branches to avoid falling. Gwen crept through the undergrowth alongside him and the two of them edged cautiously down the side of the cliff.

'Hold on as you go down.'

Swinging from one branch to the next, and without a torch, they had to guess where they were putting their feet. Suddenly, the ground gave way under Lynnford, a rush of soil and stones falling down the slope. Both legs slipped under him, pulling him down until his hand, grasping a branch, with his arm stretched out fully, caught his fall. In the silence, the noise of breaking branches and falling earth seemed dreadful. It quickly died away, and all Gwen could hear was Lynnford's breathing.

Lynnford steadied himself, recovered his breath, and they continued. Their descent was now more of a scramble as they were forced more and more to slip down, sliding the remaining distance. Almost at the bottom, Gwen took hold of a branch to steady her balance. The dry wood cracked under the pressure of her hand, and she fell the remaining six feet or so, slipping past Lynnford and hitting herself against a small tree. The shock took the wind out of her.

'All right?' Lynnford asked, slipping down after her.

Gwen nodded and sat up. She mopped her forehead, panting lightly.

'We're lucky not to have twisted an ankle, or worse, broken a leg.'

She leaned forward and slipped the knapsack off her back. Placing it in front of her, she undid the flap.

'Here, put this on.'

She held out a folded wetsuit.

'What should I do with my clothes?'

'Put them in this waterproof bag. You'll need them for the boat. I'll leave mine here. I can pick them up on my way back.'

Lynnford opened up the knapsack he had been carrying and tipped the contents out onto the ground. A small black revolver caught his attention.

'What's this for?'

'Peter thought you might need it. Put it in the bag with your clothes.'

Lynnford hesitated. 'I don't know.'

'They've already killed one person, Robert.'

'That was a mistake.'

'You don't know for sure. Take it! You don't know how desperate they are. And, if you hope to take over the boat you may find you're outnumbered.'

The rocks were cold under their bare feet as they picked their way across them to the water. The *Sea Bird* was floating, almost motionless, in front of them, and so close that Lynnford felt that he could just as well climb aboard without even having to get his feet wet. *Some hope!* The water rippled around its hull. Closer to them, it was spilling over the rocks as it rose; disappearing each time as the swell sucked it back down.

'It's not going to be easy to clear the rocks.'

'Let me go first, Gwen.'

Lynnford sat down on the rock, the water rushing over his legs.

'Can you hear anything?'

'No, they're still not in the cove. But we need to hurry.'

Lynnford attached the bag to a cord that he hung loosely around his waist so that it wouldn't impede him, and then he let himself down into the water, keeping close to the rock. Gwen followed him.

'Are you ready? Let's go when it's high again. Let the swell take you out and swim like mad, otherwise it'll bring you back onto the rocks.'

Gwen nodded.

'Now!'

And they plunged into the foaming water, pulling forward with their arms at full stretch and their legs pushing hard. The water fell, hung still for a few moments and then rose up again, forcing them back but not as far as the rocks. It fell again and they continued to swim hard until gradually the pull of the undercurrent relaxed. Lynnford rolled his head over in the water and spotted Gwen some yards away, swimming easily towards the yacht.

From in the water, Lynnford threw his bag up onto the yacht, and then reached up, catching hold of the edge of the boat's deck. As he pulled himself out of the water the boat leaned over towards him.

'Careful, Robert!'

But the roll of the yacht had given Lynnford the chance to reach further up, grab hold of the railing, and quickly pull himself aboard. The boat tilted heavily towards the water again as Gwen climbed on board after him. She kept her eyes fixed on the open entrance to the cove whilst Lynnford set about picking the cabin lock for the second time that day. In a few seconds he had released the mechanism and opened the hatch. He then got out of his wetsuit and put his dry clothes back on.

'Don't worry about that.' Gwen pointed to the wetsuit. 'I'll take care of it. You'd better get down below straight away. I'll clear up here before I go.'

'Fine. Listen Gwen, keep an eye out in case anything goes wrong. If nothing happens tonight, don't forget to come and get me out in the morning.'

Gwen closed the hatch behind him and Lynnford heard her fit the lock back in place and move around the deck.

Two or three minutes later he heard a splash of water as she slipped back into the sea and began to swim off, but not before tapping a friendly farewell against the side of the yacht.

TWENTY-SEVEN
ON THE BEACH

S hielding the torchlight under her jumper, Gwen looked at the time. Eighteen minutes past twelve. She'd decided not to wait at the bottom of the cliff and instead, once back on the path, she'd hurried down to the beach. She wanted to witness for herself the unloading of the munitions. She moved slightly to make herself more comfortable, holding down the sharp grass with her hands to avoid scratching her face, and looked back up the road that led down into the cove, and of which in the dark she could discern no more than several yards past the farm gate. The sound of a distant motor had caught her attention, still very faint.

Two tiny lights, no bigger than pin heads, flashed at her, it seemed, and then disappeared. The engine noise, now clearly distinct, continued to increase. It would be on the beach in any minute. Suddenly, the lights reappeared, the size of saucers now, progressing steadily forward. She slipped back down the sand dune and held her breath. Seconds later, a vehicle rumbled past her along the track, through the sand dunes and onto the beach. The engine cut out and the silence returned. Gwen crawled back up the sand dune and looked down.

The vehicle was there, slightly to her right. It was a van and, surprised, she recognised the blue baker's van in which Kenny made his deliveries. It was parked at the end of the track. There was no sound or movement at all. They must be sitting tight in the cabin, waiting for a signal from the *Sea Bird* or from Jacobs in his dinghy. She guessed they could not go any further for fear of the wheels sinking into the soft sand. Already, the chassis was very low down, almost touching the ground, and she imagined the crates of guns inside, still not fully able to believe it. Her anger at Peter Knight had gone but a confused sense of disappointment and sadness still hung heavily within her. Sam at least she could be proud of, but who else? She looked back up the road again. A gentle wind was blowing off the water, making the treetops break the solitude of the night air with the soft rustle of their drying leaves. She shivered slightly.

A light flashed out from the middle of the cove, almost directly in front of her, or so it seemed. It flashed on and off again. The reaction from inside the van was not slow in coming. The door opened and somebody got out, accompanied by the voice of a man still inside.

'Hurry up, Kenny. Get a move on.'

'Okay, okay.'

The door slammed shut. The figure of a tall man walked out from the side of the van and stood in front of the bonnet.

He held out a torch in one hand and quickly flashed the light on and off. The light out in the cove responded immediately. The man with the torch turned his head round, and Gwen recognised the face of Kenny. Kenny shouted out to whoever he had left in the cabin.

'They're coming over. Let's get the gear out.'

Gwen wondered whether the baker knew what Kenny used the van for in his spare time. Most likely he was getting his own cut! The driver's door opened again, and she recognised Pengal, followed by another man. With a start, she realised that it was the man who had been watching her shop earlier in the week. She followed their movements in the dark, listening as she lay flat on the sand. The back doors of the van were opened and, one by one, several crates were lifted out and stacked one on top of the other. This done, the men began to carry them out onto the beach. She turned her head to one side, resting her cheek on the cool sand to release the crick in the back of her neck.

'Careful, not too close,' warned one of them.

'Don't worry, the tide's going out. Can't you see?'

'All the same it's still damp.'

'As you like.'

Kenny and Pengal stopped, and they let the box carefully down on the sand. The other man brought a smaller crate. They then made several more trips to the back of the van until they had deposited five wooden crates on the beach. The three men then stood together beside them, waiting, not speaking; looking out into the blackness that was broken only by the water that ran up the beach in a white froth.

'They're taking their time,' Gwen heard Kenny comment and watched as he turned his back on the water and sat down on one of the crates and lit a cigarette. A little pinprick of light glowed in the dark as he filled his lungs with smoke. Still, she began to wonder, what was happening aboard the yacht? Had they discovered Lynnford? But she doubted it. She would have heard the fireworks.

Three or four minutes later the steady sound of oars splashing in the water floated through the darkness and suddenly the bow of a rowing boat with the squat form of Captain Jacobs, his back to them, emerged as if from another world, followed by a second boat with Tabby at the oars. Kenny jumped off his crate, throwing the cigarette into the sand, and joining the other two as they rushed forwards to help pull up the boats and ground them in the soft sand.

'Quick!'

Jacobs started issuing orders.

'Let's get this stuff aboard. I don't want it left hanging about on the beach any longer than necessary. We've already wasted too much time.'

'Nobody's going to see it down here.'

'Don't be too sure,' he snapped back.

'And Kenny, don't light up on the beach again or you won't be smoking much longer.'

'Don't joke. You couldn't see anything with your back to us.'

Jacobs did not bother to reply. Instead, he reached down and took hold of one of the crates.

'Come on, Skinner and you two, help out. A large crate

and the small one with Tabby; a large crate in my boat and Pengal, you'll come with me.'

'What for?'

Something in their plans had obviously changed.

'Don't argue! I need you on the yacht to help us in getting the large crates aboard. We'll be quicker.'

The two rowing boats loaded, they were hauled back into the water until they were once again afloat, Tabby in one, Jacobs and Pengal in the other. Kenny and Skinner were left on the beach with the two remaining crates. Jacobs gave out his last instructions as he pulled back the oars. 'Keep an eye out whilst I'm gone.'

'Who for? Nobody's going to come down here at this time of night.'

'Just do as I say, Kenny. I'm watching you.'

And the two boats disappeared once again into the darkness.

Kenny took out his packet of cigarettes and offered one to Skinner.

'What about the captain?'

'Damn him. Just keep your back to the sea.'

Gwen smiled despite herself as she watched them huddle down on the sand behind the stacked crates, smoking their cigarettes like two schoolboys. As the time went by and the cold began to eat away at her she almost wished she could have joined them, at least for the company. Finally, Jacobs and Tabby were back on the beach, their boats loaded with the last two crates, and with Jacobs giving out his last instructions.

'Skinner, I'll bring back Pengal and then take you over. We'll sail at first light.'

'So you are going with him, Captain?'

'Yes, Kenny. As I said last night, I want to make sure everything goes right at the other end. It's our first time. I won't be gone more than a couple of days.'

'What about the woman?'

'Put her in the back of the van and dump her somewhere on the moor. Don't worry! She won't want to hang around once she learns the other man on the *Sea Breeze* is dead as well. She'll be happy enough to save her skin, and in the boat if she makes it back to Westcliff.'

'I hope you're right.'

'Just make sure you do it and not Pengal.'

'I might as well come over with you now.'

'No, Skinner. Stay here and keep Kenny company. I'll be back with Pengal, and then I'll take you over.'

Something soft brushed against Gwen's leg. What was that? She looked down to see a dog at her feet resting its muzzle against her trousers. She held her breath, realising that there was little she could do to stop the dog from barking should it start, and prayed that the animal would lose interest and leave her alone. But the dog seemed happy enough to stay with her and made no move to leave. A sharp whistle, however, pierced the air. The dog's head shot up.

'Toby, here boy!' a man's voice whispered.

The dog left Gwen immediately and trotted away, letting her follow it back several yards until she came to the top of a sand dune, looking once again down on the van. A man was standing in the middle of the track looking at the back of the van, the dog leaning into his legs.

'Come on, Toby, this isn't for us.'

The man turned round and walked back up the track. Gwen watched him go, taking no notice of anything but the track ahead of him. She recognised the man's outline straight away. *Frank Hope!* He pushed open the gate to his farm and disappeared with the dog. The way was now clear, and Gwen did not waste any more time. She had already decided what she was going to do. Lynnford could look after himself, but she needed to find the woman from the *Sea Breeze*. What she had overheard didn't inspire much confidence as to her fate. Surely, they couldn't run the risk of her walking into a police station. Except perhaps the one in Westcliff!

Slipping down the sand dune, she walked quickly up to the van and, crouching down, crept forward until she got to the bonnet. Kenny was walking back to the water's edge to rejoin the man who she'd heard Jacobs call Skinner; no doubt reassured after he must have come over to the van on hearing Frank Hope's whistle and seen him walk off. *Good.* She returned to the back of the van, opened the door and looked inside. Empty. Everything had been unloaded and taken aboard the *Sea Bird*. With luck they wouldn't bother looking in the back again. She crossed her fingers.

A footstep behind her made her pause but before she could turn round a lightning pain thudded through her head and she fell to the ground, unconscious. Somebody lifted her and dropped her limp body onto the bare metal floor of the van, accompanying the release of her weight with a soft exclamation of contempt.

'You were told not to interfere, you and your meddling husband.'

The man closed the van door softly and walked quietly to the front of the vehicle. He recognised the two men standing on the beach, talking. He stopped where he was and waited.

'Here they are.'

Kenny turned to Skinner and added, 'It's going to be a cold stint, Skinner. Better you than me.'

Skinner said nothing.

The boat's bow hit the beach. Kenny and Skinner hurried forward as Pengal jumped out.

'Where's Tabby?'

'On his way back to the cave.'

The voice of Jacobs barked out.

'Just get in, Skinner, and we'll be off. Here, you can take the oars.'

'Good evening, Jacobs.'

The man standing beside the van had walked up and now stood two or three yards away. Kenny and Pengal turned round in surprise. Jacobs looked up, still sitting in the boat.

'What are you doing down here? It's not your business.'

'I'm afraid it is. Get out of the boat.'

'Like hell! Pengal!'

But Pengal hesitated, uncertainty clear on his face, looking from one to the other. Time enough for the harbour master to display his revolver.

'You don't need to think, Pengal. Just back off from the boat. You too, Kenny. Skinner! Get Jacobs out of the boat.'

This time Pengal's uncertainty changed to confusion.

An oar already in his hand, Jacobs sitting helplessly in

front of him, Skinner brought it down with a blow on the man's head.

'Don't worry about him, lie down.'

The harbour master pointed the gun at Kenny and Pengal, their mouths open in astonishment.

'Now! Face down, before I shoot.'

A loud splash accompanied the fall of Jacob's body in the water, pushed overboard by Skinner, who quickly set to turning the boat around. The harbour master rushed over to him, keeping the revolver pointing at the two men lying on the beach and hauling the floating body of Jacobs onto the wet sand before climbing into the boat.

'Get rowing, Skinner! And don't any of you make me shoot. I will and no mistake.'

When they got up, the rowing boat had disappeared. Jacobs, still lying in the ebbing water, rolled over onto his side.

'What are we going to do?'

'Get him up and get back in the van.'

Pengal spat out his anger as he walked off, leaving Kenny to drag Jacobs back onto his feet.

TWENTY-EIGHT
RED SKY IN THE MORNING

A few hours earlier, while Gwen watched the events unfold on the beach, Lynnford was lying on one of the berths in the bow-end cabin of the *Sea Bird* waiting for the consignment of arms to be loaded aboard. Trapped below deck by the hatch that Gwen had padlocked from the outside, Lynnford could do no more than follow with his ears and wait patiently for his chance to act.

Listening intently to every sound that broke the still night air, he heard quite soon the sound of two outboard motors purring softly still some distance away. Jacobs and Tabby had each taken a dinghy from the cave, he guessed. And then the sound was cut sharply, no doubt as the two boats entered the cove and Jacobs wanted to avoid attracting attention. Eventually, Lynnford heard the quiet splashing of oars approach the yacht and then the soft thud of a rowing boat against its side. The yacht rocked slightly as either Jacobs or Tabby stood up in the rowing boat and steadied himself by holding on to the yacht's railings. And then whispered voices, co-ordinating their movements; Jacobs telling Tabby to hand him some boxes from the dinghies once he was aboard the *Sea Bird*. This done a few minutes later, Lynnford heard Jacobs climb off the yacht and back into his boat and then followed the sounds of the two rowing boats receding into the silence.

A little while later the two boats returned, this time with a third man and he recognised the rasping cough of Pengal, later wheezing heavily as he stood up in the rowing boat and lifted himself aboard the *Sea Bird*. Clearly the crates they had now brought over from the beach were a lot heavier and required two of them in the dinghy to lift them up to the *Sea Bird* and, with the help of Pengal already aboard, transfer them onto the yacht. Three boxes were brought aboard, which made five in total, calculated Lynnford but there had to be still more, he guessed, as Jacobs and Tabby once again rowed off, this time leaving Pengal to pace up and down the deck of the *Sea Bird*, no doubt waiting for their return.

'That's the last of them.'

Jacobs and Tabby had returned and handed up to Pengal two more crates. Jacobs addressed Pengal, 'Let's get you back to the beach. I'll sail her out with Skinner.'

'Don't you trust him?'

'Let's say that two's safer than one, and I want to keep a good eye on my investment. As I said, last night.'

Lynnford heard Pengal laugh and then break out into another bout of coughing as he climbed down into the rowing boat.

'And what about me?'

'Take your boat back to the cave, Tabby,' Jacobs replied, adding, 'Remember, Tabby, don't use the motor until you're well out of the cove. Better still, use the oars all the way. You're in no hurry.'

Lynnford followed the sounds of the two sets of oars pulling away, leaving him alone in the *Sea Bird* once more. The crates were still up on deck. Once the hatch was opened to bring them down, he would have to be ready to act at a moment's notice.

Eventually, the rowing boat returned, and a man jumped up lightly onto the yacht, tying up the rowing boat astern. Skinner, guessed Lynnford, whoever he might be. Certainly not Jacobs! Whilst he was doing this the second man, Jacobs no doubt, climbed aboard, and taking hold of the padlock, unlocked the hatch and drew across the bolts.

'Let's get these crates down. They're no good up here.'

The muscles in Lynnford's body tightened involuntarily, listening attentively to the sounds of the footsteps descending the steps at the other end of the yacht, heavy under the awkward load. But it wasn't Jacobs' voice! He closed his grip around the hard handle of Peter Knight's revolver. Should they come up to the bow end he would have no choice but to take them both straight away, but even with the gun he knew he would not have an easy advantage in such a confined space.

He let out a slow breath of relief when he heard one of them order the other to stack the crates evenly amidships and in the cabin at the far end of the yacht. The final crate was, however, brought down and placed just outside his cabin; banging against the door as it was lowered roughly into place.

'Careful, you idiot! It's not a box of toys.'

Yeats! Surprised, Lynnford now recognised the voice that had been teasing him since the return of the rowing boat. The harbour master? What was he doing aboard and what had happened to Jacobs?

'Go up on deck, Skinner, and see if you can see anything.'

Lynnford strained his ears and a few minutes later he heard the faint sound of a motor starting and then gradually fading away. What was Gwen up to? He imagined her watching the yacht, close by among the rocks. The sailor came back down the steps into the cabin.

'They've gone.'

He scraped back a chair and sat down.

'What do we do now?'

'We sit and wait.'

'Shouldn't we set sail?'

'With the wind coming off the sea?'

'At least move her so they can't find us.'

'We'll take our chances.'

'I say we move her.'

'As you want. Take her into the middle of the cove, between the headlands. There's still anchorage there.'

Skinner shot up on deck and shortly Lynnford could feel the night breeze coming in from the open sea tugging at the sails tacked across the cove. When he came back down, the harbour master was studying a chart.

'It'll be dawn in a few hours, and the wind will have changed. Make something up in the galley. There should be something for us to eat there.'

Lynnford followed the sounds of the sailor as he moved

across the cabin to the kitchen and drew open the little hatch door. The cupboards and drawers banged open and shut.

'What do you want, then?' Skinner's voice snapped, clearly not happy with his chore.

'Make a sandwich. Something,' Yeats replied, adding after a pause, 'Use your loaf!'

'Yeah, very funny.'

Some minutes later Skinner returned and dropped a plate on the table. His mouth was full when he spoke.

'So where are we heading for?'

'We take this course.'

Yeats drew his finger across the chart.

'How long will it take us?'

'Maybe half a day if the wind is favourable. A day at most.'

'What's the forecast?'

'Fair, with a strong south-westerly. Possible isolated storms.'

'We need to check it again. There'll be someone at the pick-up. He'll be on the lookout for us during the afternoon. If we arrive early, we can drop anchor just outside the bay. No one will see us. It's completely deserted.'

'It's all right.'

The man was still eating.

'I know the place.'

The harbour master rolled up the chart.

'That's fine then. Your instructions are clear. You scuttle the boat and go on as planned with the others. The attack on Valera during the Royal visit must look like a bungled ambush of the Irish Republican Army that's taken out the wrong target. So it's important you leave behind some of the weapons and explosives so that they can be traced back to the break-in at the naval stores in Portsmouth.'

An assassination! Had Sam suspected this? He doubted it. Not even Peter Knight. According to him, everyone believed Captain Jacobs to be running guns for the Irish Republican Army. Why were they now involved in a plot to assassinate Eamon de Valera, the Irish prime minister? Who were they working for?

'There'll be one or two IRA sympathisers in your group. Make sure they never learn the true target and leave them behind so that they get picked up by the police.'

'How will I know them?'

'You'll be told.'

'Payment?'

'Final payment on results. The money will be in this deposit box in Liverpool. Whatever you do, don't hang around in Dublin. Take the ferry and cross the water as soon as you can.'

'And you?'

'I can't come back, not after holding up Jacobs and his men at gun point. Evans wouldn't hesitate in doing his job for once and getting one back for his cousin.'

So, that's what's happened to Jacobs, concluded Lynnford. *He's been double-crossed by the harbour master or at the very least had his consignment hijacked and diverted to perhaps something even more sinister. The Irish Republic thrown into turmoil, and, in the north, the Irish Republican Army discredited. For the benefit of whom,* he wondered. Still, he could not resist the creeping smile across his face as he imagined the print presses of *The London Herald* stamping out his story on the front page.

'It's Pengal who'll you need to fear most now. He'll treat you as a traitor.'

'You're probably right but quite by chance a nice little retirement present has just fallen into my hands. Somebody was foolish enough to trust me. But that's another story.'

What could that be, wondered Lynnford. *It'd have to be worth a lot! Has he somehow, finally, got his hands on the Exmoor Jubilee necklace? Bribing someone in the police station to take it out of the safe for him?* The chair scraped back. Some steps and the harbour master's voice again.

'Whisky?'

Lynnford felt that he could do with some himself. A bottle and glasses rattled on the wooden tabletop followed by the sound of liquid splashed carelessly into the glasses. The two men clinked a toast. A few moments later Lynnford recognised the sound of a pack of cards being cut in two, bent back and shuffled. Nothing was said as one of them dealt the cards. The game went on quietly until Skinner announced triumphantly, 'Royal Flush!'

The two men spent the rest of the night playing cards. As he couldn't do anything with them both below deck, Lynnford was obliged to sit back and wait. He lost count of the number of rounds of cards that the two men played, and he was half asleep when the footsteps of someone walking above his head brought him to.

A pale morning light had imperceptibly filled the cabin. He looked out of the porthole. The night had faded away, and the clouds with it, leaving the faint shape of a white moon still hanging oddly in the dawn sky. On the other side of the cove, behind his line of vision, the sun was rising and as it rose, a red glow was spreading out across the sky in front of him; a pale pink stain, speckled with light blue and white flecks. Red sky at night, shepherds' delight; red sky in the morning, shepherds' warning. As he repeated the short rhyme to himself, he wondered whether mariners had a similar saying. Such magnificent colours: could a storm really be brewing?

Someone else started to climb up the steps out of the main cabin, joining his companion outside on the deck. Now was Lynnford's chance. He rolled off the bunk bed and placing one hand on the round doorknob and the other flat against the door, softly pulled it ajar. He peered through the gap. Nobody was there. The crate was still there, across the doorway; about five feet long, two feet wide and eighteen inches deep. The sides were smooth and closely nailed down. He cast his eye over the other crates stacked up in the main cabin, leaving room only for the table at which Skinner and the harbour master had been sitting during the night, only a few feet away from him.

Three crates, small, square, half-sized tea chests, had been placed together. Lynnford tested the lid of one of the boxes. It lifted easily in his hands. Looking inside, he could see nothing but straw. Putting down the lid to one side, he dipped his hands into the straw, feeling around. His hand quickly came in contact with a hard oval object, the size of his hand. There were about five or so others close to each other. Lynnford recognised them by touch only too well. Grenades! He did not have to take them out to be sure; he had seen enough during the War. He dug his hands down deeper and went through a second layer. There must be ten or twelve in this box alone, he calculated. He replaced the lid and took the top off the next chest. Its contents were identical. He pulled out one of the hand grenades and inspected it closely, examining the markings. Naval munitions. Perhaps two or three years old, but still very dangerous. The haul from the Portsmouth break-in. Turning round, he looked at the crate in front of his cabin. From its length, he judged, it must have guns, possibly rifles. But there was too much for a single ambush, surely? *What else was planned*, he wondered. He put everything back and returned to his cabin, closing the door behind him.

He climbed onto the berth and looked out through the porthole, his mind racing ahead. Looking up at the sky, he noticed that a string of white clouds had appeared, rising above the crest of the cove and scudding across his line of vision out towards the sea. *Well, the wind has picked up*, he thought. They won't be wasting a second now. And as if in echo to his thoughts, footsteps ran along the deck above his head and scampered back. Both men were working quickly, each knowing exactly what had to be done.

He listened carefully. He knew that he had to act quickly. He must stop them before they got out into the open sea. He reopened the door to his cabin, and climbing over the crates, passed down towards the steps. He had only to wait for one of them to come down and grab him from behind. But he could not wait too long. Somehow, he had to attract their attention. Firing the revolver was too dangerous. He went into the galley and taking up two tin plates banged them together loudly. The noise deafened him but went unnoticed by the two sailors on deck; the clatter being lost in the sounds of the unfurling sails as the strengthening wind began to blow loudly through the rigging.

Just as he was beginning to get impatient, he heard one of them heading directly towards him and two plimsolls followed quickly, one after the other, down the upper steps into the main cabin. Yeats! Lynnford shrank back into the shadows behind the steps.

The harbour master landed at the bottom of the steps but before he could turn round Lynnford had struck him smartly on the back of the head with the butt of the revolver. The harbour master gave a gasp and collapsed under the force of the blow. Lynnford moved quickly. He bent down and rolled the man over on his back. Tucking his arms under the man's arms, he raised him off the floor and dragged his limp body, its legs stretched out in front, away from the steps and towards the second cabin in the stern of the yacht. He pushed open the door that had been kept free of crates and dragged the body inside. He was halfway through the doorway when he heard the footsteps of Skinner approach the open hatch, ready to descend into the cabin below.

Damn! He's going to come down too. Did he hear something? Lynnford let go of the harbour master, dropping the body on the floor, and jumping over it, rushed to the steps, knowing that it was too late to take Skinner by surprise. Unfortunately for Lynnford, the sailor was already down the steps and had seen him. Taking in the prostrate body of the harbour master, he did not bother to ask any questions and, not hesitating a second, struck out with his leg, kicking the revolver out of Lynnford's hand, sending it clattering across the tabletop and onto the floor. Lynnford lunged forward, grabbing hold of the man's neck with both hands, and forcing him back against the steps. Skinner gasped as his back struck the wooden steps and Lynnford's weight fell on top of him, his eyes open wide at Lynnford's grip on his throat. Recovering quickly from the shock, Skinner used his free hands to take hold of Lynnford's forearms and started pushing back against them with all his strength to force open Lynnford's hold. For a few seconds they remained locked like this until Lynnford felt the sailor twist suddenly to one side, offsetting Lynnford's balance and giving him the chance to push away his hands. In a flash, the sailor had struck a punch across Lynnford's face that sent him staggering back across the cabin. Luckily, the edge of the table stopped him from falling, keeping him on his feet. In the meantime, Skinner had got to his feet but had not fully recovered his balance before Lynnford came back and struck him with his right fist, sending him reeling back against the steps, where he slipped and fell to the floor.

He's stunned, rejoiced Lynnford, panting. He stepped over the crumpled body and bent down, examining him more carefully. So this was Skinner! The man he'd seen with Yeats in The Blue Harp. They'd certainly pulled a fast one on Jacobs and his crew!

TWENTY-NINE
INTO THE STORM

Lynnford now had the two of them, and it had been easier than he had expected. It had all fallen into place. He had the yacht under his control and still in the cove. Hopefully, Gwen was still waiting for him. He had just to secure Yeats and Skinner to make sure that they could not cause any more trouble.

The light footfall on the wooden deck made him look round sharply. The harbour master was back on his feet! And holding a knife in his raised arm, he was ready to bring it down on him. Lynnford ducked to one side but not quickly enough. The blade ripped through his sleeve and pierced his left arm, just below the shoulder, sending a searing pain through his body. Involuntarily, he grabbed hold of it with his other hand giving Yeats the opportunity to exploit his advantage and strike him hard on the head. Lynnford did not lose consciousness immediately, but fell down, dazed, onto his knees. Two hands grabbed him roughly from behind. He felt a thick rope drawn around his chest and pulled tight, strapping his arms to his body so that he could not move, and he felt the blood cut off.

'Tie his wrists as well, Skinner. Don't take any chances.'

The sailor must have regained consciousness. He could see the harbour master standing in front of him.

'Put him in the cabin and take the crate out. We'll get rid of him once we're out at sea, so that nobody will find him. Here, he'd just get washed up on the beach.'

The two men lifted Lynnford and carried him into the cabin where only a few minutes earlier he had tried to drag the harbour master. He felt the hard knock of the floor as they let him drop. One of them lifted his head and he felt the sharp pain of the man's fist before he lost consciousness.

*

A dull pain shot through his arm. Lynnford leant back and opened his eyes. He had rolled onto his wounded arm, and, like an alarm clock, the pain had brought him back to his senses. He knew where he was straight away. The yacht was running with the wind. He could not hear either of his two captors, but he guessed that they were both on deck. How far had they got? He had no idea how long he had been unconscious. The yacht seemed to be gliding surprisingly smoothly through the deep choppy water.

He looked down at himself. Trussed up like a chicken! His arms were pinned down at his sides by several turns of thick rope. He was lying on his back. He rolled over onto his other side and was able to wriggle his hands, although they had been tied together at the wrists behind his back. They were feeling numb from the lack of circulation, but by flexing his fingers a little he was able to bring back some of the sensation, at least in his hands.

Pushing his legs up and down, he moved crab-like across the floor until he reached the door. There, lying with his back flat against the door and pressing hard, he used all the strength in his legs to push himself upright. His arm was aching, and the sleeve was covered in blood.

Recalling the menacing words of the harbour master before he had passed out, he looked around the cabin. He needed to get out of this mess as quickly as he could. There was little to help him. If only he could get hold of a knife. There must be one in the galley. He looked down at his legs, bound with several turns of rope at the ankles. He wasn't going to get very far like that, and he kicked out with his legs in frustration. To his surprise, the rope gave a little. *Amateurs*, he exclaimed to himself. He separated his feet to see how far they could go; two or three inches, not more, before the rope held firm. He tried to push off the rope with his feet, but it was too tight and the slack would not let him bring back his foot sufficiently.

He got onto his knees, folding his legs underneath him and leaning backwards. Then, lowering himself back onto his ankles he felt the rope in his fingers. Fumbling along the rope, he searched for the knot. He found it almost immediately. They had tied his legs from behind, but the knot was now tight after the yank he had given the rope with his legs and his fingers slipped hopelessly around the hard knot. Still, bringing his feet closer together, his fingers found the slack in the rope and, stretching it, he was just able to ease it over his heels. The ring of rope slipped off his feet. Slowly, Lynnford pushed himself back onto his feet. His legs still felt weak, and he steadied himself for a few minutes against the cabin door.

All of a sudden, the yacht keeled to the port side, and he was pushed hard against the cabin door. They were changing course. Lynnford crossed the cabin and pushed his face against the porthole to see where they were. At first he could see nothing but deep, grey troughs of water. The sea was changing drastically. But looking sideways, towards the stern he could just glimpse sight of the two headlands on either side of Sandy Cove. So they were already some way out. And it looked as if they really were in for a storm.

The sky seemed to have fallen down low over the water leaving room only for the now dark clouds to squeeze through, almost touching the waves below, and blown along by a wind that was rapidly increasing in strength. That had made them change course, but they were not going to be able to stay out of it for long. Far off, a grey cloud splintered an isolated sun into shafts of translucent yellow light that shot into the sea.

Lynnford turned away from the porthole. He had to get free of the ropes that still tied his hands and arms. He did not fancy his chances being left like that should the yacht go down. He had to get out of the cabin somehow. He turned his back to the door and gripped the handle with both hands, tied together at the wrists. The door clicked open.

It wasn't locked! He gasped in surprise and relief. He brought the door open and peered into the main cabin. It was clear. He passed through the cabin as best he could with his arms still strapped to his sides, leaning against whatever he could as the boat swayed, and stepping from one support to the next. Once in the galley he quickly found a knife in one of the drawers. Holding the handle in both hands with the blade downwards, he moved the blade slowly up and down against the cord tied around his wrists until it broke and fell away.

Now turning the knife so that the blade was pointing upwards, he slipped it between his back and the turns of rope. Pressing outwards with the blade, the rope soon gave way as he cut the sections one after the other. Shrugging off the rest of the rope, and letting it drop to the floor, he massaged the circulation back through his arms and chest.

The revolver! He remembered Skinner kicking it out of his hand and recalled the sound of it falling on the floor after having slithered across the tabletop. He bent down and peered under the table. It was still there, lying forgotten. He picked it up and stuck it in the waistband of his trousers.

The yacht was beginning to pitch quite heavily now. Lynnford grabbed hold of the handrails and climbed up the steps. He had not thought out exactly what he was going to do but hoped that their surprise in seeing him free and on deck would help him to quickly master the situation.

Yeats was seated in the stern, occupied in manipulating the mainsail that was blowing out at full stretch and making the ropes strain. On seeing Lynnford emerge out of the hatch his face opened in surprise and an oath escaped his lips as he shouted out a warning.

'Skinner! Quick, he's got out.'

Something prevented him from getting up, and Lynnford quickly realised that the storm that was overrunning them was forcing him to devote all his strength to steering the yacht through the racing waters that were now rising and falling dangerously all around them.

'Skinner!' The harbour master cried out again and Lynnford could see the frustration in his face, realising that his words were being lost in the wind as he sat hopelessly bound to his seat, holding the sail and perceiving the inevitable approach of Lynnford towards him.

Lynnford realised that Skinner must be up on the bow, and he looked over his shoulder to see him struggling with the foresail. The sailor's feet were pressed against the rails for support, and he was holding onto the mast with one hand whilst trying to bring in the wet canvas with the other. It was not raining but he was already soaked from the spray as the boat kept bringing him down into the breaking waves of the deepening troughs of grey water. He had not heard the harbour master's warning, lost in the wind and spray, and blown away like the cries of the seagulls. But he had seen Lynnford coming out of the hatch and despaired between the terrible choice of abandoning his task, and surely giving the yacht up to the mercy of the winds, or letting the stowaway take control. Seeing the energetic signs of the harbour master, he reluctantly let go of the sail and started back towards Lynnford, gripping onto the sides of the cabin, treading carefully so as not to slip and desperately trying to reach Lynnford before he could steady the aim of his revolver.

A wave broke suddenly across the side, drenching Lynnford and forcing him to buckle over. The bow dipped down again and then rose as he straightened up in time to witness the wind whip the abandoned foresail around the struggling sailor, taking him by surprise and knocking him off balance. The bow keeled sharply and with a cry of horror, the sailor fell plunging overboard, lost from sight as the yacht rose again on the next wave racing behind it.

Lynnford looked towards the harbour master. He had seen Skinner disappear and was now clearly alarmed. He was left alone with Lynnford holding a gun in his hand. Letting go of the mainsail, he crossed the deck and lunged at Lynnford before he could steady himself. Lynnford slipped on the wet deck, and fell, his head hanging back down the open hatchway, the gun lost below deck. Immediately, he felt the weight of the harbour master jump on him and two hands grip around his neck. Trying to push him back, Lynnford realised that his left arm hanging limp was completely useless; the wound had opened up and the strength was gone. Yeats was squeezing the breath from his lungs, panting and wheezing hard. *But he must be exhausted*, thought Lynnford, and with a last effort got his right hand under Yeats' face, pushing hard against the chin with his open palm. The yacht rolled, lifting the harbour master's weight off him, and Lynnford struggled free with a kick of his legs that sent Yeats reeling back across the deck.

Taken by surprise, the harbour master sat up, forgetting to pay attention. The beam cracked back freely, striking his head with a sharp blow. Knocked out, he collapsed on the deck without even having realised what had hit him. Lynnford pulled himself up, ready to defend himself from another attack. But the body remained still. 'He's knocked out!' Lynnford gasped, short of breath, and with a mixture of relief and worry for his own safety aboard the yacht that was now plunging through the water without a crew to control it.

Rain had started to fall and black clouds blocked out the light. The boat was pitching heavily in the water. Behind him, he could hear the loose foresail whipping in the wind and before him he could see the mainsail swinging dangerously to and fro across the deck. The yacht was speeding through the water, and it seemed to him that only good fortune was keeping it afloat. He had only one good arm, he was drenched and weak, and even if the sea had been as still as a pond, he would still have had no idea how to sail a safe course.

THIRTY
LYNNFORD IN DISTRESS

ynnford stared out along the deck and over the stern of the yacht. The flapping mainsail broke up his view of the flat coastline, now far off and lying low at the fringe of a huge grey sky.

The sun had disappeared, and the strong wind was driving along a light rain. He tried to get to his feet, realising that he had to do something. But with only one good arm he found it difficult to steady himself against the chaotic motion of the boat. His wet feet slipped on the deck, and he fell down, landing painfully on the shoulder of his injured arm. A sharp pain went through his body. He pushed himself back up against the cabin wall.

Strange, he thought and looked around. The yacht was still pitching heavily and uncomfortably, but it seemed to have lost its pace. He had the impression that it had completely lost its own power and was now only being buffeted along by the uncertain currents that chopped and changed. Of course, the sails! There was no-one to trim them to the wind. Worse, they were being tossed about by the wind in all directions. At any moment it seemed to him as if their wild movement would topple the yacht over on its side and throw him into the cold water. He had to get the sails down somehow. But he recalled the sight of Skinner struggling with the foresail before he was blown overboard. At least Skinner had known what he was trying to do. *There's got to be a trick*, he thought. But with the beam swaying violently to and fro across the deck, he knew that he was not going to have much of a chance to find it out. If only he could just secure the beam. The best thing was to crawl across the deck. Lynnford tipped himself down onto his good side, and then onto his stomach. With his good arm he stretched out in front and with the other lying limp at his side, he pulled himself slowly along the wet surface of the deck, keeping his head and eyes down as he crawled forward. The timber creaked as the beam swung terrifyingly over him, the noise seeming to pierce through all the other sounds thrown up by the sea. The deck continued to heave up and down and a constant stream of water ran down the deck, changing direction with every rise and fall of the boat.

As he crawled past the prostrate body of the harbour master, Lynnford checked his pulse. He was still breathing! And then suddenly, without warning, the yacht tipped over very low on its port side towards the breaking waves, and a sheet of water ripped over the deck, showering him as it passed over to the other side. He grabbed hold of the thin railing just in time as the boat righted itself, pushed back by the next heavy wave that sent the harbour master slithering along the deck before colliding with the cabin wall.

The open deck was only eighteen feet or so long, but it seemed an eternity before he reached the stern and the cockpit where the harbour master had been sitting with the yacht's wheel in both hands. Still outside the small cockpit, Lynnford reached up with his hand and grabbed hold of the nearest handle to the wooden wheel. Yet he did not get the chance to lift himself up before he heard a loud voice boom out, it seemed as if from nowhere.

'Ahoy there!'

Startled, Lynnford looked back along the deck, thinking that Yeats had suddenly regained consciousness. But he was still lying there, motionless.

'Ahoy there,' the voice repeated. 'Is anyone aboard?'

The bow dipped, thrusting up the stern. Lynnford held on tightly to the wheel handle with the hand of his good arm. Still lying flat on the deck, he could see nothing but the grey water. Then, just as the stern was about to come down again, he turned his head over to the other side in time to see another boat, almost parallel to him, before it was lost from sight.

'Are you in trouble?' the voice boomed out again, seemingly larger than life.

He must know I am! I must get up, thought Lynnford. And, holding onto the wheel for support and keeping it steady, he slipped into the cockpit where with one last effort, he pushed himself up onto his feet. Holding steady with his good arm, he looked around and could now see the other boat quite clearly. A lifeboat. The coastguard from

Westcliff! He sighed with relief. The coastguard was holding a megaphone to his mouth. Lynnford let go of the wheel and lifted his hand, waving it wildly in the air.

The coastguard lowered the megaphone. He seemed to be speaking to someone standing behind him, after which he raised the megaphone again and shouted out, 'Mr Lynnford, is that you?'

Lynnford shouted out in reply but his voice was lost in the wind. The coastguard consulted with the man behind him again. This time the discussion seemed more animated, as if they were trying to agree what to do. He put the megaphone to his mouth again.

'Mr Lynnford. Are you alone?' And added, 'If you are, raise your hand.'

Lynnford raised his hand again, not knowing how to explain the presence of the harbour master. But this time the falling boat, knocking him off balance, forced him down onto the seat.

'I can see you. We're going to try and come alongside. Don't do anything. Just follow my instructions.'

The lifeboat circled the yacht and edged up until it was only a few feet away, running in parallel and close-to like competing horses in a steeplechase. Lynnford could now see the other man with the coastguard.

'Sam!' he shouted out as soon as he caught sight of his friend, wondering what on earth he was doing there, standing next to the coastguard, and almost lost in a set of waterproof oilskins.

'Here, Robert. Catch hold!'

And Sam threw out a rope. But Lynnford was unable to

move quickly enough, and the rope slithered off the yacht and into the water, trailing down the side of the lifeboat.

'Sam, my left arm's gone. I can't catch it.'

'I'll try again.'

Sam coiled up the rope and this time threw the coil firmly towards Lynnford. It landed almost in his lap.

'I've got it.'

'Hold on!' came back the reply and whilst the two of them held on to the rope the coastguard took up a boat hook and stretched it out over the intervening gap between the lifeboat and the yacht, hooking it around the yacht's railings. Pulling hard, he brought the two boats together so that they were almost rocking side by side.

'Here. Give me the rope.'

Sam handed him the rope and stepped up onto the edge of the lifeboat, jumping over onto the yacht, grinning.

'Good to see you, Robert. Let me have that.'

And taking the rope away from Lynnford, Sam lashed it firmly around the yacht's railing, giving him a friendly pat on the shoulder once he had finished.

'Everything's fine.' But noticing the body of the harbour master still lying on the deck, he exclaimed, startled, 'What happened? Is he dead?'

'Just had a nasty knock, that's all. He's still breathing. Don't worry Sam! I'll look out for him. Just get us back onto dry land as quickly as you can. It's good to see you again.'

'Right you are!'

Too exhausted to do much more, Lynnford looked on from where he was, slouched in the seat of the *Sea Bird*'s cockpit, as Sam and the coastguard busied themselves in securing the boats together and then carrying the unconscious body of the harbour master over into the lifeboat, held in place by its helmsman.

'Can you stand up by yourself?'

Sam was now standing over Lynnford as the coastguard occupied himself in bringing down the sails and stowing them away.

'We'd better get you across. Then we'll put the yacht in tow.'

Lynnford stood up and leant on Sam's shoulder. The boats were still rocking in the water but the wind had begun to drop and the sea was not as rough as it had been. Sam helped him cross over and step down into the lifeboat.

'You'd better let me look at that wound.'

Lynnford let him remove the shirt. A deep cut ran from the shoulder down to just above the elbow.

'I'll clean it up and put on a bandage, and that should do until we can get you to a doctor.'

The coastguard jumped back into the lifeboat, calling up to the helmsman, 'I'll take the wheel. You get out some blankets to cover up Mr Yeats and give one to Mr Lynnford.'

The helmsman nodded and once he'd handed over the wheel turned to Lynnford, 'Are you all right, sir?'

'Much better, thanks. You turned up just in time. I thought I was going to have a cold bath any moment.'

'It was close, but you'd probably have been fine. Look, the storm's blowing over.'

The helmsman pointed up at the sky that was beginning to clear.

'Still, it was touch and go in Westcliff. We had problems getting volunteers out on time. Luckily, the coastguard and Sam Mortimer were on hand.'

'Lucky indeed, I didn't know Sam could sail!'

'Anybody else aboard?'

Lynnford nodded.

'A sailor called Skinner. He fell overboard some way back.'

'How far back was this?'

'How far back?' Lynnford shook his head. It seemed an age now. 'Five, ten minutes. I can't say exactly.'

'He'll have to take his chances. We must get you back as soon as possible. I'll radio Westcliff and see if there's a fishing boat that can come out. Now the storm's dropped, it should be safe enough.'

Sam added, 'We'll look out for him and come out again if necessary.'

'Yes, of course we will,' the helmsman confirmed before calling up to the coastguard, 'I'll take her over again, now.'

The lifeboat started to vibrate as the motor increased in power and the lifeboat executed a large arc in the direction of Westcliff harbour. Lynnford looked at his friend.

'But when did you get out, Sam? And how?'

'Just a few hours ago and all thanks to Frank Hope.'

'Frank Hope!'

'So it seems. He spotted Gwen being bundled into the back of a van down in the cove and driven off by Jacobs and his crew. He called the police station and luckily Evans wasn't on duty. Smith and another constable took the initiative to give the house in Tenby Street a visit. They were all there, Jacobs, Pengal, Tabby and Kenny, but said they knew nothing about Gwen until Smith took them round to the van and opened up the back, where they found her lying stone cold. Don't worry, she's all right.'

'How did she end up there?'

'Not sure. Frank Hope said he didn't recognise her assailant. Jacobs and the others all swore blind they knew nothing about her. And they wouldn't admit to the gun running either. Evans hit the roof when he heard his cousin was sitting in a cell.'

'So, how did you get out, then?'

'Gwen offered not to press charges provided whoever had set fire to the harbour master's office owned up. Apparently, that fairly put the cat amongst the pigeons. But it didn't take them long to abandon Tabby to his fate, allowing Evans to call through to Overcombe and have me released and brought back within the hour.'

'So Tabby's sitting in a police cell. What about the others?'

'Sergeant Evans let them out.'

'Didn't Gwen tell him about the weapons?'

'Of course she did! But the guns are aboard the *Sea Bird*, aren't they? There was nothing in the house in Tenby Street to incriminate them. Without solid evidence, there was no chance that Sergeant Evans would keep his cousin locked up.'

'So we need to get the boat safely into harbour.'

'That's right. It was lucky you ran into the storm and it held you up, otherwise nothing would have held up the *Sea Bird* from sailing right into the open sea and away.'

'Lucky for me indeed, Sam!'

'The coastguard spotted her in distress. I'd just arrived back in Westcliff when I heard the lifeboat station siren. For some reason the lifeboat station couldn't get its volunteer crew down to the harbour quickly enough, so the coastguard and I volunteered. To tell you the truth, I'd have jumped aboard the lifeboat anyway!'

'You knew about the gun running when you sent me your telegram, that's right, isn't it?'

'I'd heard rumours around the harbour so with the shooting I thought the *Sea Breeze* was involved, somehow.'

'Well, you certainly unearthed a can of worms, Sam, and no mistake.'

'Here, drink this hot tea.' The coastguard had brought out three mugs, the hot liquid steaming in the cold air, and handed one each to Sam and Lynnford.

'That smells strong,' Sam commented before taking a sip.

'I added some of the boat's Navy rum.' The coastguard grinned. 'We'll be in Westcliff shortly,' he added, before rejoining the helmsman.

Lynnford continued his conversation with Sam.

'Did they find anyone else in the house? A woman?'

'Mrs Chessington, you mean?'

'Yes, if that's who she is. She must be the second Mrs Chessington because the first one died in 1938. She was on the *Sea Breeze*.'

'No, she wasn't there. Gwen said she had been hoping to find her. That's why she was going to jump into the back of the van.'

'So?'

'Her passport was in the house in Tenby Street but no sign of her.'

'Her passport? How did that get there?'

'Jacobs said he took it from the *Sea Breeze*. He also had the passports of Johann Overmann and Alfred Chessington. Overmann was the sailor whose body was found in Sandy Cove and Gwen told me you'd found the body of Chessington up by the old house.'

'But they have her somewhere, Sam. Gwen was right to be worried about her and she's at risk now Jacobs and his gang are free.'

'How's that?'

'She's a witness to Overmann's murder. The only one! We need to find her as quick as we can once we're ashore. If only there was somebody in Westcliff harbour who we could radio. Somebody we could trust.'

'Constable Smith?'

Lynnford shook his head.

'Not with Sergeant Evans watching him. He's not going to forget in a hurry that it was Smith who arrested his cousin.'

'But Evans wouldn't harm the woman, would he? Even if Jacobs killed her, surely not?'

'He's been covering up the fact that Overmann was murdered ever since the body was found, Sam. And everything else, it seems. He might be tempted, in order to prevent her from testifying against Jacobs or give him a free hand to do so.'

'That's a serious charge, Lynnford.'

'So let's hope it doesn't get to that, then,' Lynnford

replied grimly before calling out to the coastguard, 'You picked the body out of the water, didn't you?'

'Eh? What's that?'

'The Dutch sailor in Sandy Cove, last Monday. You fished him out, didn't you?'

'Yes. What of it?'

'You must have looked at the body once it was on deck. You saw the bullet wounds.'

And to provoke the coastguard, Lynnford added, 'The bullet wounds to the head.'

'No, in his back. What I mean is—'

'What you mean is that you turned a blind eye and left it to Sergeant Evans. Let's hope you recollect what happened more accurately when the time comes. For the moment, let's hope for your sake that Mrs Chessington's still alive, safe and sound.'

'He's on the quayside with Constable Smith, waiting for us. He's just radioed through.'

'That's good to hear. Let's hope so.'

The coastguard turned back, returning to his watch over the sea ahead, but his embarrassment was apparent.

'And there was nothing else in the house, Sam?'

'No, apparently it was completely empty. Just an ordinary house. Hey! What's happening?'

The lifeboat had suddenly begun to lose power.

'The helmsman's seen something in the water,' the coastguard answered, picking up the boat hook and running up to the bow. Sam stood up and looked over the side.

'There's someone in the water. Looks like he's only just about got the strength to keep himself afloat.'

The lifeboat had stopped, and the coastguard was leaning out over the water, holding out the boat hook at full stretch. The man in the water raised his hand and grabbed hold of the pole.

'Throw him a belt, Mortimer.'

Sam reacted immediately and the orange and white belt smacked the water just next to the man.

'He looks like your man, Robert.'

'Skinner?'

Sam nodded.

'Give me a hand.'

Using the boat hook, the coastguard had steered the man in the water towards the stern and was now leaning over the side to drag him aboard. Sam leant over alongside him and, grabbing hold of a shoulder each, they lifted the man out of the water, over the railings, and onto the deck of the lifeboat. Water streamed out of his clothes. He was shaking with cold.

'Take off his wet clothes and get a warm blanket around him. Is this your man, Mr Lynnford?'

Lynnford nodded as Sam busied himself in following the coastguard's instructions.

'When you can, Mortimer, can you rustle up a cup of tea? Better put some rum in it as well.'

'You'd better keep him away from the harbour master, Sam,' Lynnford added.

Mr Yeats, who had been placed on the bench running along one of the sides of the lifeboat, had still not made any sign of regaining consciousness. However, his hands and feet had been carefully secured by the helmsman, who reassured them, 'Only a few more minutes and we'll be in harbour.'

THIRTY-ONE
EVERY POCKET HAS A SILVER LINING

A small group of people lined the quay in front of the burnt-out shell of the harbour master's office, looking down onto the lifeboat. A couple of men broke away to secure the mooring of the *Sea Bird*, the yacht rocking slightly as it banged against the large rubber tyres hanging down the wall, the coastguard shouting out instructions.

'We need two stretchers.'

'Who have you got down there?'

Sergeant Evans had pushed his way to the front of the group and was making efforts to get aboard. The coastguard replied, 'Mr Yeats. He's in a bad way, and a man we picked out of the water.'

'What's he doing here?' Sergeant Evans indicated Lynnford.

'Mr Lynnford was on the yacht.'

'So, now we know what you're really about then. Hijacking boats!'

It was difficult to know whether the policeman was being serious or simply making a bad joke as he cast his eyes around the deck, adding, 'It'll have you locked up for some considerable time, Mr Lynnford. Time enough to give you something serious to write about.'

'This isn't their boat,' Lynnford replied, referring to Skinner and the harbour master. 'It's *The Dolphin*. It was stolen from Whitehaven harbour a few weeks ago.'

'Really? And what were they doing with it?'

'Take a look down below. But first, you'd better get them seen to. They're both in a bad way.'

'They can wait.'

Sergeant Evans strode over to the hatchway and descended into the cabin, followed on his heels by Sam, who had picked up Lynnford's warning not to let the sergeant out of his sight. A few minutes later they reappeared. They were quiet and the sergeant in particular looked grim.

'This is a bad business,' he commented, speaking more to himself than to anyone in particular and shaking his head.

'Smuggling is one thing, Sergeant, but gun running is quite another,' Sam added, coming up on deck after the policeman and as if echoing his thoughts.

'Get them seen to now!'

Sergeant Evans made a sign to the nurses from the ambulance waiting up on the quay and then addressed two of his constables, referring to Skinner and Mr Yeats, 'Keep a close eye on them and lock them up as soon as they've been attended to.'

Before he could issue any further orders or say anything

else two black Wolseley motor cars rushed onto the quay almost as if they were a cavalcade.

'The county chief commissioner and the superintendent from Overcombe, sir,' Constable Smith whispered, almost unnecessarily, in Sergeant Evans' ear as two senior police officers emerged from the cars, readjusting their caps, and escorted by several uniformed and plain-clothed police officers. The sergeant brushed his constable angrily aside.

'I can see who it is, Constable.'

'I hear you've intercepted a gang of gun runners, Sergeant.'

The chief constable appeared to peer down on Sergeant Evans and spoke with a condescending tone that was both congratulatory and interrogatory.

'Yes, sir. Possessing and trading firearms without the appropriate certificates.'

'I think you'll find it's far more serious than that, Sergeant. According to my information, this shipment was intended for the Irish Republican Army. Were you aware of that, Sergeant?'

'I haven't had a chance to question them yet, sir.'

'It seems, from my information again, that it's a matter of common knowledge in Westcliff. Is that so, Sergeant?'

'No, sir, it's most definitely not.'

'Well, whatever, Sergeant, they'll be charged with possessing firearms and ammunition for the purpose of enabling other persons to endanger life or cause serious injury to property contrary to Section 22 of the Firearms Act 1937. It carries a maximum prison sentence of fourteen years, but I assume you know that.'

'Yes, sir.'

'I'll leave it to you then to question their accessories.'

'Their accessories?'

'Yes, I understand you had all of them released, apart from one, after the raid on the house in Tenby Road or Street.'

'Tenby Street, sir. They weren't involved in the arson attack.'

'No, but my information implicates them clearly in the gun running. So get on with it!'

'Yes, sir!'

'By the way, you'll find them all back in Westcliff police station. In the meantime, my officers will secure the munitions aboard the boat.'

'Yes, sir.'

'Oh, and by the way, Sergeant.'

'Yes?'

'Convey my thanks to the newspaper man, Mr Lynnford, for having risked his life last night in bringing these men to justice. Commendable!'

'Yes, sir.'

Sergeant Evans gave a salute and took hold of Constable Smith, telling him, 'Let's see what Jacobs has to say, Constable.'

Aboard the lifeboat, Lynnford and Sam watched the sergeant and constable disappear along the quay. The coastguard also walked off behind them.

'So, where did the county chief constable get his information?' Sam asked.

'Peter Knight, I imagine. My impression is that the whole affair made him sick.'

'Peter?'

Lynnford nodded and continued, 'But Yeats and Skinner were involved in something altogether more sinister.'

'Isn't that enough, running guns for the IRA?'

'That's what Jacobs thought he was doing but it wasn't what Yeats had in mind.'

'Which was?'

The assassination of the Irish prime minister.'

'Eamon de Valera? You're not serious?'

'Most certainly. Yeats effectively stole the arms from Jacobs and hijacked the *Sea Bird*.'

'But the prime minister's murder would create political turmoil in the Republic.'

'Not only that; the intention was to leave sufficient clues of involvement by Irish nationalists as to have them blamed for the assassination.'

'It beggars belief! How did old Yeats get himself mixed up in such a thing?'

'No idea.'

'Shouldn't you be telling this to the county chief constable?'

'The police, of course, but not the local police. I'd prefer to leave it in the hands of Scotland Yard. I'll call Detective Chief Inspector Sheffield in London as soon as I get to a telephone.'

'Come on then and use the one in the shop,' Sam suggested, adding, 'and best leave now whilst everybody seems to have forgotten about you. Evans has just disappeared with Constable Smith. And I think the coastguard went with them.'

'Let's go then.'

And the two friends stepped out of the boat and started walking along the quay towards the promenade.

'I've been meaning to ask you.'

'Ask me what?'

'What was it that you took out of Yeats' coat pocket just before we got into harbour?'

'You mean this?'

Lynnford stopped and held out a hand-sized cloth bag, the draw cord hanging around his finger, a smile on his face. Sam nodded.

'Every cloud has a silver lining, Sam, or a pocket in this case. This, I believe, is what the harbour master thought was going to be his retirement nest egg. I overheard him talking about a retirement present to Skinner during the night. I noticed he had something in his pocket when you and the coastguard carried him off the *Sea Bird*.'

'What is it?'

Lynnford drew out the contents of the velvet bag, and with it Sam's amazement.

'The Exmoor Jubilee. A diamond heirloom of the Stewart family who owned North View House.'

'The large house in Sandy Cove, up on the headland?'

Lynnford nodded and continued, 'It was given to Jennifer Stewart, on her marriage to Alfred Chessington, that's the first Mrs Chessington, and when she died he must have sold it. It was stolen last summer. Not by Chessington. He may have commissioned the burglary or most likely he heard the thief had it for sale. There's no information to tell us exactly what happened and now he's dead. Maybe Pengal will tell us.'

'Pengal! You know him?'

'Unfotunately, yes. Our paths crossed more than once in the last week.'

'I wouldn't believe a word he says.'

'No, you're probably right but on Thursday he took something very valuable to London and left it in a safe deposit box. Where? I don't know but I have the key and the person who wants whatever Pengal left in the box has my telephone number.'

'That's a dangerous game to play, Lynnford. And you know what Pengal left?'

'Not exactly but I suspect it was the money in cash that Chessington handed over to Pengal for the diamond necklace.'

'But you don't know for sure, do you?'

'No, I don't. We may never know for sure unless Pengal can enlighten us.'

'Well, I think you'll have a long wait for that!'

'Possibly.'

'And Yeats, how did he get his hands on it?'

'If Pengal did hand over the necklace to Chessington then I believe Yeats was somehow involved. He was seen with Chessington a couple of days before in Tower Port and he was involved in some sort of physical altercation with him on Sunday evening on the terrace of North View House just before Chessington's fatal fall on the path down to Sandy Cove. One of his coat buttons was found in the turn-ups of Chessington's trousers to prove it. When he fell, Chessington had the necklace, or at least its velvet pouch, in his hand. The necklace had fallen out and Constable Smith found it a little distance from his body.'

'Yes, so Yeats may have known that Chessington had come to Westcliff to collect the necklace but how did he get hold of it in the end?'

'He was there when we discovered the necklace next to Chessington's body. My guess, given the way Westcliff works, is that he was able to bribe somebody in the local police station to take it out of the safe where it had been placed and hand it over to him. But it's only speculation, though! Evans told me that he'd reported the loss to his superintendent in Overcombe and that it was being investigated. So we should find out soon enough.'

'And what are you going to do with it?'

'Take it to London and hand it over directly to Scotland Yard. It was originally stolen in Mayfair, so it's their case. They can sort out its loss in police custody with the Overcombe police. That's a separate matter.'

'And Anna Chessington in all this?'

Lynnford suddenly stopped, putting his hand to his head.

'Sam! I'd forgotten all about her.'

'Who? Mrs Chessington?'

'Yes. Come on! How stupid! I've just let Evans walk away.'

'Does he know where she is?'

'Of course! Jacobs will have told him.'

'But where are you going to start looking?'

'The tower at Tower Port!'

In a flash, Lynnford recalled again the conversation in the kitchen in Tenby Street that he'd overheard.

'They had the arms stored there. She isn't in their cave or in the house in Tenby Street, or in North View House, so she must be there. It's the only place I can think of. Come on!'

The two men rushed along the remaining yards of the quay and towards the ambulance parked on the promenade whose crew had released some minutes previously the harbour master and Skinner into the custody of the two police constables to whom Sergeant Evans had assigned the task of taking them to the police station.

'Get in!' Lynnford shouted at the surprised crew and a third policeman who had been talking to them.

'We might just stop a murder yet,' he yelled at them.

'And your arm looks like it needs attention!' countered one of the nurses as the ambulance doors slammed shut and the vehicle shot off with Sam directing its driver.

THIRTY-TWO
THE RACE TO TOWER PORT

ergeant Evans slowly released his foot from the brake pedal, still smouldering with the angry surprise that had shot through him only moments earlier when the coastguard, sitting beside him, had wrenched the steering wheel out of his hands. His action had caused the police car to skid off the road with a suddenness that had almost had its bonnet smashed into the telegraph pole standing in the middle of the verge. Behind the stationary car, a deep furrow of wheel tracks now lay embedded in the ground, tracing its short, chaotic course.

The two men stared straight ahead, gazing motionless through the windscreen, the sergeant saying nothing for an instant until with a vehement swipe he smacked the steering wheel hard with his fist. The horn blared out inadvertently.

'What for heaven's sake are you playing at?'

'It's gone too far, Evans. You've gone too far, to be precise.'

'If we don't get there before them, she'll tell them.'

'What are you thinking you'll do? Are you mad?'

The police officer stared at the telegraph pole in front of him, his fingers holding the hard wheel, their nervous grip translating his torment.

'Well?'

'I don't know.'

The admission seemed more one of failure than guilt.

'You can't help Jacobs. You never could. The sailor had been shot in the back. You knew that.'

'We all knew it! You and Yeats, my God, whatever he's been up to. The doctor. All of us.'

'It was your job.'

'You seemed happy enough. Letting things go.'

'It was your job, Evans. Not mine. I picked him out of the water. You should have got to the bottom of it.'

'And have the whole town against me?'

'So what have you gained? You saw what was in those crates.'

'I didn't know.'

'No one will believe you. And do you think it would have stopped there? And the woman? She wasn't just going to walk away.'

'She didn't see anything.'

'Oh no? So that's why you were going at breakneck speed just now to get to her first.'

'She'll put us inside.'

'No, she'll put your cousin inside and whoever pulled

the trigger. Tabby, or was it Kenny? Kenny, I can't believe it was him.'

'But he's family.'

'You can't help your cousin. He's got you into this mess. You'd better get yourself out of it whilst you still can. You saw the county chief constable and the superintendent just now. They're breathing down your neck. You don't want to end up in Princetown prison with Jacobs, do you?'

'Prison!'

'If you're lucky, you'll only lose your job.'

'And you keep yours!'

'You've always got your old boat.'

'Back to fishing?' the police officer snorted. 'I'll be a laughing stock!'

'Get a grip of yourself, Evans. Look! They've already caught up with us.'

The sound of the approaching vehicle made the sergeant glance up into the rear-view mirror.

'No thanks to you.'

And he watched, completely at a loss, as Lynnford, Sam Mortimer, and one of the constables that had accompanied the superintendent from Overcombe police station got out of the ambulance and walked towards them.

'You wouldn't be heading towards the tower at Tower Port would you, Sergeant?'

Lynnford peered down at Sergeant Evans, with a glance at the coastguard.

'And you, sir, I'm surprised to see you with him. Or am I?'

'The woman from the *Sea Breeze* is in the tower, Mr Lynnford,' the coastguard hurried to reply.

'Mrs Chessington? I've already guessed that, no thanks to you.'

'I didn't even know there was a woman until just now.'

'Didn't you? But Sergeant Evans certainly did. Didn't you, Sergeant?'

The police officer remained silent.

'The key, Evans. Can I have the key that Jacobs gave you just now at the station?'

'What key?'

'The key to the watch tower at Tower Port. That old door will take some breaking down without it.'

Sergeant Evans stretched into his trouser pocket and pulled out the key, which he handed to Lynnford in his open palm.

'Well, I think this is proof enough, Sergeant,' Lynnford declared before turning to the coastguard. 'Can I trust you to take the sergeant back to Westcliff?'

The coastguard nodded, lamely.

'Good. The constable here will accompany you, just to make sure.'

*

Lynnford, Sam, and the nurse and driver from the ambulance walked across the wild grassy space towards the tower. It still appeared abandoned. Lynnford took them around to the old wooden door. The key turned easily in the lock. He gave the door a little push with his hand, and it opened inwards, revealing a dark, circular chamber, the light from outside not penetrating much beyond the threshold.

A yellow beam of light shot out from behind Lynnford, lighting up the space in front and creating a strange, illuminated canopy around them that cast the rest of the chamber into yet darker shadows, dissolving and reappearing elsewhere as the ambulance driver moved his torch from side to side. There seemed to be little of interest on the floor; only some empty crates stacked up here and there along the wall.

A stone staircase took them up to the floor above. Here, daylight penetrated the room through the narrow slits cut into the wall. But its aspect was little different, with empty boxes scattered here and there; the only sound had been that of a rat scuttling away as they had mounted the steps.

'Well, whatever else, it looks like they've cleaned up here,' Sam remarked.

The second floor was no different except that the door leading to the next flight of stairs was locked.

'She must be up here.'

Lynnford rattled the handle.

'Break it down.'

The door splintered open under the weight of the ambulance man's heavy boot and the four of them ran quickly up the stairs.

Arrested in their movement, the filtered light revealed a woman lying on a low camp bed, fully dressed in a rough woollen jumper and canvas trousers, except her feet were bare and strapped to the end of the bed, her hands likewise. She turned her head slowly towards them. Her eyes were covered by a bandage that went around her head. Her mouth was free, but she made no attempt to speak.

'See to her!' Lynnford ordered, breaking their momentary inertia.

The nurse went over to the bed and carefully began to remove the bandage and the straps. She examined the woman's face whilst Sam rubbed the woman's hands and feet.

'She's been drugged, but otherwise she seems fine. It looks as if the drug's wearing off,' the nurse declared.

'They must have come over each day to feed her and send her back to sleep,' Lynnford observed.

'That's what they must have been doing on Wednesday afternoon when I met them outside the tower.'

'Since Sunday, that's almost seven days since she was taken off the *Sea Breeze*,' Sam interjected.

'How long were they thinking of keeping her?'

'No idea. Can she stand up?'

'I doubt it,' the ambulance driver commented, adding, 'We'll get her onto the stretcher. It shouldn't be too difficult getting her out. I'll go down and get it.'

*

Later that day Lynnford was standing on the platform at Westcliff railway station, shaking hands with Sam and Gwen Mortimer, his left arm carefully bandaged and his train for Exeter about to leave.

'Are you sure you have to go back this evening? You've only just come out of the hospital. You should stay at least until tomorrow.'

'I'm afraid not, Sam. Monday's another week. The editor's already getting jumpy about deadlines.'

'But he's got your story.'

'Two even! The Exmoor Jubilee burglary and the Westcliff arms smugglers but he's insatiable. It's never enough. That's how *The London Herald* keeps going. He needs another story for Tuesday. I just have to find it!'

The whistle blew, as the station guard called the last passengers to board the train. Lynnford leant out of the window in the carriage door.

'Keep in touch, Robert.'

'Look after your arm,' added Gwen.

'And don't worry about Anna Chessington. She'll be fine with us until she's well enough to leave.'

'Be careful. She might not want to leave!'

THIRTY-THREE
SAILING HOME

L ate one afternoon, a week on, Lynnford, back in London, was sitting at his desk, the typewriter in front of him. A postcard of a windswept coastline was pinned to the wall. Best wishes from the Mortimers, hoping that Lynnford's arm had healed, and informing him, with some ironic regret, that they had another lodger. A parrot! Polly the parrot had been released from police custody into the care of Anna Chessington, who was still with them.

Lynnford's left arm was still in a sling, forcing him to type with only the forefinger of his right hand. An expression of frustration hung over his face as his finger passed furiously over the keyboard.

'Ask Mabel Wainwright, or someone from the pool,' Max suggested, wearily. He was looking on hopelessly, unable to concentrate himself. 'You can dictate to one of them.'

Lynnford hunched his shoulders and carried on without a word. Someone knocked at the door.

'Come in!' Max called out.

Jack Worth appeared in the doorway, holding a manuscript in his hand.

'Kombinski's sent this down.'

As Jack placed the paper on Lynnford's desk, Lynnford stopped typing and picked it up. It was the copy he had sent up only an hour earlier. A postscript to the events in Westcliff with the appearance of Mr Yeats, Captain Jacobs and four other men in St David's Street Magistrates' Court in Exeter on possession of firearms with intent to harm and smuggling charges. A thick blue pencil line ran through the title that he had given it:

ARMS GANG BLOWN AWAY BY A SEA BREEZE

Next to it Mr Kombinski had scribbled a small note: *Not bad, but leave the headlines to me, Lynnford.*

He stared at the note for a few seconds, letting his author's anger burn out. The harbour master's plot to kill the Irish prime minister was not going to appear in print, anyway. A D-notice banning its publication on national security grounds had been slapped on it by the government that not even Joseph Irvine, *The London Herald's* proprietor, had been able do anything about. So what did the headline matter? Yeats and Skinner were happy enough to plead guilty to gun trafficking, together with Jacobs and his crew, but they would fight the much more serious charge of possession with intent to harm. Tabby had also pleaded guilty to arson and manslaughter and the others to kidnapping Anna Chessington. He handed the note back to Jack.

'Take it back upstairs and tell him to do what he likes with it.'

And as if the matter were closed, he took up his hat and headed towards the open door.

'And what about the safe deposit key that Jack picked up from the Old Bailey? Any news?'

Lynnford paused in his stride and turned round to face Maxwell.

'Some. They've found the box. It was in a bank in Shoe Lane in the City, close to the Old Bailey where the key was left.'

'There must be a tidy sum there.'

'Not so much as we thought but still a fair amount.'

'How's that?'

'It wasn't payment for the stolen Exmoor Jubilee necklace. It was only payment for the burglary.'

'So Chessington was behind it?'

'Yes. He commissioned the burglary and arranged to collect the diamond necklace in Westcliff. The money he handed over to Pengal was the agreed payment for the job. Whoever did the burglary instructed Pengal to take the necklace down to Westcliff and come back with their money and leave it in the safe deposit box, which he did.'

'Pengal must have told you this.'

Lynnford nodded.

'He's hoping it will reduce his sentence on the charge of possessing firearms with intent to harm should he be found guilty, but he still won't say who did the burglary.'

'Doesn't Anna Chessington know who it was?'

'She denies knowing anything about the necklace. She'd never heard of it before.'

'You believe that?'

'Maybe. But anyway, whoever is waiting for the money that Alfred Chessington handed over to Pengal must have smelt a rat and they're not going to take any risks. At least, not for the moment.'

'But at some point? Wouldn't it be nice to catch hold of the individual?'

'Chief Inspector Sheffield is keeping an eye on who visits Pengal whilst he's on remand. Hopefully, the person who wants the key will make an appearance there.'

'And where is the necklace now?'

'It's been returned to its owner, the Mayfair banker. What do you expect?'

'Nothing really. Just, it seems a bit hard on Anna Chessington. She's lost her husband and all that money he paid to have the necklace stolen. And for all that, she still doesn't have the necklace her husband surely intended to give her.'

'But the necklace was never his to give. It belonged to his first wife's family who gave it to her and Alfred Chessington on their marriage. And on her death, he sold it. About the money he then paid to get it back, well, really, he shouldn't have resorted to criminals to get back the necklace.'

'I suppose what Pengal says is true?'

'No doubt about it. Still, the police aren't going to prosecute her for the burglary. They accept her story. She was an innocent party. So they might return the money to her, but the case is not yet closed, and there's the unpaid burglar out there who could come knocking on her door should he find out she has his money. She needs to be careful. Better she forgets about it altogether.'

'Well, there you go. I'll stick to betting on the horses.'

'You do that, Max. But you should be careful too. Anyway, I'm off now. If anybody wants me, I'm dining with Victoria at Oscar's.'

The door closed behind him and the sound of his shoes running down the steps echoed in the stairwell.

*

Late in the month of November and under a pale winter sun, the *Sea Breeze* is once again under sail, an early morning wind already ruffling her sails as she passes out of Westcliff Harbour. At the helm, Anna Chessington is on her way back home to the Netherlands, a splendid blue-feathered and yellow and red-breasted parrot perched on her shoulder. Turning, she waves at Sam and Gwen Mortimer, standing together at the end of the quay, leaning on the railings and looking out to sea.

'She's a pretty widow, for all that,' observes Sam dryly, taking the pipe away from his mouth and knocking the ashes out against the railing.

'Pity, she could have stayed, and made something of the old house rather than giving it to the National Trust.'

Sam shakes his head.

'I don't think we'd have kept her attention for very much longer. After all, we're not much more than an ordinary seaside town even if you're living in a big house with grounds and a view.'

Behind them, workmen have eventually set to rebuilding the harbour master's office, and the sounds of banging, scraping, sawing, machinery and heavy boots crunching grit underfoot fill the air. Still, Mr Evans, having been discharged from the police but still having been able to pull some strings to be appointed Westcliff's new harbour master, is in no hurry for them to finish, having installed himself quite comfortably in The Blue Harp with a fine view of the harbour before him, and the bar even closer to hand.

A lonely and forgotten figure up on Watchman's View is also surveying the scene. Frank Hope, his hands in his pockets, smiles quietly to himself as he watches the *Sea Breeze* sail away, thankful that no-one is interested any longer in what goes on in Sandy Cove.

This book is printed on paper from sustainable sources managed under the Forest Stewardship Council (FSC) scheme.

It has been printed in the UK to reduce transportation miles and their impact upon the environment.

For every new title that Matador publishes, we plant a tree to offset CO_2, partnering with the More Trees scheme.

For more about how Matador offsets its environmental impact, see www.troubador.co.uk/about/